WHAT THE WATER REMEMBERS

ELYSE WELLES

RUNNING WILD

EARLY PRAISE FOR
WHAT THE WATER REMEMBERS

"*What The Water Remembers* is a must-read for ghostly mysteries done right! With an eerie, vividly drawn setting in an old home steeped in long-buried secrets, Welle's spine-chilling debut will keep you turning the pages well into the night."
— Kimberly Patton, author of *The Knowing*

"Simply put, I loved this book. Elyse Welles' *What the Water Remembers* is my type of ghost story: thoughtful, well-written, suspenseful, yet cozy. Her characters are multifaceted and diverse, and their relationships are genuine. I was delighted that the book touches on many of my favorite things. I am with Kendra, the main character, as she juggles being a writer and needs a day job. I'm there with her, touring old houses, discovering quirky antiques, daydreaming about decorating, and cuddling cats. Although I am not a witch, Elyse Welles makes me believe in magic. She weaves it into the story gently, sharing Kendra's reluctance to overwhelm her family with her powers while ensuring readers understand the beliefs behind her actions. The story gets darker as Kendra unravels a century-old mystery linked to a deadly flood in her new, small-town home. Welles draws you in with her balance of warmth and suspense, ultimately delivering a satisfying, emotionally resonant ending. It's a wonderful escape for those who enjoy their mysteries served with new knowledge and a cup of tea."
— Sarah J Makowski, author of *Bitches in Bonnets: Life Lessons from Jane Austen's Mean Girls*

"Nancy Drew meets Practical Magic — Welles expertly weaves a charming small town with a tragic past, a history-sleuthing witchy heroine, and some ghosts who raise more questions than answers into a can't-put-it-down cozy mystery."

— Heather Wildflower, creator of @heather.wildflower

CONTENTS

"Foreboding sudden of untoward change
A tight'ning clasp on everything held dear,
A moan of waters wild and strange,
A whelming horror near..."

Florence Earle Coates
May 31, 1889

Lynn does a smart tip-toe-lean forward, like a kid trying to think of how to explain a frog in their lunchbox. Her fringe falls across her eyes as she settles back on her heels and says, "They have relocated. It's expected to be a short sale." She has mastered the chipper tone of a salesperson. Smiling and turning to the rest of the home, she beckons to the stairs behind her. My temple flickers, and out of the corner of my right eye, I see a silver sparkle float past, winking out on a door at the right, adjacent to the front door. Interesting; familiar. I watch the door, hoping it – or they – will reappear.

I look at Lynn, who is seemingly oblivious to the sparkle. She nods exuberantly to the door, gesturing a pixie hand in permission.

I smile wide as I swing the door inward. The ceiling seems to slope toward the back of the room, an illusion of the tall bookcases along the walls. There is a beautiful writing desk across the room with its back to a large bay window. The shelves are filled with books and classic Victoriana: astrolabes and phrenology skulls, a globe in the corner by the door. The only thing missing is a butler's bell on a tray next to a ficus.

Walking around the room and scanning book titles, I circle the desk and wheel out the chair, sinking into it. The sun from the bay window has warmed its charmingly-cracked leather, a faded red with a border of brass studs. Looking out at the room, through the door, across the atrium, I can see myself in the mirror, my brown eyes staring back at me. I'm starting to look like my mother did – I'm almost as old as she was when she died.

My mom was the first sparkle I ever saw, about a week after the funeral. I was so young I thought it was the tooth fairy. But I'm not seven anymore. And I've seen the sparkles of ghosts many times. I've found that every ghost has its own feeling. It's

Chapter 1

NEW TO ME

A FLUORESCENT LIGHT FLICKERS ABOVE THE stretcher rolling Maude Henderson down the hallway toward the elevator. We're taking her to the operating room. Our mood sputters in rhythm with the eerie shadows in the corridor. The elevator doors grind open slowly, then the IV pole clatters ahead of the stretcher, wheels clunking over the divide. My nurse, named Ginnie, and I lean over the stretcher's handrails to squeeze in on its sides, our narrow butts pressed firmly against the walls. Maude moans and writhes with another strong contraction, a reminder that babies wait for no one.

We spill out of the elevator one floor below, tugging and pushing to get the stretcher and IV pole out. It's 1988, not 1968. This should not be happening. The stretcher lurches in front of us as we push into the space to put on shoe and head covers. I leave Ginnie and a nurse there while I hustle to scrub at the sinks. They move Maude into the OR.

Maude screams, "Help me! Help me!"

I hear Ginnie growl like a mama bear at the nurse. "Just wait a minute, dammit! Let this contraction pass, and then she can move under her own steam!"

By the time I've gowned and gloved, Maude is paralyzed, intubated, and quiet under general anesthesia. We cover her body except for her belly, protruding through the surgical drapes and painted copper with betadine. Quickly, I cut through the skin, fat, and fascia and separate the muscles. I'm poised with a fresh scalpel to make an incision across the lower segment of the uterus. And then the shit show begins.

The baby's legs are locked, extended straight out, almost like the knees are completely missing. They won't bend or rotate. I can't position him to deliver from the breech position.

"Come on. Just turn for me, baby, so I can grab that shoulder," I say, coaxing him.

Phyllis Whitehead, our pediatrician, chimes in from the corner, "Just take your time. He's still connected to the placenta and getting plenty of oxygen. Relax, no need to hurry." She had entered the OR while Maude was being anesthetized. Phyllis was trying to tamp down the rising panic in the room while she checks her equipment by the Ohio bed, the standard platform heated to warm the baby, where she'll give the baby the once-over.

No torque, no bend, no angle is working. I'm sweating hard with the effort when the uterine muscles contract vise-like around the baby's head. The scrub nurse dabs my brow to wipe the sweat threatening to drip onto the operative field. But there's no point in continuing to struggle. The scrub nurse hands me the scissors, and I cut upward through the middle of the uterine muscle, almost over the top of the fundus, practically splitting it like an avocado opens around its pit. This maneuver is standard technique when the head is stuck. I ignore the blood spurting from the incision's edges as I scoop the baby's head out.

The scrub nurse grabs a towel to dry him as I flip him over my arm. He's floppy, legs dangling motionless from the hips. His chest isn't moving against my palm. I lay him on the drapes while the scrub nurse snatches up another dry towel and rubs the baby more aggressively. I suction his mouth. Phyllis steps up with her arms extended to receive him bundled in the towel. I throw the suction bulb in with him. In an alley-oop lob to avoid contaminating the surgical field, the transfer is awkward with the baby's outstretched legs trailing. Phyllis runs to the Ohio bed where she starts rubbing with another dry towel, trying to stimulate some reaction. Maude's abdomen is filling with blood.

But I'm in control from here on. As I suction blood and fluid out of the abdomen, I hear a little mewl and then some more. Phyllis is working her magic on the baby while I'm doing mine. I lift the uterus out of the abdomen so I can see the incision better. I stitch the vertical section first, pulling the thick muscle back together. By the time I close the horizontal section, I've created an inverted T with the cross bar spanning the lower part of the uterus.

This hellscape was unimaginable during my training. Although this is North Carolina, our meager community resources are more akin to a struggling South American country. Apparently, the clinical settings where I trained represent only a sliver of what exists across the land. How had these three brown-skinned women—Maude Henderson, Phyllis Whitehead, and I, Laura Hampton—intersected on such barren terrain in this operating room at this county hospital named after the vice president of the Confederacy, Alexander Stephens?

Earlier in the day, I fielded a call from an ob-gyn resident at East Carolina Medical a couple hours away in Greenville.

"Hello, this is Dr. Laura Hampton," I answered matter-of-factly.

"This is Dr. Jason Wilson," he began authoritatively. "We sent one of our patients, she's thirty-eight weeks, to your L&D for possible rupture of membranes. Because she lives near you, we wanted to save her the trip to our place if it's a false alarm."

I was covering "unassigned" patients that weekend, meaning any woman coming to L&D who didn't already have a doctor on staff. Saving her the four-hour round trip seemed admirable, but if it were me, given the distance, I would have gone ahead and delivered her anyway, even if her membranes weren't ruptured. Dr. Wilson had bristled at my suggestion despite my seniority.

When I saw Maude standing in triage, I immediately recognized her face, although I couldn't recall her name. I had diagnosed the fetus with congenital arthrogryposis, a syndrome where the joints in the extremities become frozen and immovable. The condition is rarely fatal, but affected children will develop a range of handicaps. Because our facility lacks the appropriate support, we had referred her to East Carolina in the first place.

The rarity of the diagnosis had sent me scurrying to my textbooks to review the disease because I'd never seen it before. I silently cursed the East Carolina resident for failing to mention the condition. If I'd known, I would have tried to contact Maude before she came and redirected her to their hospital.

A puddle formed at her feet as she explained that her doctors had sent her to us. The telltale bleachy aroma eliminated any need to test for amniotic fluid. More disturbing though, Maude wasn't feeling the contractions that appeared on the fetal monitor once she'd been settled into a bed. I had hoped they were irregular uterine activity close to term, even though most women will go into labor within forty-eight hours after their water breaks.

Here's where things get complicated. A federal statute dictates that every hospital must treat women in labor as an emergency, so Maude is ours unless East Carolina officially accepts her transfer. And we are responsible for the outcome, good or bad, until she reaches there.

We're in a bit of a bind. The only way to know if Maude's cervix is changing is to put eyes on it using a speculum. Digital exams are a no-no when membranes are ruptured. Since the amniotic membrane acts like a steel barrier to protect the fetus from the outside world, even a pinhole opens the uterus and fetus up to all sorts of bacteria happily multiplying in the vagina. The bacteria can hitch a ride to the cervix on our sterilely gloved fingers, potentially causing the infection of both mother and baby.

Organizing a hospital transfer is kind of like untangling a strand of Christmas lights, so I deferred the cervical exam until absolutely necessary. The mild contractions kept coming, in an unpredictable march toward a known end. Babies come when they want.

East Carolina gave us a hard "no" when we asked if they could send an ambulance for Maude; after all, she was their patient. We hoped to avoid not only the delay for the Stephens County volunteer paramedics to gather, but also the possibility that the single ambulance might already be in use. Even if it weren't, they wouldn't be too thrilled to leave the county for at least a five hour trip.

Finding the nurse needed to accompany a laboring patient in the ambulance was another stumbling block. We had only one nurse and one nursing assistant on L&D duty. No nurse on a Saturday on-call list would answer her phone, even if she were watching TV right beside it. Ginnie is the exception, and she's the one on L&D today.

Sure, we could have made a call to request a helicopter medevac, which has its own nursing team, but there wasn't time. This ragtag patchwork of individual actors available to transfer a fetus in utero was going to lead to the inevitable result; Maude would be delivering with us.

With each phone call, Maude's contractions were growing stronger, a nascent time bomb ticking down. I called Dr. Whitehead to let her know that we would be performing a C-section for a breech once the OR team was assembled. But gathering the team required more phone calls, including the nurse anesthetist, a substitute for the anesthesiologist the hospital hadn't had on staff for a number of years. I had my fingers crossed that Maude's labor would be protracted; that its trajectory would exceed the average ninety minutes it takes to prepare for a C-section at this institution.

And so, it was in this unnecessarily risky fashion that Isaiah Henderson came to be born in our OR, slightly traumatized by the delivery, but he did well in Dr. Whitehead's care. She was able to transfer him to UNC within a reasonable amount of time. Because he hadn't needed to be intubated, his care was less labor intensive for Phyllis than it could have been. Isaiah's mother had needed a blood transfusion for the excessive bleeding she'd experienced, which unfortunately, still carries a risk of HIV and hepatitis. The extension of her incision into the dense upper uterine muscle means that Isaiah's future brothers or sisters will need to be born by cesarean. It's a precaution since the scar from an inverted T-shaped incision could rupture in a future labor. Maude, only twenty years old, will find her reproductive choices limited by the number of C-sections she can have. Each surgery carries an increasing risk of potentially life-threatening complications.

No one died, but I continue to question if this is the best care I can offer. Maude and Isaiah are casualties of the nexus of a host of circumstances that are dependent on the will of other people completely outside of their control or mine. I continue to chafe at these limitations, frustrated that I am master only of my own piece of the puzzle.

Chapter 2

IT AIN'T COMIN' UP ROSES

T HIS ISN'T OUR FIRST FORAY into the South. Without warning, Aaron, my husband, had dragged me kicking and screaming from NYC in 1979 when his new job with a labor union relocated to Nashville. Back then, I liked to think of myself as a sophisticated Manhattanite, consumer of the arts featured in the pages of the *New York Times*. Mine was imitation from afar, like most New Yorkers, cobbled together with discounted tickets and shopping, not Bloomingdale's or Tiffany's. I dreaded the prospect of saying goodbye to the museums, the dance and theater like Alvin Ailey, Martha Graham, the Negro Ensemble Company in Harlem, Broadway, and Off Broadway. And the restaurants in Little Italy and Chinatown and the Village that offered the widest variety of food I had ever seen. Even quiet mornings with the Sunday *Times* would become a fond memory.

I could hardly breathe at the prospect of exchanging all that for a place where the fate of an interracial couple was perturbing if not downright terrifying. The thing that made it bearable was the new group of women who, like me, believed in expanding equality for women. We fought for protections against domestic violence, sexual abuse, and prejudice against homosexuals and lesbians. Many of them I met while tending to our new daughter Abbie and settling our four-year-old son Damian into preschool. Then I started at Vanderbilt Medical School while Aaron got busy trying to organize workers at furniture factories across the region.

In a city like Nashville, we were able to judiciously shelter our family within a cocoon spun from university-associated friends and a neighborhood nestled near the campus. But we're in the boonies. For me, this move comes with a hard-to-shake, unquantifiable threat of danger. If the KKK, in full regalia, could collect donations on Nashville's Music Row in the middle of the day, what does this hamlet have in store for us?

Weavers Crossing, NC, home to Stephens Memorial, stands at the intersection of my career with Aaron's. As the one location where we could work in the same town, this place was our parachute after my Plan A for a Maternal Fetal Medicine fellowship crashed like a plane blown out of the sky. But a single exit off an interstate highway is a harbinger of a less than expansive town.

Nestled in a region known as the armpit of North Carolina, the settlement remains an updated version of the archetypal textile mill town now bypassed by cars that carry elderly snowbirds from New York to Florida. When the town's boundaries were extended to include the highway's on- and off-ramps, it added a second traffic light. Both are flashing reds. Neither is downtown.

This, then, is quite a change for me, the daughter of parents who crossed the Ohio River in the 1950s to deliver their children from Jim Crow. Cincinnati was a promised land of desegregated education for two Negroes with masters' degrees seeking the American dream. In their minds, a good education was the ticket to that house in the suburbs with a well-kept lawn, picket fence, and two-car garage.

My parents raised me as a middle-class kid destined to go to college, the embodiment of the best our race has to offer. They believe that we can show white people that we deserve equality by performing at our finest in spite of the obstacles placed in our way. That hasn't worked yet, but there's still hope, maybe. What's another century or two?

I met Aaron Hampton, a nice Jewish boy from Long Island, in college. We were an unlikely pair; me, a leading light in the Black Power movement and him, caught up in the left wing of the Anti-Vietnam War movement. Our politics coalesced in a socialist group naively theorizing that a working-class movement fighting to seize power from self-aggrandizing capitalists would understand that anti-Black racism was antithetical to their common interests.

Certainly, it wasn't a path my parents wanted me to follow; the politics more so than the choice of husband. His family, though, was apoplectic over the prospect of a shvartza joining their clan. But that's a story for a later time. In the end, the heart wants what the heart wants. We married and, when the revolution didn't happen, settled into the beginnings of a middle-class life, he as a public school teacher and me as a research lab technician.

Needless to say, the Hamptons' migration into the South is an ironic reversal of my family's journey out. Now on the cusp of the twenty-first century, very little has changed except the laws on the books. White Southerners fought long and hard to leave those laws buried and unenforced on the local level. Quietly, towns like this one still maintain the customary relationships refashioned after Reconstruction, built on the denigration of Blackness. In fact Ronald Reagan counted on it to sweep into the presidency.

The civil rights laws of the '60s were no match for clever circumvention through nonenforcement employed across the South. In my experience, most whites are okay with a few "exceptional Negroes" being allowed to rise to economic, if not physical, security while the bulk of African Americans remain bypassed by the fruits of the economy as well as political power. Amazing, really, that so many folks like me have kept the faith that somehow, someway, someday, equal access to opportunity will come, despite centuries of bondage and another of State-sanctioned terror. We've protested and marched, boycotted and suffered the wrath of police violence. We've tried begging and praying and rioting and self-defense, lawsuits, sit-ins, voting, and running for office. As a group, we have got to be the most hopeful human beings on the planet. In Stephens County, Black people seem conditioned to the status quo, less concerned with rights than worn out from trying to make a life day to day.

Unlike the snowbirds who depend on the rise and fall of the thermometer to trigger their flights, the Hamptons' trek is an uprooting, a displacement. The two traffic lights in town never turn green. Red is stop; go is an assumption alternating in the darkness between reds. There is no yellow for caution. Is that an omen?

We've settled in a multicultural neighborhood, a true oddity in an area where divisions are bathed in the stench of Jim Crow that floats like an undertone in the paper mill's stinky exhaust. Certain neighborhoods here, not unlike the rest of the country, are reserved for people of a certain color. The majority of Afro-Americans live in poorly maintained trailers and shacks scattered across dirt-road laced hills and fields in the surrounding counties. Whites and Blacks may be neighbors, but they're usually separated by intervening fields where their lands border but their houses don't exactly sit next door to each other. I'm sure their interactions are cordial, though, because the white neighbor knows that he gets to call the shots, and the darker neighbor must find a way to be satisfied with whatever he can squeeze out.

Dr. Phyllis Whitehead, a fellow Antioch Associates provider, was one of the first people to welcome us to the neighborhood. Her family lives on the next block, and we're hoping for a budding friendship between her daughter Geena and our Abbie, both the same age. Dr. Dwight Goodwin, another Black ob-gyn in a rival practice, lives nearby as well. Even more extraordinary are a couple of East Indian physicians who also have close-by homes. Imagine that—our own little international medical enclave, no doubt facilitated by the higher incomes that come with the profession.

Chapter 3

BEGINNINGS

T HE STREETS ARE PRACTICALLY DESERTED at this early hour. I could have slid through the flashing red light without tapping the brakes, a habit that never leaves a Manhattan driver. To my left, the road leads to the interstate entrance, lined with the kind of establishments that travelers crave. A McDonald's, belching out the familiar aroma of its fries that overwhelms until subsumed by Colonel Sanders' eleven herbs and spices to be followed in turn by all manner of fast food joints. They're all just beginning to make their biscuits and prep their breakfast menus. Next to the highway, a Howard Johnson's and an all-you-can-eat buffet, situated below an extra tall sign that's easily seen from the overpass, offer a different option for those who want to stop when the road gets dark and prefer steam tables to fryers.

The street's a little damp from an overnight rain, but a smattering of drops isn't enough to bother with the windshield wipers. It's only a five-minute drive, maybe the best thing about Weavers Crossing. Most of my world revolves around three places: my house, the hospital, and the office, a few more minutes away.

"How are you feeling today?" I call out to Mamie Lucas, the new mother of a baby girl, her third, as I stroll into her hospital room.

"I'm good, Dr. Hampton." She smiles back, sitting on the edge of her bed.

"How's your breakfast?"

"Oh you know—it's hospital food."

"Lie down for me so I can check your belly."

"I can't wait to make a pot of cheese grits when I get home. And those powdered eggs." She screws up her face in mock horror, pointing at the tray.

"Mmm, grits sound soo good," I kid as I press around Mamie's belly button to make sure her uterus is firm. I'm running on the two cups of coffee I drank as soon as I got out of bed. I seldom eat breakfast, exchanging the prep time for a few more minutes of sleep. Sometimes on the weekend, I make pancakes or waffles as a treat for me as much as for the kids. Mostly, my coffee intake streamlines my day to eliminate eating until I inhale my dinner at night. I drink my coffee black so I can have it anywhere, anytime. At one point, I had a twenty-cups-a-day habit.

Once Mamie assures me that her bleeding has slowed and she's feeling fine, I encourage her to breastfeed, pointing out that it's cheap and convenient. What's not to like about no bottles and no need to get out of bed in the middle of the night? The added bonus is that she can eat the extra eight hundred calories a day that it takes to produce the breast milk and still lose weight. But

Mamie isn't buying it, like most of the mothers I suggest it to. They don't know anybody who breastfed, including their own mothers. More importantly, it's embarrassing. I'll keep trying, though, because it's worth pursuing the special bond between mother and child that feels more intimate than bottle feeding, even if I'm only occasionally successful.

"I guess the immunity you pass to the baby, which helps keep her from getting sick, isn't going to convince you either." I laugh. "Just three weeks is enough to make a difference." She doesn't answer.

"We need to talk about what you want to do for birth control before you leave tomorrow, so think about it. If you want to use birth control pills, I'll give you the instructions for when to start after you get home."

Mamie looks at me quizzically. "Oh, I'm not even thinking about having sex."

"My experience has been that it's better to be prepared than to take a chance that you're thinking differently a few weeks from now."

"Are you sure I should be going home tomorrow?" she asks quietly, trying not to seem disrespectful. "I stayed longer last time. My mom won't mind keeping the kids for a few days. And I can use the rest." She chuckles as she leans back, hands pressed into the pillow behind her head.

"Girl, we're not doing anything for you here. You're fine. The nurses won't keep bothering you at night, and you can have your little girl all to yourself. You just said you wanted to make that pot of cheese grits. Even though I'm new here, I've been doing this a long time. It's really healthier for mothers to be up and around instead of lying in bed. That only increases the risk of having blood clots. I'll see you tomorrow."

My routine postpartum visit, done hundreds of times during my residency at McCune Smith Hospital in Philadelphia, is complete. Mothers with kids at home, like Mamie, were sometimes less enthusiastic about having to resume daily chores. First timers were sometimes afraid to be left on their own. But many warmed to the prospect of early discharge, particularly those with childcare issues. I figure the same will happen here where longer hospitalizations are the routine.

My usual is not the norm here. The nurses don't like getting women out of bed and walking on the first day after a C-section either. Or helping moms up to use the bathroom instead of a bedpan. They're fearful that feeding cesarean patients early will result in some massive bowel obstruction. They're not comfortable with a less than five-day stay, as if something untoward will happen without their oversight. My written orders are followed half-heartedly, the nurses sometimes letting them "slip their mind." That's not terrible because it creates a space for me to educate. I always say, "The only bad question is an unasked one." Teaching is my North Star, like Harriet Tubman's map in the sky to freedom. Questions plant the seeds of change, one mind at a time.

In these minor skirmishes, the physician is in command. They're called "orders" for a reason. The nurses can grumble that I don't know what I'm doing behind my back, but each is beginning to see for themselves that the ibuprofen I prescribe means that my patients don't need narcotics for pain; that they complain less about being hungry; that they generally feel better. After all, nurses want their patients to do well, and what's not to like about less work?

Before I go to the office, I drop by L&D to see if any of our patients have arrived since I left home. I'm greeted by a low moan that builds to "Oh lawdy, lawdy, lawdy" as I walk past a room. The unit, a study in dreary institutional green bathed in a fluorescent glow, is completely devoid of cheer. I guess they're counting on the births themselves to bring the joy. Two labor rooms and one for triage sit off a central corridor ending in the final destination for every mother when time permits: a delivery room set behind foreboding double metal doors.

"Oh, she's not for you, Dr. Hampton. Dr. Goodwin already knows about it." Ginnie says, chuckling a little breathlessly and smelling of cigarettes as she walks up.

Ginnie pushes back a wisp of her dirty blonde hair, frizzy from the color and perm done in front of her bathroom mirror. The crow's feet around the eyes of this veteran L&D nurse crinkle as she laughs and the pursed wrinkles above her mouth paint a picture of a difficult life.

"She's only three centimeters dilated, so it could be a while. Maybe not—she's had a couple of babies already. You'd think she'd know this was coming."

I bristle at the joke. Within it lies a kernel of disrespect for this mother-to-be, the kind that can intrude on a caring nurse-patient relationship. It's not that Ginnie isn't dedicated and efficient. She can be empathetic and kind. But she can also be harsh and severe when she thinks a patient needs disciplining. She's been wrangling the unruly ones like children for years with her tough love. But that's the thing—they're not children; they're grown women, often the heads of households. Without thinking about it, Ginnie has infantilized Black women like most of the whites in town do. Just another way of saying they can't take care of themselves or their children or, by extension, accomplish anything in their lives. Of course, she's blind to what has been to her a fact of life, a remnant handed down from the antebellum era. Ginnie's doing the best she knows how, and she's always willing to go the extra mile.

From this point on, Ginnie's in charge. She's the one who will check the cervix and, when the mom's complete, start her pushing. But not too much, because she's got to put the mother-to-be on a stretcher and gather the IV bags for the trip down the hall to the delivery room. Inside, she has to get the mom to scoot onto the delivery table, hang the bags of IV fluid on the poles, position the stirrups to hold the mom's legs apart, and position her bottom at the edge of the table. If a woman has had other children, it makes more sense to do most of the pushing in the delivery room because a few pushes can be enough. Once the head nears the vaginal opening, Ginnie still has to get into her own gown, sanitize the perineum with betadine (an iodine-based disinfectant), and then throw the surgical drapes over the mother's abdomen, legs, and butt.

Somewhere along the way, depending on where she thinks the doc is located, she pages the OB to let them know that it's time to leave the office or the operating room or get out of bed to catch the baby. All in all, it's a complicated dance, timed for the doc to arrive as the hero to save the day. Not uncommonly, the intricate machinations result in a birth performed by the nurse, no matter how many times she asks the mom to blow or pant because, as I've said, babies come when they want. Most nurses like that, and the doc gets paid anyway, so he doesn't mind.

"Well." I say with a laugh. "I'm on my way to the office. You know how to reach me. Fingers crossed, it won't be later today."

After I say it, the joke makes me wince. There's nothing I'd rather do more than this job. Sure it's hard on me and my kids, but I've chosen this life. Ginnie doesn't know me well enough yet to know I didn't mean to imply that I don't love what I do.

I'm running behind almost as soon as I get in the office door. I hate for patients to wait when they have an appointment. It's one thing if I'm doing a delivery, but then I'll ask if patients would prefer to reschedule. Long waits are too much like our resident clinics, not like a private office I'd want my mother or sister to go to.

The practice isn't super busy, even with the recent gift from the North Carolina legislature that extends Medicaid coverage for prenatal care to all low income women, employed and unemployed, after they've made one prenatal visit. Lawmakers were embarrassed that the state was dead last in the nation in infant mortality. Their response was a prenatal care program that could push their ranking up a couple of notches. Forty-eight is less obvious than fifty.

The fly in the ointment is the requirement for the one prenatal visit. In rural counties like ours, it can be a nonstarter. Navigating the network of unmarked dirt roads that wash out in heavy rain or turn to ice during occasional cold spells is, for many who don't have vehicles, a barrier. Some women may be able to hitch a ride with a friend, but often they still have to pay for gas, straining their already meager budgets.

Daisy Halstead came in last week at what turned out to be six weeks before her due date. As a veteran mother of three, she didn't think that what we offer was worth the cost of the gas. But unbeknownst to her, this time she has gestational diabetes. Beyond the threat of high blood sugar to her health, diabetics usually have big babies whose shoulders can get stuck during delivery or will require a cesarean without labor. At this point we can't make much of a difference in the baby's weight, but by regulating Daisy's blood sugar, we can make sure that the newborn won't have low blood sugar at birth (known medically as neonatal hypoglycemia).

As for working women, they can't get time off during the workday beyond their thirty-minute lunch break, so they have to lose a day's pay for a doctor's visit even if they do have a car. The same is true for the dads. Having trained in Philly with its easily accessible transit system, the obstacle that transportation presents is something I never anticipated.

The truth is, I'm a middle-class kid who couldn't imagine the kind of poverty I see around here. My relatives all have jobs and pay their mortgages on their own homes, contrary to common assumptions about people who look like me. Nothing grandiose but well kept. They all have indoor plumbing. They own cars and appliances and TV sets. Of course when I was growing up, I knew kids who were poor, but their urban poverty didn't hold a candle to this Southern rural destitution.

Chapter 4

A PLACE TO DIE

I **WANT TO BELIEVE THAT COMING** to work at Antioch Associates was a marriage made in heaven. Less optimistically, it's more an arranged marriage for a distraught woman with a large dowry facing a less than exemplary set of suitors. Antioch's star, a practice desperate to find backup for a family practitioner who can't perform cesareans and gynecologic surgery, had aligned with mine, an ob-gyn resident frantically searching for employment at a designated National Health Service Corps (NHSC) site before my training came to an end. Their current Ob/Gyn, Dr Barbara Edwards, was approaching the end of her NHSC obligation and was scheduled to move on to a more permanent situation. I would be replacing her if I signed on.

This was not the ending I'd envisioned when Aaron and I made the decision to swap my medical school tuition for a four-year NHSC obligation to provide care in a "medically underserved population" (a euphemism for the poor). The prospect to forgo an estimated $150,000 in student loans was a no-brainer for a couple with two children and a mortgage. A stipend to make up for lost income was the cherry on top. I figured that since my goal is to serve the poor, particularly people who look like me, a medically underserved area was exactly where I was destined to practice. But that was before I understood anything about academic medicine and made the choice to specialize in ob-gyn.

However, during residency, I discovered an alternative way to fulfill an NHSC stint—a two year fellowship that, while extending my term, would position me to realize my now fully baked plan to join a medical faculty. There I could return to the laboratory research that I loved before medical school while I would train ob-gyn residents and set about reforming medical care delivery. Ambitious, I know, but I have come to appreciate my skills as a teacher and power to persuade, long deferred from my more politically active years as a youthful revolutionary.

My delicately crafted, multifaceted fellowship plan crumpled in the face of political maneuvering within the labor union that cost Aaron a job. Despite feeling unmoored, I scurried through a rapid-fire series of interviews for jobs at unfilled NHSC sites. And they were all abysmal. At one, newborns lay on the floor on mats, as if the bassinets where white babies were sleeping comfortably in other area hospitals hadn't yet been invented. In all these places, medicine from a bygone era was being practiced—a horrifying thought in these years of Reagan prosperity.

For me, it was just more evidence that the president is too busy bringing down the Berlin Wall to divert attention away from the Republican party's continuing demonization of Black people back home. His twin wars on drugs and welfare are designed to build walls around the very people he's intentionally buried under a mountain of rhetoric that slaps laziness and criminality onto Black faces. Of course, African Americans' mere thirteen percent of the population belies the reality that there are vastly more white people on "the dole," repudiating the Republican party half-truths. But you never hear anything about them! Naturally, it infuriates me that current political efforts, from the federal government on down, are meant to ensure that Black people stay outside the circle of empathy that would make solutions to inequity possible. It's a fantasy to think that voting can make a difference when neither of the two parties, and there are always only two, has the interest of my people on their radar.

The current political climate mingled with the circumstances surrounding all the sites I'd visited rekindled my zeal for transformational change in this country. Throughout my medical training brimming with the inequities of skin color, I have watched the routine denigration of all women, but especially those who are not white, by physicians and staff in every setting. I know there's a better way, a path that can be crafted by brown women's hands, so often scalded by the perverted, white, sexist perspective that dominates the specialty. Misogyny is embedded in the professional language, the procedures, and standard ideas about the mechanisms of disease. In this space, I represent Black Woman Power, quietly chipping away at the pillars of the established order. I'm giving expression to a voice long written out of the narrative. I may not be able to do it on a grand scale, like we fantasized in my revolutionary days, because conditions aren't ripe. But, maybe I can contribute, one woman and baby, one colleague, one nurse at a time. And I'm looking for others to join me.

Almost from the moment Joyce Fowler extended her hand to greet me for my interview, I knew I had found a kindred spirit. An electricity was in the air, niggling at the hairs on the back of my neck. Her shoulder-length red hair and freckles shout of an Irish warrior ready to do battle for what she holds sacred. The fact that she's a couple inches taller than me only magnifies the effect. As one of the founding members, she has quietly expanded Antioch from two family practitioners to include ob-gyns, the latest being Dr Edwards, and a pediatrician, Dr Whitehead, in an effort to uplift the level of medical care in Stephens County. And so I'm looking forward to an effective collaboration with a physician I really admire who also happens to be a woman—and white, since, by their very nature, words from darker-skinned mouths are often destined to be ignored. This locale is not the setting I'd envisioned for the start of my career arc, but right now, it's what I've got.

$\mathfrak{J}$ust before noon, a nurse's aide pops her head in my office.

"Dr. Hampton, Fanny has a blood sugar of 280. Fanny Hoskins. She's in room two."

"Is that postprandial or fasting?" I'm asking if the blood was drawn after she ate or before she'd eaten anything.

"I'm not sure," the aide ventures. "I think she ate something this morning."

Either way, there's no universe where Fanny's blood sugar isn't too high, meaning she has some form of diabetes. Gestational diabetes can develop in as many as one in ten women in a population that is overweight. Still, in a place where women seldom get medical care between pregnancies, we can't be sure that diabetes hadn't gone undiagnosed before pregnancy. Since the treatment is the same for both, and the diagnosis of preexisting disease must wait until postpartum, it's irrelevant.

I'll have to scramble to keep Fanny's blood sugar from rising into diabetic ketoacidosis range, DKA for short. The danger there is that tipping the mother's acid-base balance into the acidic zone instead of slightly above neutral interferes with oxygen diffusion across the placenta to the fetus.

"Hi, Fanny. I'm Dr. Hampton," I begin with a cheery flourish. "Sorry to have kept you waiting. How are you today?" These words are meant to keep the urgency I feel from eliciting concern right away.

"I'm fine." Fanny smiles back almost as brightly as her red headband. Her green eyes and freckles on a tortilla-colored face cast an intriguing spell, a combination that reminds me of a high school friend I lost touch with long ago.

"Can you hop up on the table so we can measure your belly and listen to the baby's heartbeat?"

Fanny is short, probably around five feet, kind of a butterball at twenty-four weeks into her pregnancy. I grabbed her elbow to help her lift up on the small extended footstep at the exam table's base, one I'm sure she can't see. I ask the usual questions about fetal movement, bleeding, discharge, and pain as I'm extending the paper tape measure over the top of her belly bump, pressing down to find the firmness of the fundus at the top of the uterus.

After listening to fetal heart tones, I launch into some preliminaries about gestational diabetes, but not too far ahead, because I think it's important for a physician to be at eye level with her patient for more serious discussions, not towering over her when she's lying flat on her back.

In my office, I lay out the treatment plan like a military commander. First, admission to the hospital where it will be easier to lower her glucose quickly. Then, over the next couple of days, use frequent blood sugar checks, determine the appropriate amount of insulin she'll need. Luckily, because she helps her grandmother with her disease, this isn't completely foreign territory.

Fanny is probably reeling from the news that suddenly her pregnancy isn't going to be like everyone else's. Nevertheless, time is short, and there's a ton of information to get through, so I push on.

"I know this is a lot to take in, Fanny. Do you have any questions?" I feel guilty that we're moving at such a rapid pace. "You'll have more time to get those answered while you're in the hospital." I wonder if I sound as harried by the clock as I feel.

Fanny looks shell shocked and almost whispers, "Can I go home first?" She looks down at her belly. "I need to get some stuff."

"Sure, sure. What time do you think you can get back? I'll call over, let them know you're coming, and leave orders so they can get a room ready. I'm not on call tonight, but one of the other providers will check in on you. I'll see you tomorrow morning."

I rub her back as I hug her, trying to signal that I feel her dismay and, hopefully, to reassure her.

"Don't worry. We do this all the time."

"All the time" was a bit of an exaggeration; we did it all the time in Philly, but Fanny is my first Stephens admission for out-of-control diabetes. The nurses aren't used to my kind of strict regimen, so I'll have to run roughshod over them. There will be lots of phone calls tonight.

My schedule is going to be seriously thrown off by this encounter of more than an hour. I'm the first to admit that in trying to explain things from several different angles, I use too many words and dominate too much of the conversation, but my intentions are to help patients actively participate in their own care through better understanding their condition. As part of that effort, I'm very intentional about speaking in plain language while including the medical terms so women will recognize them when they hear them again. I think that "medicalese" is used by a lot of docs as a barrier to good patient communication—a device to remain distant from their patients, discouraging questions and shortening encounter times in the process.

Patients are astute enough to know that their questions are better received and answered by nurses, dieticians, and aides who know how to speak their language. Not that it doesn't come with a side of moralizing and a sprinkling of soft admonition like one gives a child, even from them. But that's to be expected by both sides in this dance that is a medical encounter.

Kelly Paxton, a physician's assistant in the office with me today, has saved my bacon. While I've been yammering away, she has been fitting some of my patients in between hers. She's like a soft-hearted kindergarten teacher who listens intently to everyone. A native South Carolinian, her Southern drawl hints at wealthy origins, somewhat in contrast to an openness that makes people want to unburden themselves to her. Kelly isn't one to rush in to fill a quiet moment, so her patients tend to do the talking. Her curly naturally blonde hair seems at odds with her extraordinary thoroughness and efficiency, not that blondes aren't smart, thorough, or efficient. She is heaven-sent.

Sure enough, when I call the nurse on antepartum, the aide has been checking Fanny's urine for glucose levels, not the blood I ordered. Just crazy; urine checks were abandoned at most hospitals in the 1970s. Those lost data points almost defeat the purpose of the hospitalization. Unsurprisingly, I also have to instruct the nurse on how to use the sliding scale to determine the proper insulin dose for a specific elevation in blood glucose. For instance, if the level is 230-250, five units of insulin is needed. Easy peasy; no hesitation, no calls to the doc to check.

This morning, already three cups of coffee into the day, I find Fanny on her side in her hospital bed, her back toward the door, crooning into the phone on the bedside table. She's speaking softly as she laughs with the person on the other end, bathed in the sunlight that highlights her cheeks as it streams through the window.

"Did you finish your cereal? Okay, good. Shirley will come over later, but I have to go now. I will call you back in a little while. It won't be long. Just watch the TV until I call. I love you. Bye." She hangs up and shifts onto her back.

"How was your night?"

"Okay, but I miss my little boy."

"Oh, was that him on the phone?"

"Yes, ma'am."

"Who's looking after him?"

"The lady next door looks in, but she works at night, so she couldn't keep him. He's by himself."

"How old is he?"

"He's almost six."

Panic grips my chest. A five-year-old left alone for a night. How many ways can that go wrong?

"You don't have anyone he can stay with?"

"No, ma'am." Fanny looks as if she's bracing for a scolding as she sinks further into her pillow.

"He's not old enough to be home alone," I blurt out. "Why didn't you tell me yesterday? We could have worked out a different plan." My panic is vibrating around the edges of the words.

"I wanted to do the best thing for my baby. I didn't want you to think . . ." Her voice trails off as the covers drift up around her chin.

My reply spews like water from a Super Soaker. "I am so, so, sorry. Let me review all your numbers, and I will get you out of here as soon as I can. I have to calculate the dose of insulin you'll need to give yourself in the morning before breakfast and again before dinner."

Faster and faster they surge. "You'll have to get your prescription filled, but we can give you the vials you used here to take home. Have you had your insulin yet? Did they show you how to mix your insulin and give yourself the shots? Did you talk with the dietician? If not, we can fill in more information over the phone when you get home. I can have Kelly Paxton, our PA, call you and go over the information. You've talked with her before."

Fanny's eyes widen, the whites overwhelming the green as her lids creep open. But I can't stop.

"Come back to the office in a couple of days so we can look everything over. Be sure to write your blood sugars in your logbook. I'll give you a guide that tells you how much more insulin you need to take when your readings are too high. Remember you need to eat three meals a day with one or two snacks; otherwise your blood sugar may get too low. Have they told you what to do when your blood sugar is too low? If you feel light-headed, check your blood sugar before you do anything else. We'll send you home with a glucometer, lancets, strips, and prescriptions for supplies. I'll go get started on the orders and come back in a little bit. I didn't know about your son. I'm really, really sorry."

Fanny looks as if my sanity has taken a wrong turn. I need to get out of the room to breathe. My heart is racing at the speed of an express train. Why didn't I know about her child? I knew she'd given birth before, but a simple question got lost in the urgency of a new diagnosis, a lot of verbiage, and a sense of impending doom. Damn, I have screwed up big time. It's unconscionable for me to place a child in danger. This is a friggin' disaster.

I sit down in the doctor's dictation room, not to dictate but more to stop my thoughts from ricocheting between where I'd gone wrong to the worst possible outcome. My heart is gasping for more oxygen; my hands are shaking. Time is wasting. I need to get started calculating and writing scripts. Fanny must have been desperate when she went home, scrambling to try to reassure her son, get the neighbor on board, and make food for him to eat for a couple of days. Why had I been so oblivious? I had failed to ask the relevant questions.

I hadn't given childcare issues much thought—ironic since my own struggles felt desperate as we cycled through a slew of live-in nannies essential to maintaining my residency work schedule. We had to deal with sudden departures, unannounced absences, and theft, but however inconvenient, Aaron could fill in the gaps. My despair pales in comparison to women like Fanny whose lack of resources means that without reliable caregivers, they have to choose dodgy relatives or neighbors or Child Protective Services, whose mandate is child removal, not temporary care. There is no middle ground.

Under Child Protective Services, every mother must go through the standard procedures to have her children returned, even if she has only been hospitalized for a couple of days. That means months of visits and hearings before her children could be home again—a process that leaves a permanent stain on her record. She will be vulnerable to a subsequent removal until her children reach age eighteen. Quite a few of our mothers know from their own childhoods how unsafe foster care can be. It goes without saying that Child Protective Services more aggressively pursues brown-skinned mothers, automatically assumed to be less capable and more irresponsible. It's no wonder mothers would rather take a chance on a stay-at-home-alone, keeping their kid on the phone until they fall asleep.

By the time I return to her room, Fanny is cooing once again into the phone. She's smiling now as she hears the words "home soon," as if she hadn't believed me before. I apologize again for not offering to try an alternative if hospital admission wasn't feasible— this time, though, in what I hope is a more professional manner.

"It's okay, ma'am. You were doing what you thought best. Like you said, it's going to be fine." Fanny is beaming now as she eases her legs over the edge of the bed.

I'm not quite sure how to communicate my contrition. I worry that the anxiety I caused may have increased her blood sugar during the hospitalization. Throughout the rest of the day, I'm doing a walk of shame. Fanny Hoskins has put me on notice.

I've learned since my arrival that locals call Stephens Memorial Hospital a place where people go to die. That reputation still hovers from the days when the textile company-built Weavers Crossing. The company doctor's job was to keep people working. A worker had to be nearly limbless or dying to be admitted. These days, on labor and delivery, almost all of our patients are African Americans, like the majority of the county. Few of them work in the mill where mostly white women make trousers. Ironically, since the union organized the mill, the women who work there can now avoid the reputed death trap because their insurance allows them to join other middle-class white women who drive thirty-five miles south on the interstate to the hospital in Rock Creek. That hospital doesn't accept Medicaid, guaranteeing a more exclusive, lighter-complexioned clientele.

The hospital's reputation from the not-too-distant past isn't completely undeserved today. Sometimes I wonder what I would do if one of our kids or Aaron got sick. I'd probably hit the interstate too, lacking confidence in Stephens medical staff. Or maybe I should head straight for the University of North Carolina in Chapel Hill. I've got my fingers crossed that because we're all healthy, we won't have to cross that bridge. Still, accidents, especially with children, happen unexpectedly.

Most of our patients have no insurance when they're not pregnant, and so, for the most part, they don't get much care except in emergencies. So when they come in for prenatal care, we may have to diagnose and treat medical problems they may not know they have. It presents a significant challenge, but I'm energized to try to meet it.

I'm kicking myself that Fanny got less than my best. I now realize that if I'm not careful, the thoroughly modern Dr. Hampton can commit unintended errors through careless omissions and oversights. To err is human; not learning from errors shouldn't be. I don't want to become part of Stephens's notoriety; I want to be part of the solution.

From here on, questions about children and childcare will be squeezed into my banter with every patient while I'm measuring bellies and listening to heart rates. And I'll incorporate it into preoperative discussions. I've already started writing up a standard routine for outpatient management of diabetes, which does frequent monitoring and self-administration of insulin at home. We'll provide the instruction in the office and loop ancillary personnel into tracking the necessary parameters. I'll become more willing to negotiate with a patient if they can't quite meet more stringent management requirements. It should not have taken an incident like this one to kick-start the process. Thank goodness, this time nothing untoward happened. In the future, I promise to do better. I'm just happy that a small practice like ours can change on a dime without much fuss.

I'm discovering too that my friendly yet casual demeanor isn't enough to circumvent an established deference to the title "doctor," particularly for people whose lives and livelihoods demand they use patterns of submissiveness to get through the day. In contrast, Philadelphians are more cynical and self-confident; they just talk back. Maybe some were encouraged by the idea that their relationship with a "student doctor" was going to be short lived. I once had a heroin addict, without a trace of embarrassment, show me the most accessible vein in her body to draw a blood sample. And another who strutted up to me and yelled "f@#k you" right in my face. I can't imagine anyone being so bold down here. For one, they're just more polite. Beyond that, I find that people are reluctant to share information, as Fanny admitted, for fear of being ridiculed or maligned as uncaring or incompetent or worse.

Since all the ob-gyns in town are brown skinned, shared skin color is insufficient to overcome such constraints. Patients feel a sense of racial pride in the individuals who've become physicians in a world that's stacked against them, and they want to respect that. At the same time, our status as members of the Black middle class make it more difficult for patients to share intimate details, particularly those they fear will be judged as less than admirable. A long history of antagonism within the Black community is encapsulated in the term "boojee," a pejorative shortening of "bourgeoisie" with all the connotations of snooty arrogance. Integrated into these class issues are the ob-gyns' northern origins.

These tensions, quietly simmering behind the scenes, are not insurmountable. I believe that the trust will come as people get to know me better, to see the dedicated care I can provide and the good medical outcomes that will result.

Nothing in this environment excuses my recent oversight, but it does provide an opportunity for some soul searching. I may have flown close to disaster this time, but I will double my effort to create a clinical practice where people can feel comfortable to speak up and understand that I'll listen without judgment to whatever they have to say. First, I guess I have to talk less so they can talk more.

Chapter 5

A BIT OF HISTORY

1985

I WAS A SECOND-YEAR RESIDENT ASSISTING on a hysterectomy when the surgeon, a third-year, accidentally lacerated the ureter. Although it's a potential complication listed on the operative consent, this mistake presented a rare opportunity to learn how to repair it. My excitement built until the fourth-year resident, Josh, scrubbed in to take over, relegating me to the role of observer. Even that possibility was lost when he asked me to go talk to the family to explain the delay. I lamented my loss all the way to the room where Mr. Anderson was waiting. After introducing myself as a member of the surgical team, my ID badge fully visible on my white coat worn over scrubs with booties covering my shoes, I explained the extended surgical time and the implications for his wife's recovery. The husband merely nodded. I promised the man I would return later.

Afterwards, as we approached, Mr. Anderson ran up to Josh, frantically fuming that the surgery had gone far beyond our predicted forty minutes.

"What happened? Why did it take so long?" Spittle projected alongside the husband's rage.

"I apologize for any miscommunication," Josh calmly replied. "We asked Dr. Hampton to update you during the surgery," he continued, in the practiced neutral authoritative tone expected of the consummate physician he wasn't yet.

"We didn't see any doctors," the husband bellowed back. "The only person who came in was a cleaning lady!"

Dumbstruck, I froze, breathless in anticipation of a rejoinder.

"Again, I apologize, Mr. Anderson. I understand how worried you must be. Let me put your fears to rest," Josh soothed, as his intro to the explanation of the surgical mishap that I had already given.

How absurd! How would a housekeeper know anything about hysterectomies and ureters anyway? It was completely fantastical—Anderson's refusal to accept that people who introduce themselves as doctors actually are doctors, regardless of their complexion. Denial, one of the brain's most powerful devices, literally erased reality.

I guess the finely linked mail in my suit of armor allowed a stray shot to penetrate the periphery. But even a flesh wound stings. Silly me. I started out thinking I would learn ureteral laceration repair firsthand and ended the day learning yet another way to be told I didn't belong. I can't say that I was disappointed exactly, in Josh's collusion; my level of expectation had cratered long before that. Despite my cynicism, I guess there must have been an enduring sliver of hope, buried somewhere deep inside my core, that someone, someday, would rise to the occasion.

Quietly, I patched my armor, swept the incident into my collection of wicked deeds, and plowed forward with increased vigilance. In my head, I generated schemes to sidestep the pitfalls as if any maneuver would ever succeed outside of whitewashing my skin.

Medical school firmly reinforced the lesson that you are what they, meaning the people in charge, think you are. When your skin is dark, the first barrier is demonstrating that the original misconceptions were inaccurate. Imagine trying to dodge the "War on Drugs gang member" persona by being well spoken or well dressed. Or sounding earnest enough to circumvent the scam artist illusion. Or working tirelessly to circumvent the "Welfare Queen" image. In fact, one of my classmates, knowing I had two kids, joked that he originally thought that I'd been a high school dropout teen mom on welfare who went on to a GED and college before medical school. How far away from my story can one get? And he thought he was a good enough friend that he wasn't at all apologetic or embarrassed to admit his imaginings.

There are also weapons to combat the oldies-but-goodies still holding sway long after the days of Uncle Tom's Cabin. Obviously, the Angry Black woman falls flat when you remain calm in every situation. The Jezebel temptress can be defied by plain all-business demeanor, and a skinny, uncaring woman can put the Mammy caregiver fantasy to bed.

However, I came to the school carrying my own false impressions. Since I was ten years older than most of my classmates, I had expected to be viewed as wiser and more experienced. Unfortunately, my youthful appearance didn't make that readily apparent; some class members looked older than I did. And the faculty seemed to firmly believe that experience outside medicine was irrelevant. My invisibility became increasingly intimidating.

And then there was my version of New York City Afro-chic, a curly natural hairdo. The faculty saw me as simply unkempt and grubby, far afield from their standard of professional appearance, a precise replication of the best of whiteness. Before I ever opened my mouth, the physicians responsible for evaluating my performance consigned me to a ghetto back alley.

First impressions count enormously in a fishbowl like a medical school. It took me a while to realize that what I thought represented my unconventional approach to the world meant something quite different in that environment. They didn't want unconventional; they wanted exact replication.

During those four years, trainees traveled across multiple rotations in different settings where we started over and over in a whirlwind of new people, patients, faculty, nurses, fellow trainees, and associated medical personnel. We were always colliding with the same set of stereotypes filtered through new sets of eyes. We are, I think, all viewed through hundreds of different lenses, each with its own tint, an amalgamation of the accumulated shadows and highlights of the observer. In all of them, to be Black is to be wrong.

Straightening my locks created more confusion because I didn't match the first-year photos circulated to the wards to facilitate identification of new students. If they managed to identify me as a med student, they often couldn't figure out which of the other nine Black students I was.

"Hey, Pauline. Can you write orders for room 204 to get a CBC with diff?"

"You mean me? I'm Laura Hampton."

"Hey, Linda. Did you get the results on the twenty-four-hour urine in room 515?"

"Did you mean me—Laura—or somebody else?"

Linda was short, and Pauline was unusually tall; Linda, light-skinned with a neat bun at the base of her neck, and Pauline, pecan colored with long straightened hair. Among ourselves, we'd mimic our y'all-look-alike encounters in an effort to make banana bread out of too ripe fruit. Being a brown blob is difficult but not unique to medicine. Cops and accusers in police lineups do it all the time with more dire consequences. Just as importantly, it never mattered what any of us carried in the overstuffed pockets of our white coats; by default we were orderlies or housekeepers or clerks—any position that didn't require an education. It was high praise to be mistaken for a nurse.

So, as I step onto the landscape of Stephens Memorial, my five-foot-six, 120-pound frame is prepared for battle. My skin is the color of a perfectly baked muffin top. I'm not gorgeous, but I'm not bad looking either. I don't own or know how to apply eyeliner or mascara or lipstick. I dress neatly but more casually than the men in suits. I seldom wear a white coat except over scrubs. I almost never look in a mirror after pulling my hair back into a ponytail in the morning. I talk and walk quickly at a pace that most Southerners think is too fast. In essence, I am, at almost forty, a no-nonsense plain Jane ready to get down to work. Except there's no Black stereotype for that. If experience is any guide, I'm acutely aware that the physicians on staff won't catch any of the specifics; for them, I'm a question mark in a place where everyone's supposed to fit neatly in a box.

In this arena, challenges about my gender are likely to become equally as prominent. Drs. Whitehead, Barbara Edwards, and I are the only Black women physicians on staff, and we'll soon be down to two when Edwards moves on. Dr. Fowler is the only other female physician with privileges. In a place where real women are expected to wear makeup and plenty of it, smile politely, say "yes, sir," and remain quietly in the background, I wonder how the others have managed. I think Joyce, unburdened by skin color, just keeps pushing ahead despite the opposition.

The big difference from previous settings is that the medical staff here is very stable, without the same shuffle of personnel that I experienced during my training. And I understand the rules. The new kid on the block is supposed to wait their turn and let the grown-ups take charge. But those docs aren't in charge of me; I'm my own independent provider on par with them. Other than that, there's nothing very surprising here. The battlegrounds of color, gender, and even youthful appearance are the same in medicine as in the world beyond. I am who I am, and I won't bend to the nonsense. They will find that Barbara Edwards and I are very different people.

By now, I'm well-rehearsed in molding my square peg into a round hole without compromising the real me. Outward facades are meant to project a certain image, and I've trimmed mine to one that shouldn't interfere with the advancement of my medical career. I'll have to keep impatience and frustration in check to make the kinds of changes I have in mind. Hopefully, the smallness of this hospital means that when they get to know the professional Dr. Laura Hampton, I'll be able to get things done.

"**G**ood morning," I say as I pop my head inside Barbara's door.

She reminds me of molasses, both in skin coloring and movement. Her head swivels slowly to orient her glasses toward the door, like Rip Van Winkle on first awakening. Her lips part in a less than enthusiastic response. "Good morning," thuds back at me, flat and unaccompanied by a smile.

"Anything happen last night?" I ask in an attempt to hit a more conversational note.

"Nothing," Barbara answers as her focus shifts back down to the papers on her desk, her glasses sliding down her nasal bridge. She brings her cup of tea to her lips as if to dismiss me.

I hesitate. Should I press on? Nah, maybe later. The short and compact Dr. Edwards moves through her routines more like a sixty-year-old than a thirty-something, a pace that seems strangely out of place in the semi-urgent chaos of L&D. We've had surprisingly little interaction since my arrival. She didn't volunteer to introduce me around the hospital; Joyce did that. Maybe she's just shy. To me, she seems worn down, barely hanging on by her fingernails until her moving date.

Barbara's residency training at a small hospital in Connecticut where the faculty were all in private practice left her unprepared for the challenges of the poverty she faced here. She had hoped for a not-too-busy, low-risk practice, and that's where she's headed now.

She isn't a sharer, so I've picked up this information from the staff. Their most common impression of her is temerity, hands-down.

I'm the exact opposite. I'm passionate and can be boisterous. I get angry, but the professional Laura Hampton tries never to show it, always cognizant that the Angry Black Woman trope overshadows my every move, sitting just within reach for others to dismiss me. I'll admit that I'm not always successful in burying my wrath at strategic moments; it's a work in progress. I've been bullied enough to know that is not something I want to be. However, I can be intentionally intimidating when I need to be, and that isn't the same thing.

My mind is always going a mile a minute. I'm full of ideas, and that's what drew me into medicine. The intellectual challenge, the thrill of answering the whys and wherefores. Not that the idea of service isn't important. Anyone would have to be stark raving mad to work this hard and sacrifice so much if they didn't want to take care of other people. My vision of service is in a broader context, a three-pronged approach. Not simply direct patient care through prenatal diagnosis and counseling as a perinatologist, but also investigating the causes, prevention, and treatment of diseases. And lastly, training physicians in ways to deliver the best, most unbiased and compassionate care. This sojourn is a detour from the main event to come.

The basics of gynecologic practice are annual exams, pap smears, pregnancy testing, sexually transmitted diseases, and contraceptive visits, none of which require much thought. Dr. Edwards seems to enjoy this autopilot mode that follows well-trod recipes for diagnosis and treatment.

For those surgically inclined, you need to see a lot of women to find one who requires a hysterectomy, although wielding a scalpel to sculpt and slash tissue holds no particular attraction for me. Barbara seems to prefer the office to the operating room as well. I'm not knocking any of this. There are different roles for different people, and all slots need to be filled.

Overall, I'm enjoying settling into the office. There's a lot of girl talk with our almost exclusively female staff and providers. We gossip about the usual stuff—who's doing who, our kids, TV shows, hairstyles and recipes we often sample as treats we bring in. It's supposed to be fun, but Dr. Edwards never seems to enjoy herself.

Chapter 6

MY BREAD AND BUTTER

"**H**I, SORRY FOR THE WAIT.** I'm Dr. Hampton. How can I help you?" A café-au-lait-colored chin tilts upward toward me, but not far enough to meet my eyes.

"Lula . . . Lula Hubbard," the thin woman mumbles, almost inaudibly.

"What brings you in today?" I try again, leaning forward. Lula pushes back slightly as if to blend into the walls. She's wearing a faded floral print dress, the violet in the flowers now mostly blue from multiple washings.

"I wanna know if I got somethin' from that man." This bold statement comes out flatly, with brown-flecked downcast eyes highlighted against the green scarf tied around her head. The statement should contain defiance, and yet it doesn't.

"Are you having any vaginal discharge or bleeding? Any sores, itching, or pain around your vagina or anus?" I launch into an initial battery of questions looking for symptoms that would suggest infection.

"No."

"Any of your partners have sores or a discharge that you could see?"

"I don't never get to look at that. I got none of that stuff. Jus' come in to get a check."

"Are you using condoms or other barrier methods of contraception?"

"No. Had my tubes tied." She's not one to waste words.

I move on from risk assessment. "Okay. I'd like to do a pap smear, the test that screens for cervical cancer at the same time. We can do an HIV test as well. It's important because the virus travels with other sexually transmitted diseases. We have to do a blood test for syphilis anyway. You can think about it while you get undressed." I turn to step out for some privacy while I try to knit a story together.

Lula's chart is thick enough to indicate that she's not new to the clinic. She's twenty-six years old with three young girls followed by "getting her tubes tied." We don't really suture the fallopian tubes; we cut out a section so that an egg can't be fertilized by sperm traveling through the uterus into the fallopian tubes.

Okay, contraception or a pregnancy test aren't a concern. If Lula's worried about sexually transmitted diseases, could she be a prostitute? Her demeanor betrays no hint of a self-marketer who promotes her own body; but then again, I'm not a potential customer. No judgment—just a search for social circumstances to inform the clinical. Can an entrepreneur of the body enforce the use of condoms? The threat of no condom, no action is probably less effective when a customer can easily find somebody less strict. Besides, there's the loss of payment and the risk of physical assault. Although condoms should be free from the Health Department, the director in Stephens County, an abstinence-only adherent, refuses to distribute them. We try to fill in as best we can with free condoms in bowls strategically placed around the office and in the bathroom.

I'm well aware that some element of coercion underpins many intimate encounters. We've all half-heartedly engaged in a sexual encounter just to avoid a fight with a partner. Our natural desire to confirm our attractiveness through sexual intimacy can mean compromising what we want for who's available. Unfortunately, a lot of my patients seem to find themselves in this predicament. Hell, that's true for friends as well. Still, "that man" doesn't sound like someone Lula's happy with; but maybe that's because he's been unfaithful. I didn't see any history of past infections, but she may have been treated somewhere else.

I don't have much to work with yet. If there is some element of coercion involved with Lula's seemingly simple request, I don't feel like I have the rapport to begin to explore it yet. If I haven't broken Lula's shell thus far, I'm not sure we can get there before we must face the dreaded pelvic exam. My hope is that our shared gender can soften the tension, but it's not the kind of exam during which you have idle conversation. I get it; I've known the same dread in my own gut. Nevertheless, the pelvic exam, the ob-gyn's unique area of expertise, is essentially my bread and butter. Every woman who isn't pregnant is going to get one, and pregnant women will have at least two.

Having had my own legs splayed on the table, I can testify that there is no drape that can cover the nakedness of a woman's most intimate core. The vulnerability is inherent in the position itself, known as dorsolithotomy, towered over by a strange man between your legs, fingers poised to insert inside your vagina. The drapes are meant to imply some sense of protection, a privacy boundary that does not protect against the onslaught of unseen hands armed with spiked instruments that stretch and probe and prod a woman's innermost places. We know there will be pain— one that can bring news of a fault in our bodies.

As medical students, we were taught never to say "spread your legs" to a patient, the salacious connotation being inescapable, even for female physicians. This centerpiece of my specialty sprang from the minds of eighteenth-century male chauvinists determined to dominate women. There's no way that a man would submit to such indignation. There's a reason the prostate exam, a male's most intimate, is performed standing, facing away from the examiner. From an anatomic perspective, a prostate exam could just as easily be done in the dorsolithotomy position, but physicians would never have considered that.

After doing thousands of "pelvics", the exam is now a set of reflexes implanted in my muscle memory. To make it somewhat more tolerable, I have tried to evolve my own techniques from what I would like done to me. I use communication to let my patient know what I'm doing and when. I dent the drape downward between her knees so I can see how she's reacting and she can see me, even though she's usually got her face turned away or her eyes closed. I hope my steady stream of dulcet-tone chatter will coax her into the muscular relaxation that's so necessary to lessen the discomfort, the best one can hope for. At the same time, I'm watching her for clues to her discomfort, so critical for setting the pace of my intrusions.

Lula is sitting on the edge of the exam table, the paper gown held tightly together in a fisted grasp. I want to seize this opportunity to perform the complete physical that her chart indicates she hasn't had in a while, although technically a targeted assessment would suffice. Lula is reluctant; she didn't have it on her previous visits and doesn't want anything she doesn't need. I reassure her that it's part of a package that won't cost any extra.

Begrudgingly, she submits. As I begin the breast exam, we both tilt our heads away—Lula at the unwelcome intimacy, me concentrating on the variation in tissue layers below the tips of my fingers. Our diverted gazes are a small concession to the exposure of Lula's nakedness. Then I tackle the other elements of a basic physical: her thyroid, lungs, heart, and abdomen.

We stutter step through the complicated dance of repositioning. She must scoot her bottom down to the table's edge without seeing it under the drape. I mark the spot with my hand, reassuring her that she can stop when she hits it. I've got one eye on her face, crinkled and averted as if she's praying to be somewhere else, her eyes clamped shut. With my other eye, I'm checking below the drape. I'm trying to keep her calm and relaxed. Advancing a speculum against a tensed butt and thighs is like a mother trying to force a spoon into a willful toddler's mouth. It can be forced, but it's not pleasant for either of them.

There are no lesions, blood, or discharge. Lula's cervix glistens pink surrounded by a moist vaginal mucosa visible between the lips of the speculum. All normal. Aiming to get the speculum out as fast as possible, I rush through the required cultures and include a sampling of cervical cells in case I can talk her into the pap.

"We're three-quarters done," I say before coaxing her, as I stand, to relax her abdominal muscles. Relax, despite the pressure I apply to help sweep her ovaries down into the space behind the vagina while I elevate her uterus with the fingers on my other hand. Everything feels normal. Basically, my humble effort to sweet talk my patients through a pelvic isn't just for them—it's for the both of us. I don't want to be hurting people if I can help it.

When we talk in my office afterwards, I caution Lula that while her exam appears normal, only the cultures can rule out infections. Pelvics can't detect precancerous cervical lesions either. Lula's response is quick. She didn't ask for a cancer test, and she can't afford one. We move to HIV, far more dangerous when a woman unprotected by a condom must rely only on a man's word about his sexual activity.

Lula shoots back, "Don't know nothin' 'bout that."

She seems momentarily angry at my prying but then quickly composes her face into a neutral facade. Even though she looks like she wants to be anywhere other than here, I surge forward with the details of HIV testing. We encourage women to use our lab services for HIV even though the state health department *supposedly* provides free, anonymous testing. Supposedly, because the lab technician and nurses who work there know practically everyone in the county and are as well connected to community gossip as the telephone wires running through the hair salons to Sunday church service. Sometimes I've gotten an earful during my turn in the beautician's chair. Just asking for the test at the health department shakes the grapevine. Names and partners drop from limbs like snakes hunting their prey.

I can't guarantee that HIV tests done through the clinic's lab will remain private either. While our staff is bound by rules about patient confidentiality, seemingly innocent conversations in bathrooms or parking lots containing medical information can unknowingly set the rumor mill spinning. Our staff know a lot of people in the community, an advantage that helps us fill in knowledge gaps about circumstances outside our medical purview. But some valuable information can slip out without knowing it.

"Now sex has the power to kill," my big finish draws no reaction.

Instead, Lula seems to have surrendered to a process that has trapped her in an endless loop. "We all gonna die of somethin'" comes out, flat as a pancake.

The unfortunate truth is that the HIV epidemic among women is being largely ignored while Larry Kramer and gay men are "actin' up" in protests against the federal government's blind eye toward the disease. In the meantime, women who have sex with men who have sex with men are quietly acquiring and dying from AIDS. Others become infected from transfusions or IV drug use. In Philly, when we began seeing HIV-positive tests in our population of pregnant drug addicts, the hospital quickly adopted universal precautions, which meant treating all patients as if they were infected with the virus. Without testing, we had no way to know. Because L&D is deluged with gallons of bodily fluids and blood during the normal course of labor and delivery, we went from cloth surgical drapes and gowns to disposables in the blink of an eye. None of us was interested in getting a fatal infection before our careers had even begun. Very quickly, we began offering HIV testing as part of our prenatal lab panel.

Thankfully, the reality of HIV's threat to mother and fetus hasn't yet penetrated Stephens County. We're lucky that no prenatal tests have been positive yet, but we've transitioned to disposable drapes, both in the office and at the hospital.

I make one final suggestion to Lula—a stop to see our clinic social worker, Allison Murray, about payment options before she leaves. Really, it's more to explore any state or local services that might be available to cover pap smears. Maybe there's something new. I still have the cervical samples, so if Allison could find a way, Lula might consent. I'm counting on Allison to establish the kind of rapport that I haven't. She's another northern transplant who came south with her ex-husband and stayed for the weather. And the gaping need.

Allison's optimistic energy radiates from her physically fit frame. The divorced mother of two sons has become increasingly available to extend her range of duties since they left home. One is a plumber who lives in nearby Virginia, and the other is heading off to UNC Chapel Hill. The bloom of bright red, green, and yellow flowers across her dress complements and extends the joyfulness that swings out of her long, straight, strawberry-blonde ponytail as she talks. But it's her way of sharing vulnerability that patients seem to respond to. I don't think they think of her as a friend exactly, given the constraints of relationships across color lines, but I think she represents, in a way that I don't yet, a known member of the community who cares deeply about it. They trust her because she's helped other people they know.

Far more complicated than a matter of character or quality of care, every physician walks in the footsteps of the ones who treated that patient before. There are institutions standing behind us. People here have personal and family histories that make them wary of medical providers. That isn't something that can be overcome in one visit or two or even three. They're always on alert for a slip up. I want to believe that over time, I'll approach Allison's level of credibility.

Beyond the institutional distrust, I'm a northerner, but even if I were a southerner, I'm not from around here, not even from North Carolina. That's more important to my patients than I could ever have imagined.

Their fierce loyalty to *this* place and *its* people is difficult for me to fathom. I've underestimated how their allegiances frame the way county residents approach others and, for that matter, live their lives. Some people are proud that they've never traveled more than fifteen miles away. I can't understand why anyone would want to limit their world to such a tiny space.

The differences in my speech, dress, and assertiveness that mark me as "boojee" to some residents carry another set of assumptions. They're suspicious that I look down on them and their circumstances, but I can only learn more if they help me. It'll just take time.

Allison understands that here, social circles are as tightly knit around a family core as argyle socks, each embedded within well-developed support networks that radiate from the churches and social clubs across several generations. That's what makes Allison so good at her job. I'm on the outside looking in.

Discarding a pap smear just wasn't done during residency. Because they're so central to the fight to eliminate cervical cancer, rates of the disease here are high, primarily because the monitoring that paps provide isn't happening. Without insurance, most women who no longer need contraception or prenatal care disappear from gynecologists' offices. In Philly, because of its importance, every encounter for any complaint was evaluated with a pelvic and a pap. No woman escaped our grasp. But here, a patient's going to be billed by the lab even if the medical encounter, charged on the clinic's sliding scale pegged to income level, requires minimal payment.

Money was never part of resident or even faculty considerations. We never knew what anything cost or who paid for it. But cases like Lula's have brought me front and center with some existential choices around financial considerations—to do the best practice or to do what the patient can afford.

I have come to understand I should at least ask first. Lula would have complained about doctors always charging people for extra stuff they don't need when she got the bill. The choice between feeding her children and cancer screening is obvious to her, no matter what it means for her distant future.

For this visit, the pap smear is destined for biological waste.

Chapter 7

DOES IT ALWAYS HAVE TO BE ABOUT COLOR?

S INCE BARBARA EDWARDS'S QUIET DEPARTURE, I've been alternating after-hours calls with Joyce Fowler. On her nights, I can be summoned for operative interventions. The workload isn't burdensome, so I'm not unhappy to wait until a second physician can be recruited. My one beef is the worry about having a couple of beers when I'm on backup, but truthfully, it's only an implied restriction because few requests have come my way.

As I watch my kids careening around the backyard pool, I'm soaking in the warmth of the moment, time to spend with them after I come home from work. I was always so exhausted during residency, even near the end when call responsibilities were lighter. By then, though, I was frantically studying for the board certification exam. My children's lives whizzed by in a haze.

Now, thanks to a summer warmth that extends into autumn, long after our pool in Jersey would have been covered, we can play. They pull me into a Super Soaker battle before I head in to start dinner. I'm almost untouched until Kyle, our youngest, moves in for a sneak attack and the others gang up on me at the end.

"Everybody's homework done?" I ask as I towel off.

"Of course." Damian chuckles in a know-it-all kind of way.

"I'll start dinner. You guys hit the shower to wash the chlorine off before we eat."

My question about their homework is perfunctory really because school poses little challenge for them. From my observation, my oldest could probably teach some of his classes. Worse still, some of his teachers don't speak proper English. That annoys me to no end. My mom always says that children should use proper English at all times. I'm only slightly more relaxed. To my mind, they need to know what's appropriate even if they don't use it in everyday conversations. The way we speak shapes how others see us, be it teachers or employers or the general public. The best prepared people understand that they can pick from a smorgasbord of grammatical variants in different settings, from the informal to the more formal. You don't talk to your friends the same way you talk to your professors or your boss. Anyone who is brown or yellow or red recognizes these language shifts as the essence of what's called code switching.

Code switching—the art of looking, talking, and acting as much like white people as we can when they're around—is an essential tool for Black people in white spaces. We've got to make people feel comfortable so they can forgive us for our skin color as much as they can. From the grocery store to politics, code switching is the key to getting served or keeping a job or getting a promotion. The cops, of course, are an exception. There, we must grovel, and even that doesn't usually help.

I consider myself a master code switcher, a veteran inhabitant of predominantly white environments since junior high, extending even to my bedroom. My parents embrace the practice without ever naming it, understanding that it was part of their path to success and what they hoped would be equality. My mother, an English major, is a stickler about proper grammar and the building of an expansive vocabulary. She knows that improper English is yet another cudgel used to define Black people as uneducated and unqualified. She forcefully corrected our errors and still does. Almost as if encoded in my genes, I also correct my children's sentence structure, tense, and pronunciation.

Aaron, on the other hand, is unconcerned, often wandering into grammatical errors himself. Nobody in his family tree has a grammar gene. The further his journey takes him from the classroom, the more the language used around him becomes his own. I wonder sometimes if he even remembers what's correct and what isn't. But then again, code switching isn't something he has to worry about.

I've always loved school. So I'm beginning to worry that Damian, marooned in this wasteland of faulty grammar, could lose his enthusiasm for school. If he was bored with the more advanced class work earlier in his education, what must be going through his mind, or not, with the materials he's being presented now? I'll be heartbroken if my children come to think of the place where they'll spend the majority of their childhoods as drudgery, not a source of joy. I worry that they will fall prey to teachers who stifle students' capacity to explore their creative instincts and then discipline them into behavioral compliance with mediocrity. That's not what I want for my kids.

Aaron and I have always been committed to public schools because we were both educated in them. His years as a junior high school teacher in Harlem cemented our egalitarian belief that public schools bring kids from all different circumstances together in ways that emphasize that the world is naturally composed of all kinds of people. If some of them aren't nice, it's because of who they are, not because of some label they're tagged with. We believe that a cross section of students improves education for them all.

As we've moved around, our pursuit of the best schools has regrettably sent us into white neighborhoods—or at least they were until my kids and I arrived. But here, there are only two alternatives. First, the public school that is at least 99 percent Black. The other is the private segregation academy, founded with public funding in the '60s to circumvent *Brown v Board of Education*. I assume it's 100 percent white, which suits everyone's aspirations. Admittedly, it's hard to believe that despite substantial progress nationally in school desegregation, the institution is still going strong since this one is not unlike a lot of other Southern towns determined to keep the past in their future.

The private school, where state certification isn't required to teach, appears to offer an education even less rigorous than the county school. The bottom line is that every kid in the county suffers from an educational deficit—the white ones from a Confederacy-filtered version of the world, the Black ones from inadequate resources and low expectations piled on top of those Southern myths. Luckily, our kids are bright; they will succeed in any school because of our abundant family resources. I'm confident that they'll be fine after my stint here is done.

However, Damian's classmates, victims of limited horizons, seem to be having a corrosive effect on him. Figuring he's got the grades locked almost without trying, he's redirected his energy to his social life. This situation, where peer group sway is so disparate from parental influence, at least in terms of academic achievement, is new. Every Psych 101 professor will tell you that peer group influences become more important than parental ones in the normal course of human development. This important transition enables adolescents to rebel against their parents, a prerequisite for independence. The adolescent who doesn't rebel, at least a little at some point, becomes an emotionally stunted adult. But I don't want our son's rebellion to peel his vision of his future away from the one that our family has always shared.

That vision includes successful application to institutions like Cornell, where our children will be double legacies, or Princeton or Yale. Here, I'll just concede that I'm an Ivy League snob. But Aaron and I know firsthand the quality education those institutions provide. Perhaps more important than the classroom, you can't beat the opportunities to mingle with the children of secretaries of state or governors or ambassadors, the kind of people who will become the movers and shakers in business, politics, and government that shape the future. In a world where influence matters more than competence, those interactions are a leg up that can't be overestimated. Merely an institutional name gets people in doors where they might otherwise be barred.

Yes, I want the best future for my kids, just like everyone else. The horizons of Damian's classmates, though, seem constrained within the state's borders with UNC worshiped as the pinnacle destination. It's not that the institution doesn't offer a great education. It's the tragedy in missing out on the indulgent part of dreaming, the bigness of far-fetched and improbable fantasies.

In all honesty, I hadn't anticipated this turn of events in raising a teenager for the first time. The fear that our selection of Weavers Crossing will leave some lasting scar on my children probably has me overreacting. And yet after all the effort we've put into finding good schools over the years, I don't want Damian to blow it just as his academic performance will begin to count for college applications. Still, there's no reason to panic. I should trust my son, whom I know to be a good kid, to experiment with ideas that vary from my own.

With assurances that the homework is done, I start making spaghetti and meatballs, a family favorite. Over the years, I have tweaked the dish into my own rendition of the recipe my mom clipped from a magazine. As the first meal I learned to cook when I was fourteen, it's not the archetypical homemade Italian sauce that simmers for hours on the stove, something neither she nor I knew anything about. My sauce tastes great in as little as thirty minutes, depending on the level of hunger around the table. I make my own meatballs from scratch too. For not much more effort than making burgers or meat loaf, you get something that tastes so much better than either. The aroma, laden with memories from my mom's kitchen, is floating through my own when the kids are toweling off from their showers.

My thoughts wander to Aaron while I'm rolling the meat mixture into balls. He's probably finishing a meeting somewhere in Alabama where he's trying to organize a shop. He'll be heading out with workers to begin home visits to ask others to sign cards requesting a union election. Aaron loves these engagements, whipping up people to seize their power like a football coach before the team takes the field. Over a beer or glass of sweet tea, he'll offer them a voice in their workplace through the power to bargain. At the end of the night, long after his kids have gone to bed and the burger joints have closed, Aaron will be reheating his food in a motel microwave. If he's lucky, he might be treating himself to a local BBQ rib plate.

Certainly, as a big supporter of the union movement, I believe he's doing important work. Organizing is Aaron's reason for living. But more and more, he's missing in action here at home, not just in body but in spirit. He's more often yoked to a telephone than he is conversing with any of us. I thought my more relaxed work schedule would be a springboard to a new closeness. Instead, it's more belly flop than swan dive. I don't expect him to understand basic medical stuff, let alone the nuances. But he could at least hear my frustrations with the hierarchy, the bureaucratic bungling, the crazy regulations. It's that empathetic listener I fell in love with that I miss. The one who promised to take it all in and make it all better with a caress and a back rub. It's beginning to dawn on me that Aaron isn't going to be the one to soothe my raw edges for the duration of this four-year stint.

I put the bowls on the table where the kids are now gathering. The rule in our house is that dinner time is family time, free of interruption. By the customs replicated from my childhood, the table is the place to share our day. That first year of residency, when I'd fall asleep over a meal, Abbie would yell, "Mommy, Mommy, I'm talking to you. Wake up, wake up." I'd yank my eyelids open and try to appear conscious.

Kyle, our preschooler born during my residency, begins with an afterschool slip-n-slide game but Abbie jumps in almost before he's finished.

"Mom, Kyle says kids are calling him Chico or Jose," Abbie interrupts testily, brow knotted in a scowl.

In the moment, I'm taken aback. They've obviously mistaken his beige complexion for some Spanish speaker of unknown national origin. Kyle really browns up in the summer sun, making his ethnicity even more mysterious. But that's not the point. These kids have never seen a Mexican in the flesh; given their limited education, they probably can't find Mexico on a map.

Damian chimes in nonchalantly, "It happens. We both know it," as he looks toward Abbie. And then turning to Kyle, he adds, "It's more the kids' problem than yours."

"Yes, but it's still not fair!" Abbie fires back.

"Nobody says the world is fair. And you can't make it that way by bitching about it," Damian replies.

"Language," I warn as I shoot a stabbing glare at my eldest. But the adults in the house use those words, so the kids know my objection is pro forma.

"Yeah, whatever. My point is that you just gotta ignore the name calling. They're just trying to get at you." Damian laughs. "I'm too cute to let that stuff stop me. Kyle, it doesn't change who you are inside. You can't let it get you into payback, or they win."

"It's just dumb," Kyle pipes up. "I don't care."

In an effort to let the siblings work through it, I refrain from commenting. They're good with each other. They don't think that there's anything wrong with being Mexican; it's just not part of their own heritage. And I know it's a taunt to identify Kyle as someone who doesn't belong. I'll circle back with him at bedtime.

In the South, still home to over 50 percent of African Americans in the country, most people are either Black or white with other minorities few and far between. I was surprised to find that many Southerners barely even acknowledge different nationalities. One exception is ethnic Jews, and many of them do so quietly, frightened by the South's history of periodic waves of anti-Semitic violence. There's a strain of Protestant-based hatred of "the Jews who killed Jesus on the cross" that rears its ugly head every now and again. Anti-Semitic jokes are not infrequently shared with Aaron, the jokesters unaware that he is one.

Many Black southerners have no idea that the British hate the Irish and used to mock them using images of monkeys. Or that Italians and Poles were considered both nonwhite and repugnant when they began immigrating to the US in large numbers. Is it any wonder, given the state of their educational systems? The textbooks probably don't cover the battles between ethnic groups that preceded the Immigration Act of 1924, which set quotas to keep out "undesirables." Many African Americans around here think that white people are one big happy family united in a concentrated hatred reserved for us; that the heavy burden of prejudice is ours alone.

"**M**om, I don't care," he says as I sit on Kyle's bed. "If I don't say anything, they just go away. I've got lots of friends."

Is this evidence of my son's premature natural aplomb? Or my own concession to the inevitability of name calling? These names are nicer than those that will come. These bullies are a couple of Black kids on the bus whose message is that he's not like them. His skin is too light; he isn't from around here; he doesn't live on their side of town; he talks too proper. He's the epitome of low-hanging fruit.

As much as Aaron and I have tried to shelter our children in safe neighborhoods, I know that we can't protect them from the world's meanness. Nor do I want to. They will have to learn to cope using a range of tools. Sometimes you just walk away calmly as the superior person without a hint of anger. Sometimes it's the subtlety of a retort that may even go over their head. Sometimes it's a joke. Most importantly, one should always be more disappointed in the name caller than hurt by them. These are skills I can model. The truth is, Kyle will be going places those boys can't even imagine. More than anything, I want my kids to have the self-confidence to roll right over these haters to where they want to go. These things, only I can teach.

Almost since we first got together, my social life with Aaron was mostly his Jewish friends, at first in our left-wing political circle and later within the world of public school teachers. My friends from the lab, like the entire complement of research workers in the medical school, lacked surface melanin as well. His junior high school students in Harlem provided the only color in our lives. Shocked to learn that many of them had never been below 125th Street, we shared with them the places we had come to love all over the city outside Harlem. I knew that if his students found the way, they would love them too. Obviously as adolescents, none were potential friends for me.

I became Aaron's designated role model for "young, gifted, and Black." It's not a contradiction to be "Black and proud" and love a white man. Alice Walker, author of *The Color Purple*, and Nina Simone are two examples of proud Black women who did. I've been accused by not a few people, behind my back and to my face, of wanting to be white. Ridiculous! I have long argued that there should be no right way to be Black. If people want to sing opera or dance ballet or sing country music, they should be able to pursue those interests without ridicule. I have never wanted to be anyone other than who I am. The legacy from my slave ancestors inspires me every day to use my brown skin as a weapon for change in a society that seems to think my skin color is problematic.

But that mission requires me to shift back and forth between two worlds. I'm a pretender, an outsider who doesn't fit neatly in either. It takes constant vigilance, a tapeworm sucking my energy in quiet symbiosis. It's even more difficult when I'm with Aaron. I never know how new people are going to react to our being together, something I don't think Aaron gives a second thought. He isn't confronted about his skin color at every turn. No one has ever questioned his parental status when he's with our children while mine has been challenged repeatedly over the years. Whiteness automatically confers a culturally created perception of rightness. That old saying "if you're Black, get back; if you're white, you're alright" says it all. Where is my safe haven where I can unabashedly be the complicated being that is me?

Aaron and I have never talked about any of this. Ironic because when we fell in love, I thought we could talk about anything and everything. Over the years, we've just assumed we're on the same page. I think, though, that his page is in a different book.

Biraciality is murky territory when identities are delimited by skin tone. Thousands and thousands of people like Mariah Carey can be white unless they don't want to be. For centuries, mixed-race individuals have been "passing" as white even though it generally meant disappearing into a new location completely cut off from their families. But browner-skinned people, usually raised in enclaves on the other side of the color line, have always been considered Colored or Negro or African American or Black. Their one white parent couldn't save them from being dropped into the bucket labeled "undesirable". Simply saying that you're of mixed origin isn't enough to prevent people from reacting to you as the race they've decided you are.

My children's journey, because they look different than me, will not follow mine. They will have to decide who they want to be in the world and fight for their identity if it's at odds with who the world tries to tell them they are. If asked, they call themselves mixed because, they say, they don't want to deny either parent their due. I think of my children as Black with all its inherent risks in the world as we know it. What will their Blackness mean to them? Taunts and nonacceptance by one community or the other or both? Or a heritage to be celebrated?

The times and their upbringing are not mine. They blend more easily into white spaces, and conversely, blending into Black ones may be more difficult. I hope that by frank talk, truth telling, and role modeling I can give them weapons for their journey. I hope their battle will not be too bloody or leave too many scars. I hope my love will serve as part of their armor.

My pager startles me as it clatters on the table, a momentary surprise each time, perhaps because it happens so infrequently. This time it's a woman with vaginal bleeding. I tell her to go to the ER if she soaks through two super pads in one hour, a way to quantitate her blood loss and, in that way, reassure her that she's not bleeding to death if the pads aren't full. Otherwise, she should come to the office tomorrow as a walk-in, one of the appointments reserved for people with urgent problems. I want to spare her from what I consider the ineptitude of the ER docs, which usually comes with humiliations around implied inappropriate sexual activity and suspicions of STDs.

It's always a relief when the beeper doesn't herald a laboring patient. My nightmare is that I have to go into the hospital when Aaron is away and get stuck there until the morning. I'd be on the phone with Damian, just like Fanny Hoskins when she was hospitalized for diabetes. Except he's not six like her son; he's a teenager who knows the drill well enough to bristle at my implied lack of confidence in his capabilities. But my biggest fear is that they'll be vulnerable to some freak situation that only an adult should handle. It's not crime. My horror scenario is carbon monoxide or maybe fire. So far, fortune has favored us.

Chapter 8

NEW CIRCUMSTANCES

WE BOUGHT THIS HOUSE ON Oakdale Court because it feels almost palatial. What looks like one story from the street is actually two from the back, with a balcony that runs its full length overlooking a kidney-shaped swimming pool. The lot fills most of our side of the cul-de-sac, extending downhill to a wooded area with a creek.

The pool's deep end has been a major draw for both the kids and Aaron, who's excited to leave behind our lap pool in Jersey. He loves the large sloping lawn too, across which he finds an easy rhythm in mowing as he sweats in the sun. He says the sight of freshly cut grass is physical evidence of a job well done. This centerpiece of his weekend chores is perfect for him.

The four years we'll spend here represents a big chunk of our children's lives. With the landscape of outside amusements as bleak as it is, we'll have more time to enjoy together as a family. In that spirit, we've decided to create our own little wonderland.

We've started with a little gardening, a throwback to my life before medicine, but this time as a project with Kyle. He's a sucker for digging in dirt. I eat tomatoes, my favorite fruit (or is it vegetable?) on anything and everything. There's nothing better than a tomato picked fresh off the vine; you don't even need salt. Kyle and I have started two beefsteak tomato plants in flats that Aaron built. Since I'm the only one in the family who eats them, we'll be overwhelmed with a two-plant harvest. I'll leave some of the excess in the office break room alongside the surplus summer produce that the other people bring. And the kids and I will can the rest for the winter. My mom flash-freezes hers, so I might try my hand at that. There's still space in the flats to add cucumbers for the perfect salad; they're pretty easy to grow. I need to make up my mind before it's too late.

The house's interior is crying out for rescue from the psychedelic colors of the '70s, more work than two do-it-yourselfers could consider. Besides, our circumstances have changed, not merely because of the excess chunk of money from the sale of our house in Cherry Hill. After years of being paid as a trainee, my physician's salary feels like a windfall. I'd been so focused on improving medical care for the underserved that the financial perks that come with a job as an ob-gyn just whizzed right by me. Thinking I was joining a clinic with few resources, my almost six-figure salary nearly knocked me over. On top of Aaron's salary, we've been catapulted into a whole different tax bracket.

We have always lived well below our means because we are simple people without extravagant habits or expenditures. We grew up as bargain hunters looking to save every dime. There's no sale or discount we won't exploit. But more than that, Aaron, afflicted with an inherent fear of financial ruin, is an inveterate saver. The circumstances surrounding the foreclosure of his family's home traumatized him enough to seek a psychologist at one point. His family's move into his grandparents' home permanently shifted the dynamics within his close-knit extended family so that his father became the butt of relentless ridicule among relatives for the rest of his life. Aaron, forever trying to prove that he's not his dad, set out on a path divergent from every other member in the clan. They've honed in on accumulating more money than anyone knows what to do with. Instead, Aaron chose to work to empower people like himself, without regard for his monetary compensation. He wants to transform lives, starting as a political organizer, then a teacher, and now a union organizer.

Aaron's approach to money management does collide at times with our socialist roots. He avoids direct trading in stocks, the epitome of capitalist greed. But money markets and bond funds are also investments in the system, as are bank accounts and mortgages, for that matter. If you live in a capitalist society, there's no path to financial security outside its monetary instruments. You can only hope to hold on to your principles and integrity, knowing that you will have to make compromises. In our youth, it was campaigns to divest from companies heavily intertwined in the Vietnam War, the military industrial complex, and South African apartheid, an injustice that continues to live on. Now he cherry picks the funds in which we invest.

I leave our finances completely in his hands because it's important to him, he really enjoys it, and he's good at it. I don't have the skill set or an interest in acquiring it. I just sign our tax returns, happy that I don't have to think about it. I know nothing about our account balances or our net worth. I do recognize that our bank accounts have quietly swelled over the years.

Our move-in ready house in suburban New Jersey looked exactly the same when we moved out as it did when we moved in. Honestly, Aaron and I probably spent more time away from it than in it. We want to reverse that situation with this house, crafting it into sumptuous surroundings that the family will hate to leave.

Aaron seems as excited to begin updating the place as I. He immediately liked the contractor recommended by Sherry Walcott, the real estate agent who found the house for us. Max is tall and then some, his dark hair neatly cut but not buzzed. His bronzed face and neck mark him as a man who works outdoors. His vibe is that of a Vietnam vet who returned home unscathed to settle into his wife's hometown. He's enjoying a comfortable life with her extended family as he expands his business. His blue eyes have a little twinkle when he smiles, always subtly, never broadly. Aaron likes to think of himself as a premier do-it-yourselfer, so the two men seem perfect for male bonding, genial but not overly talkative as they walk through the rooms in amiable banter.

Our elevation to the kind of people who hire builders and decorators feels almost too self-indulgent. Our decorator, Lucinda

Jackson, is your archetypical Southern belle—blonde hair, local drawl, and all. It feels comical for me to be poring over wallpaper, paint, and tile samples with someone who looks like Dolly Parton. And yet she seems attuned to my vision. Not that I'm disparaging Dolly; I loved the movie 9 *to* 5, but country music is the only music I absolutely cannot listen to. Consequently, my car radio has been rendered completely useless, leaving me reliant on my CD player, not a bad thing because you can select what you want to hear.

I have a keen sense of what I want, although there are some moments when I employ the feminine wile that lets Aaron think my choices are his idea. I welcome his insistence on being part of every choice, as partners should. I can intuit his limits on cost and inch them along; nothing extravagant, but price isn't the most important determinant. Since the real estate market here will never have rapid turnover, we've been liberated from concerns about what will sell well, free to explore all kinds of possibilities. There's nothing we can do to make this house sell faster. Our best prospect for a buyer is probably the doctor who will eventually replace me at Antioch.

After eight years of essentially being a student, I feel like a full-fledged adult again.

In the office, my clinical practice style, a mishmash drawn from the various institutions that trained me, has been central to my design for updating the procedures and protocols followed by the PAs and staff. In that, I'm like a hungry grizzly bear that stumbled into a storage shed. After I type my regimens into my new Mac

Classic and print the WordPerfect documents, our secretary retypes them on her electric typewriter because she says dot matrix print "just don't look right." Her pages are xeroxed to be distributed between the offices where in staff meetings, we talk about major adjustments. Of course, I have the medical hierarchy at my back, but education and persuasion are the tools I choose. This is a new feeling, this being heard in ways that people like me don't often experience. I'm a boss and I like it. Maybe it's a little reward for countless sleepless nights.

My confidence springs from what I call a post-residency high, the period when we're at the pinnacle of our specialty knowledge, having just passed the written board certification exams given at the end of residency. We poured months of study into all aspects of ob-gyn, medicine, pharmacology, anatomy, and pathology. I want to share the bundle of knowledge at my fingertips with this community, not just in our practice but with others at the hospital.

For the rest of a physician's days in clinical practice, it'll be downhill from here. I'm already watching the pharmacology and pathology, unused in daily routines, slip away. Repetition is the key to retention, like tacks that keep earlier tidbits from sliding into the brain's deeper recesses. Even now, treating an acute asthma attack would send me scurrying to check medication dosages before I could write orders; I don't think I've encountered a single case here.

Similarly, the routine cases we see in daily practice will make us hazy on more uncommon diagnoses, and those patients will have to be referred to specialists. Doctors in places like Weavers Crossing will find themselves constrained by the lack of resources, further exacerbating the knowledge drain. New medications will hit the market, and our only source of information about them is the drug reps who knock on our doors. I mean, eventually there has to be a treatment for HIV/AIDS.

I hadn't understood the critical role of continuing medical education until I looked around this hamlet. Even if they wanted to attend CME courses, many physicians are missing out on new research and updated changes in practice because they have no one to cover their clinical duties while they're away. Even if hospitals could afford to buy the new equipment needed for newer techniques, the physicians who work in them will have trouble learning the procedures.

When I look around, I see this downward spiral in real time in the physicians at Stephens Memorial where the present seems mired in everyone else's past. The only path forward is a vigorous individual commitment to lifelong learning to replenish our knowledge stores. And I plan to not only generate new findings but also spread them through the medical community as a prominent researcher and educator. One day, I'm going to be up on a podium as a featured speaker at a Society of Maternal-Fetal Medicine meeting. No one can say I don't dream big.

I can't think of a better example than the case of the now retired Dr. Jenkins, the only ob-gyn in town when Joyce arrived. L&D at Stephens Memorial used to shut down for two weeks every February when he went on vacation. Of course, he was going fishing in Florida, not to attend a CME conference, but that's kind of the point. For me, the idea that an L&D would close its doors for a two-week vacation seems ludicrous. And think of the number of women he was inducing to deliver before he left. In his absence, some laboring women went to Rock Creek, but the fate of the women on Medicaid was unclear. Rumor has it that there was a smaller hospital two counties over that accepted them, but that L&D has since been closed after their only ob-gyn lost his medical license due to some unfortunate incidents involving excessive alcohol intake.

At least as incredible, it took Joyce to bring continuous fetal monitoring, the standard of obstetric care for almost two decades, to Stephens County only a few years ago. Her principal opposition was Dr. Jenkins himself, currently spending his days in sunny Florida. Is it any wonder the state's infant mortality is so high?

More directly impacting newborn loss, until Phyllis brought her expertise in neonatal practices, the hospital nursery simply put premature babies in a bassinet and waited for them to breathe . . . or not. This was earlier in the 1980s, not the 1960s when treatments were just beginning to be developed. Stephens Memorial's reputation as the hospital where people go to die was especially true for newborns whose lives hung in the balance, particularly those who came into the world before their time. Most people, Black and white, seemed to accept that one more dead Black baby was inconsequential and immutable. But not Dr. Fowler.

Now, Dr. Whitehead is called to intubate a newborn when necessary. Then she and the respiratory therapist take turns hand bagging the baby to maintain its oxygenation since the hospital has no neonatal ventilators. The intervention can last for hours while they arrange a transfer to a NICU at UNC or East Carolina or in a pinch, Richmond VA, almost a hundred miles away. Between the phone calls to arrange a transfer, Phyllis will do whatever is needed to stabilize the baby as best she can. I genuinely admire her fortitude, to endure hours of literally breathing for a baby, a dedication that is almost unimaginable. I guess she's kinda like Wonder Woman, saving a life each time she does. That picture is exactly why it's critical for us to transfer the fetus while it is still inside the mother. Imagine the chaotic disruption for moms and families to have their baby whisked away to some unfamiliar location. Despite our aggressive efforts to refer women with potential problems to other centers, we still get caught with a mom in unexpected preterm labor, and we can only hope we spring into action in time.

Chapter 9

LESS THAN IDEAL

GINNIE CALLS FROM L&D WHILE I'm seeing afternoon patients in the office. Rosa Durham is settling into early labor with her third baby. Her contractions are still so mild that she's hardly feeling them at three centimeters dilated. If a normal labor curve holds, I figure I can get through everyone waiting, and with any luck, make a quick dinner before her baby arrives. Well, eating my own dinner might be pushing it, but the kids should be able to eat.

Stopping by L&D on the way home, Rosa is now four centimeters dilated by my exam, a little behind the norm. When I can, I like to do my own assessment and review the chart. Ginnie had the Pitocin drip already mixed and ready to go by the time I wrote the orders to try to get Rosa back on track. This baby, though, feels a lot bigger than her last. The head hasn't dropped into the pelvis yet either—another red flag.

I still get anxious being outside the hospital when a patient is in active labor, but by the time the kids are heading to bed, it's clear that Rosa's labor isn't proceeding as it should. After some hours of fretful sleep where Aaron woke with each page, I head to the hospital in the early morning hours. At least one of us should get some rest. By seven a.m., Rosa's exhausted from pushing, and the baby's head still hasn't come down. I should have called it earlier because, at seven thirty, we're heading into the witching hour, when the first OR cases will start and the battle to get into the OR begins.

And there's the rub. I'll have to play "let's make a deal." All the ORs are likely booked, so it's my job to sweet talk a surgeon into letting Rosa's C-section go before his hernia repair. The surgeon has no obligation to comply, his primary concern being *his* schedule. I've found the best strategy is to make it sound urgent, but somehow, the fate of two patients, a mother and child, doesn't hold much weight. Let the games begin. Luckily, one OR case was delayed because the patient snuck in some breakfast, so Rosa is able to greet her new daughter by noon. Mother and baby are doing well.

Rosa Durham's case points to one of the larger issues at Stephens Memorial, far more important than how soon postpartum patients will be discharged. "Let's make a deal" surgical scheduling is a blatant violation of the standards of obstetric care set by The American College of Obstetricians and Gynecologists (ACOG). These impotent standards have no enforcement power beyond the fear of competition with nearby institutions and, of course, malpractice litigation. The reason is simple. In this hospital, in comparison to surgery, the ob-gyn department generates less income, so the surgeons can write their own ticket. Once again, it's the money, stupid.

In this case, the violation is the decision-to-incision interval, a recommended maximum of thirty minutes between the decision to perform a cesarean and the surgical incision. In Philly, we had two dedicated ORs on L&D and twenty-four-hour anesthesia, which allowed us to perform a stat C-section in five minutes. That's half the ten-minute window of anoxia—absence of oxygen in the blood—that causes neonatal brain damage or death. In an adult, the interval is three to four minutes, a testament to the protective low-oxygen intrauterine environment in which a fetus exists.

The decision-to-incision interval is less important when the surgery ends a prolonged labor like Rosa's. In her case, it was about six hours—far too long—but both the mother and baby were stable without any indication of difficulty. Rosa might argue that she objected to the unnecessarily long period of hurting she had to endure. But there are occasions where elapsing time in urgent and sometimes emergent conditions can mean neonatal or maternal damage or death.

Unfortunately, after-hours OR protocols are no better than daytime. Since the OR staff scatters to their homes after four p.m., we have to wait for them to return to the hospital. They're particularly prickly about cesareans for "fetal distress," which they think is an exaggeration because the baby's always fine. I'm quick to point out that that's the point. We're trying to intervene before any damage can occur. Fetal monitoring serves as an early warning system. If the baby has low Apgars, then we waited too long. Unfortunately, any neurologic damage may not become apparent until eighteen months or even later at school age, long after the OR staff has forgotten all about it.

Over time, the OR staff has gotten the idea that "fetal distress" is always a false alarm, so they finish their barbecues or watching the game before they leave home, which is for some, an hour away. It should also be noted that they don't forgo the usual liquid refreshments when on call.

Wouldn't it be great to just call overhead and have the nurses spring into action, prep the patient, and set up the OR like we did in Philly? To get a little closer to that goal, I've begun calling in the after-hours OR staff on standby in anticipation of a possible C-section. Like for a singleton breech with the potential for what's called an "after-coming head" where the baby's body, smaller and less firm than the head, delivers first and the cervix, not yet dilated enough to allow the head to pass through, traps the head, preventing complete delivery. Death can occur within minutes. Similarly, I plan for an early call for twins where the second twin can present as a breech, or the umbilical cord can prolapse in front of the baby's head. In all of these situations, failure to deliver the baby within a ten minute window would result in neonatal death, an impossible timetable to meet when the average cesarean decision-to-delivery interval here is ninety minutes.

Obviously, my little work-around doesn't approximate our situation at McCune where we had everything set up while we had the mother pushing in the OR, in which the bed converted to a table in a matter of moments. Here, maternal pushing in the operating room is forbidden. The mother-to-be is only allowed to push in the delivery room and then be sluggishly moved downstairs in our pokey elevator. Fetal monitoring has to be suspended completely because the monitors are absolutely forbidden in the OR. Apparently, nursing seems convinced that the operating room will be contaminated from germs from the delivery room. Somehow, they envision the OR as a sterile space despite the other nonsterile equipment, like the anesthesia machine and the Ohio bed for the newborn, already there.

Admittedly, I'm being passive-aggressive with the OR staff, but they're powerless to refuse. Instead they make their journeys into the hospital in slow motion or fling arrows behind my back in whispers around the locker room. Hooray, I've scaled another molehill, although these occasions will be rare because the diagnoses are uncommon. I'll have to resign myself to the fact that there's nothing I can do to dent the hospital's overall decision-to-incision time.

Sometimes when I'm tired from a stint on L&D, "Nobody Knows the Trouble I've Seen," one of my grandmother's favorites, pops into my head. It's an odd thought for a nonbeliever like me, but there's something about the raw emotion in the rhythm of the spiritual that captures the gloom I feel at my progress here. "Nobody knows the trouble I've seen" moans from the dreary walls themselves. I guess you can't turn history around on a dime.

For more than five years, Stephens Memorial has had no anesthesiologist. The hospital has failed to fill this open sore for so long that the ache among the surgical staff has quieted to a dull throb. For me, the situation is unimaginable and untenable. How is it possible, on the brink of 1990, for any hospital in the

United States to perform major surgical procedures without an anesthesiologist? My naivete has slapped me in the face again.

The hospital's solution is three certified registered nurse anesthetists (CRNAs) who require supervision by a physician. At Stephens, that becomes the surgeon of record. Blindsided by a situation that Dr. Edwards had failed to mention, I furiously refused to sign the operative records, as if that's any real protection from the insanity of my predicament. General anesthesia is outside my area of expertise, so much so that I think this puts my medical license at risk. As an obstetrician-surgeon, I have responsibility not only for the mother but also the baby if it has a problem. Just me and the scrub nurse. The unscrubbed circulating nurse responsible for getting us stuff in the OR can only call for help. The whole situation is absurd. And unsafe.

Hopefully, an anesthesia complication is so rare that it's silly to even contemplate, although it's more likely here because of the universal use of general anesthesia for cesareans. But good medicine is more about being prepared for what could happen, no matter how infrequently, than what has happened.

I think about the time when as a senior resident, I found a private patient in cardiac arrest, unconscious on the floor of her labor room. We suspected amniotic fluid emboli. We immediately rolled her into our OR just feet away, doing chest compressions on the stretcher. We started the C-section without anesthesia because, being unconscious, she wouldn't feel it. It's not easy to make an abdominal incision with someone pumping on the patient's chest. We had probably twenty people in the room before her doctor even arrived mid-operation. At Stephens, she would have died before we could get her into the elevator. We probably could have saved the baby with an emergency C-section in the labor room without anesthesia. You just need a scalpel and scissors when a patient's unconscious. The outlook for the mother would have depended on how soon the code team arrived from the ER. We don't have enough personnel, let alone expertise, on L&D to do both maternal resuscitation and a cesarean at the same time.

The CRNA can't contribute another pair of hands in the OR when she's managing the patient's vitals. If I'm tending to the patient's respirations and heart rate in an emergency, who's going to be tending to the mom's surgical concerns? Who's going to remove the placenta or handle any excessive bleeding when the scrub nurse is the only other person scrubbed? Who's going to close the uterine incision, the major source of blood loss, which we suture as quickly as possible to minimize hemorrhage? If I've broken scrub, I'll have to leave the OR to rescrub and regown. How long would it take to get someone in to help—more nursing, another ob-gyn, another surgeon, the code team? Nothing in this hospital happens quickly. A panorama of nightmarish scenarios spring easily to mind.

People reacted to my initial sense of outrage like I'd gone off the deep end—an angry bag lady on 42nd Street who roars about the wrath of God at people passing by. My protests were dismissed as irrelevant. The hospital says that as a lynchpin in the county, it couldn't shut down surgery altogether. They insist that their record of complications or medical errors has been good, although I've found no evidence that they're collecting any data on either. I'm a lone wolf howling in the wind.

Despite my outbursts, my name remains on the operative record whether or not I sign off; the chart simply appears in my basket of unsigned orders in medical records for me to take care of later. So after some more reasoned thought, I've settled on a more strategic approach that more closely approximates ACOG national standards. The organization has long discouraged routine use of general anesthesia for cesareans. Instead, safer alternatives like spinals and epidurals are recommended except in emergencies that don't allow time for either to take effect.

At McCune, the specific differences between general and regional anesthesia had been drummed into us. We had to practically convene a conference to get permission to use general anesthesia for a cesarean. And yet at Stephens, they use general anesthesia because they have always used general anesthesia.

Alternatively, I now request spinal anesthesia for my cesareans. Their simplicity, lower labor intensity, and complication rate make them a plus for the CRNAs who are, after all, under my supervision. The CRNAs have been so receptive that I hear they're offering spinals to the other OBs, and even those guys are becoming more receptive. Word spreads quickly in our little fishbowl.

These changes are such small things, and yet they loom like Godzilla. I worry that I may have splashed onto the scene with too big a bang. I may have been too aggressive about knowing and meeting the standards of care, before the interval allotted for junior Black females to bide their time had expired. I do have a more reticent side, particularly in a group of strangers, where I try to get to know the lay of the land. "Know thy enemy," as they say, and, I'll admit, I haven't been diligent about that. But because my time here feels circumscribed by refusals to try anything different at any time, impatience is winning out over quiet observation.

I always try to lead with the facts, pure unadulterated facts, in hopes that reason will carry the day. It turns out that man is not a rational thinker. We're still operating with caveman brains, honed to the "fight or flight" reaction. When a decision must be made, our neurons fire with patterns of automatic shortcuts for which facts are no match. It happens within a nanosecond without our ever knowing it. Our constellation of instinctual responses are culled from previous experiences, impressions, self-interests, visual images, and yes, stereotypes. I don't pretend to completely understand the whole process but I've read that waiting before you respond allows you to think more logically. While I have a lifetime to learn, I need the persuasive power now.

In the case of the CRNAs, I think they were surprised that someone valued their predicament rather than simply ordered them to comply. While it hasn't been all smooth sailing, I suspect our common gender, or perhaps the way we're treated because of it, has played a role in their easy acceptance. Of course, there's that medical imperative that makes me the captain in any of my surgeries. But people can greet an order with hostility or more pleasantly, and I've successfully hit the sweet spot.

This isn't to say that my frustration doesn't ever bubble over into rage that scatter-shots all over Phyllis, Joyce, and Aaron, out of sight of the problem makers. I have no respect for those buffoons whose medical incompetence disgusts me. Those sentiments make it more difficult for me to schmooze them into letting my urgent C-sections into the OR schedule. At least they can't see the expression on my face behind the docile phone voice I use to make my requests. Talk about eye rolling.

The impulse to leisurely hang out and small talk with most of these guys never crops up. And on their part, not one of those men has moved beyond a cursory acknowledgement to a perfunctory "Where you from?" that passes for introductory chitchat. Originally, I had hoped to find some common ground with the two other ob-gyns in town. Dr. Goodman's chubbiness camouflages his height, kind of like a football lineman whose muscles have turned to fat. He's the epitome of a fast-talking Sportin' Life, without the music of Gershwin. His ticket out of Antioch Associates cost a rumored $300,000, the price to terminate his NHSC obligation. On top of that, the cost of starting up a new solo practice must have created a mountain of debt. Maybe that's why money seems so important to him.

A Nigerian whose name is difficult to spell and pronounce, Dr. Nwachukwu is the other member of our department. His espresso coloring hints at his roots before his British accented verbiage exudes his pompous African male chauvinism. He firmly believes that his way is the only way. Unfortunately, he's also stupid, which means he's seldom right. I genuinely fear for the women he takes care of.

Their consistent irritation over my comments in our departmental case review meetings has trampled any hope for more congenial interactions. My intrusions automatically make every meeting last longer, an unsettling affront to their little boys' club. My arguments for long-held clinical standards are my attempt to transform a clipped rubber stamping session into a collegial forum. My words are gnats dodging swats of interruptions mid-comment and swipes of buddy talk between the two, both meant to blot out my voice.

But I have to stand up for my values, not cater to their egos, a prospect made easier by my new role in charge of peer review. Neither of them wanted to take the time, but from where I sit, I've got plenty of it. Thank goodness for the hospital's risk manager whose transcriptions put the proceedings into a confidential record. We've switched to documenting each individual opinion, rather than taking a vote that was usually two "appropriate action," one not—the other two Obs on one side and me on the other.

Our constant jousting is infertile ground for friendly relationships outside the hospital, even though Goodman lives not far from me. Neither of them is the kind of people I have any desire to socialize with. And Aaron wouldn't give them the time of day. Sometimes I fantasize about a dinner function dissolving into a food fight over a medical debate where no one is willing to concede. Our families readily join in the hostilities, flinging mashed potatoes and gravy across the room. It's worth a chuckle at low points. If only I could find the generosity of spirit to forgive and forget.

Chapter 10

HEADING FOR A CRASH

THE WOMEN OF STEPHENS COUNTY deserve the same opportunity as other women in the country to experience the kinder, gentler approach to childbirth embodied in epidural anesthesia. I brought impressive credentials with me, determined to expand labor pain relief beyond a meagerly stocked cabinet of narcotics and prayer to the Cadillac of anesthetics.

Medications in labor are generally restricted by concerns over placental passage to the fetus. Unfortunately, we have only one agent, Stadol, a combination of a narcotic and an anti-narcotic. The drug induces a foggy haze that at best makes the woman care less about the pain without actually dulling it. Because the drug acts as an antidote to other narcotics, once it's given, it's Stadol or nothing.

Mysteriously, my application for epidural privileges at Stephens has languished for over a year. Occupied with various other skirmishes, I hadn't given the delay much thought. However, the fact that my original privilege list was expanded to include circumcisions within days of the request should have alerted me that some other agenda was afoot. I was a babe in the woods back then, ignorant that there were such a thing as agendas, let alone what they might be. The intricacies of behind-the-scenes administrative maneuverings were as obscure to me as the mystery of life.

Right now, as I stand against a wall in the back of the room, I'm watching the gathering of the medical staff. A flurry of mumbled voices blend from separate conversations into a quiet buzz that fills the room. Several physicians, seated at two tables in front, face the gathering. Not every face belongs to a gray-haired white guy; two are East Asian, one an orthopedic surgeon, the other a general surgeon dressed in scrubs under a white coat. Their black hair and tawny brown faces stand in sharp contrast to the paler ones to their left, facing away from them. Their heads lean together as they laugh, their conversation in a foreign tongue divorced from the chumminess spreading through the good ole boys palling around nearby. A few men, gathering in the seats facing the tables, signal a greeting as they drop into the chairs. A couple saunter up to the front to shake hands and chat. On the meeting's agenda is approval of applications for hospital privileges, among them my own to perform epidural analgesia.

Not spying any friendly faces, I remain apart from the crowd. I don't want to prematurely celebrate the end of this ordeal, but I'm brimming with cautious optimism—not a phrase I use often. The audience begins a round of applause to welcome Dr. William Schneider, our new anesthesiologist whom I've not yet met. I hear he's come from a hospital in wintery climes, no doubt looking to coast into retirement on the substantial sums he can extract from a hospital desperate for his services.

Balding with a ring of buzz-cut speckled gray hair, Schneider is probably looking forward to boating with his wife on the lake where his pale crown will need a brimmed hat to protect him from the unrelenting North Carolina summer sun. Presumably, he's anticipating afternoons filled with tee times at the local country club. Surgical schedules generally run from seven a.m. to three p.m., and with experienced CRNAs handling the few after-hours emergencies, Schneider can count on plenty of daylight to play a round or two of golf, then meet the Mrs. for dinner at the club. Afterwards, he'll return home to sleep through his nights, uninterrupted by midnight forays to the hospital. I'll bet Schneider probably had night call rotation for emergencies where he came from. On second thought, I doubt that given the long interval without an anesthesiologist, Stephens even remembers what prevailing standards are supposed to be.

I don't have any details, but I hear the hospital did everything possible to loop him into a contract. After all, they've been looking for over six years now. While it's still early in the meeting, I can't imagine how the hospital can deny my impeccable qualifications. Trained by a nationally renowned anesthesiologist, I have extensive experience, thoroughly documented by a procedure list from residency and a letter from the McCune chair of OB anesthesia. That preparation was the result of extensive planning, beginning with my choice of residency program.

Back in 1984, thinking that epidural anesthesia might be a useful skill in a low-resourced hospital setting, McCune Smith moved up in my list of residency programs—that and the violence surrounding school bussing in Boston that scratched Harvard from the list altogether. I could never subject my children to that. At McCune, the ob-gyn residents provided the majority of labor epidurals for clinic patients by agreement with anesthesiology, while anesthesia residents dedicated their time to private laboring patients and all operative deliveries.

We would insert the epidural catheter, give the initial dose, and periodically redose as needed. Nursing would do the monitoring between doses, and the anesthesia residents would take over when we moved to a delivery room. Our arrangement allowed ob-gyn residents to meet our Accreditation Council for Graduate Medical Education residency requirement to learn anesthesia techniques. The ACGME lays out the curriculum, standards, and practices for postgraduate medical education for the US across every medical specialty. Its goal is to standardize training, specific to each subspecialty's needs, across all training sites regardless of location or type of institution.

To gild the lily, I took an additional elective rotation where I expanded my toolkit to rapid spinals used for cesareans as well as treatment of epidural complications. I even practiced adult intubations. If I hadn't wanted to establish clear boundaries, I could have performed my own spinals for cesareans instead of the CRNAs. Really, any anesthesiologist-less hospital like Stephens should have been begging for my skills.

◇◆◇◆◇◆◇◆◇◆◇◆◇

𝕴'm becoming increasingly anxious as the pace of the meeting grinds on, caution overtaking my flagging optimism. Schneider stands to announce "privileges for labor epidural anesthesia . . ."

Has my dream come true? My heart skips . . . Wait a minute. Why him?

". . . will be granted to Dr. Laura Hampton under the following conditions: One, that I monitor her first twenty procedures in my role as anesthesia department head. Two, once granted privileges, Dr. Hampton will become personally responsible for the cardiac resuscitation of any of her patients who experience cardiopulmonary complications."

With this *pièce de résistance*, he winks at me, a snicker on his lips. He wants me to know that he's in the driver's seat and I'm handcuffed in the back of a paddy wagon. His words slice through my throat like a scalpel, sending metaphorical blood gurgling into my lungs from multiple cuts. I'm approaching death.

My mind is spinning. I grab my throat in my confusion. These conditions are completely bogus. Life threatening respiratory complications from epidurals are extremely rare; I have never seen one in the hundreds of epidurals I've been involved with. In Philly, we had a designated code team scrambled from the medicine department. At Stephens, the code team is headed by an ER doctor. Why should my patients be excluded from the normal protocols? I don't think that's even legal.

Smoke is beginning to billow from my ears. I don't know if I've said what I'm thinking out loud. I have to get out of the room. Grateful that I've taken a seat in an unoccupied back row, I steel myself to stand and quietly step out, slowly and carefully, my face chiseled in stone. I close the door behind me and take the stairs two at a time up to the L&D call room where I can be alone. I splash some cold water over my face and gaze in the mirror over the sink as I dry.

I'm surprised the mirror isn't fogged by steam rising from my forehead, and yet, there's no fury that can erase my defeat. I get it now. Obviously, the delay in approving my privileges was connected to the negotiations with Schneider. My patients and I were sacrificed to the prerogatives of a shrewd negotiator who had decided to eliminate any competition that would force him to respond to the demands of obstetricians on staff. Epidurals are good enough for the women who go to Rock Creek's hospital, but not my moms. This self-interested self-promoter has tried to eliminate a potential interloper into his uninterrupted country club dinners and quiet nights. I have to concede it was a masterful stroke by a man who knows he has the hospital by the balls. It's anyone's guess what he's told the administration about epidural services. He's the king of the mountain who controls all roads to anesthesia now. No doubt, in an effort to appear gracious, he plans to keep me on an endless loop of inadequate reviews until I abandon my efforts altogether.

Many anesthesiologists would like to avoid labor epidurals, but their popularity among women in areas where hospitals compete makes them mandatory to attract patients. Since labor can last twenty, or even thirty hours—longer than almost every surgical procedure—it's a ball breaker. Charges for anesthesia during surgical procedures are done in fifteen-to-thirty-minute increments, similar to charges for operating room use. But Medicaid's flat fee reimbursement for labor epidurals, whether they last thirty hours or two, has meant that those patients in many settings are being left out. There's that cash register again; time is money.

One other big downside for epidurals: surgeries are scheduled; labor is not. I don't know if Schneider has come from a hospital with obstetric services, but here, with the CRNAs, he could preserve his tee times without disruption by having them take care of the whole ball of wax. The hospital might have to pay them more, but he could have negotiated that. If he had wanted, he could have devised a minimally invasive system. The OB who offers them at Rock Creek has established a competitive advantage across the region, even though they're only offered when he's on call one night out of three. That's a perfect example of a collaborative approach.

I'm the one willing to shoulder the extra burden of twenty-four-hour availability to remain in the hospital to maintain the epidural. I would feel obligated to stay in-house, at least in the early days. That would have meant additional nights away from my children.

And I would have been willing to take charge of educating the nursing staff, none of whom have experience with epidurals. The education around continuous fetal monitoring clearly demonstrates that nursing administration can't be trusted. The nurses will need to anticipate and react to the anesthetic's effects on blood pressure, fetal strips, and labor curves, none of which they've ever seen. All in all, it would be quite an undertaking, with no increase in my take-home pay. As a salaried employee, I'm paid the same no matter how many patients I see or babies I deliver or hours I work. Now that I think about it, I probably should have been thinking about negotiating a salary increase.

Given all that, I still think it's worth the sacrifice. There's something magical about leveling the playing field, about declaring to my patients that they matter as much as the white women in town.

Dammit! Dammit all to hell!

I would rather slit my own throat than agree to Schneider's conditions. I can see it now: Schneider will cherry pick the times he'll be available to supervise, obviously not at night, and drag out the period of time it will take to accumulate the twenty procedures. Then he'll nitpick my technique where it varies from his, as if it can only be done his way. And before you know it, I've moved on.

All the winning cards are in his hand. Since there are only two people with the expertise to judge, he and I, it's my word against the word of a desperately desired chairman of a department of one. It's hardly worth subjecting myself to endless rounds of not-good-enoughs when his objective is to shut down the possibility of epidurals altogether.

This is a power grab by a prick who's worried about controlling his fiefdom, not time or inconvenience or patient welfare at all. I'm as qualified as the ob-gyn in Rock Creek; I'm an independent contractor like any other physician at this hospital. My services don't require his involvement in any way. I deserve the opportunity to ply my trade. This is a classic case of restraint of trade.

I'm bubbling like a volcano ready to erupt. I want to scream. To cry. It hurts. F@*k them! If they don't want my services, I'm not going to cram them down their throats. I'm numb. I don't want to face another human being. "Just a closer walk with thee, precious savior let me be," rings in my ears. The spiritual, played at my grandmother's funeral, reprises a traumatic event when I was twelve. A lump forms in my throat. Man, I must be losing my mind, a heretic like me wallowing in songs about God.

Somehow, I manage to muddle through office hours, but each belly check has reignited my fury until I'm apoplectically irate again. I don't know why I expected this decision would be different from what is becoming the usual playbook. There's something about asserting my competence that seems to rankle these boys, particularly galling because it's an uppity dark face who's supposed to be grateful that they allow her to play in their sandbox. I'm good at what I do, and there's no reason why I should have to hide that in deference to the racist and sexist misconceptions that permeate this place. It's just exhausting.

As I approach Schneider's office, now calm and controlled, I take a few deep breaths to center my most rational, reasoning self. It took a couple of nights to regain my composure, commit to humbling myself, and marshal my arguments to convince the anesthesiologist to buy into bringing epidurals to our L&D—maybe some collaborative effort where I manage the annoying tasks for my patients. In my hand I held my credentials and protocols; facts and figures about reimbursement were on the tip of my tongue.

"Hello, Dr. Schneider. I wanted to talk about the protocols for my epidural privileging." I'm wearing my friendliest smile along with a blue skirt and matching jacket, not my usual slacks. I want him to think that I'm eager for his tutelage.

"Come in." He laughs as he offers his hand. "I have no idea how an ob-gyn would qualify to give anesthesia."

"I mean, we are surgeons, and we stick long needles in lots of other things. And, we've been tasked with backing up the CRNAs in surgeries for years." I chuckle, trying to keep it light. "Didn't you see my credentials on my documentation? I've done at least two hundred labor epidurals and assisted with many others." I smile as I cross my legs. "Did your hospital have an L&D?"

"Oh, I didn't look at your paperwork. And no, we were a med-surgery facility with an ER, of course."

"How did you come to your decision then? Maybe you'd be interested in some of this material I brought from McCune Hospital in Philadelphia; they're protocols and procedures from the obstetrics anesthesia division."

"Oh, observation is standard practice when new people start." Schneider doesn't lift a finger to take the folder I advance toward him. "No need for documents. I have to say that I'm not much interested in developing something new this late in my career."

"I don't understand. Then how will I be able to start?"

He let out a long pitchy laugh, almost obscene. "I don't . . . *yuk, yuk, yuk, snort* . . . see how you can . . . *yuk, yuk, snort*. If I can't certify your readiness . . . *yuk, yuk*."

"And you can't because I've performed more labor epidurals than you," I interject in a matter-of-fact kind of way, accompanied by a chuckle. It was probably a mistake, but I just couldn't help myself.

"Now you're getting it. It's more work than I'm prepared to do."

I persist in this thrust and parry contest. "Certainly, it's not new to you, just a variant on surgical epidurals. You know the techniques. All you need is the dosing regimens for agents you've probably used in other contexts. I don't think the demand will be large, especially at the beginning. Antioch Associates isn't doing that many deliveries. And the service can be run almost completely by the CRNAs. I'm sure you've found that the CRNAs are very capable."

"They are. But how many ways do I have to tell you that the hospital has done fine without epidurals, and it will continue to, at least while I'm here. I'm making a business decision that the service would be more trouble than the reimbursement it would generate."

"I have some information on reimbursement right here. We'd probably be able to attract women with insurance, a plus for both the hospital and you."

"No need."

"So you refuse to consider any possibility for a labor epidural service?" I shoot back, but not hotly or hostilely.

Schneider leans forward, looking straight in my eyes. "Not me, not the CRNAs, not you. I'm not going to let you generate interest in something that I have no intention of providing."

"You understand that's restraint of trade?" I respond, holding my ground.

"Not from where I sit. You can't access the medications from the pharmacy without my sign-off, and I can make an argument that those medications should only be used by the anesthesia department. But you'll have to make that case in court. I don't take kindly to a threat to my livelihood!"

"How am I threatening your livelihood?" I do raise my voice near the end, but manage to reel it back in. "I have no interest in general anesthesia or even spinals for cesareans. Would you consider epidurals for cesareans, with their advantages over spinals, especially in post-op pain relief? The CRNAs could do those." I'm clutching at straws, hoping a foothold might stimulate some interest among the other ob-gyns to expand.

"Spinals and generals seem sufficient for now." Schneider is savoring the prospect that he's boxed me out.

"It's unfortunate the hospital found you," I say with a straight face as I stand. "Someone who's more interested in his wallet than the patients he's supposed to care for. It's not a surprise. There are more people like you in medicine than those of us who put our patients first." I walk out the office door before he can open his mouth.

The prick had admitted to the whole gambit, without shame. My parting shot meant nothing to him. But it felt good to say what I thought to his face. And without overt malice—well, maybe a little. The threat of legal action was more spiteful than real. A suit for restraint of trade would be lengthy and costly without a positive result. I'll be long gone before it would ever appear on a court docket.

My vision for the centerpiece of Laura Hampton's contribution to the women of Stephens County had shattered into a thousand shards. I want to find solace in avoiding the additional workload and constraints on my private life, but being drawn and quartered, with muscles and organs stretched and distorted until they burst, could not have felt worse. My lips will never reveal how deeply wounded I feel to another soul.

I'm not sure that any amount of brownnosing can overcome an inherent unwillingness to accept a person as an equal colleague. They can't hear people they don't see. The chasm between the races and the gulch between the genders will remain an ever-present multiplier, barring access to the rooms where tacit agreement means that only a few words need to be said out loud to make things happen. I imagine them as wood paneled and cigar smoke filled, but since I've never been in one, I have no idea. Dammit it all to hell!

On the other hand, my goose is cooked if I concede that the way forward has been barred. While it's hard for old dogs to learn new tricks, it's not impossible. A less cynical individual than I would try to establish more friendly relationships with colleagues, if only because stereotypes can be chipped away when two individuals get to know each other as just that. Joyce is a perfect example. She started with hate mail and death threats because she, a single white woman, dared to go into practice with a family practitioner who was a Black man. That ticked all kinds of white supremacy boxes. She stuck it out, though, to become someone admired by the whole community, not just the hospital staff. Phyllis seems fairly well-adjusted, and it's not just because she's the only physician who can do what she does. I guess I'm not as forgiving as they are, and I'm struggling to maintain any desire to bridge the gap with anyone on the other side.

Have I burned some bridges with Schneider? Probably, and he seems to be the spiteful type. He can create delays around OR scheduling, for instance, but I don't anticipate much else, given that our department is pretty self-contained. And he doesn't need to; he's clearly the victor.

Once again, I made a rookie mistake, not knowing that something routine in my past required a lot more thought than I knew to launch it. The delay in privileges was a flashing yellow light I couldn't see. I got a little too wrapped up in being the heroine who would save our women from the horrors of labor, like Phyllis saves their newborns. I don't even know how many women would have used an epidural. Our mothers are pretty cautious, especially about having long needles stuck in their backs. They're not keen on trying the latest thing.

No one ever died from pain.

Chapter 11

ALRIGHT BY ME

I CAN'T COMPLAIN ABOUT WEAVERS CROSSING. I'm here because I'm committed to going anywhere Laura chooses, and I'm as good as my word. There's not much to do here, but I don't mind. I'm happy spending time with the family, and I'm focused on my work.

Originally, my job was supposed to be servicing the union local in town. I have to thank their leadership for thinking that I was a spy from international headquarters in New York trying to control them. So New York shifted me to working for the international. So here I am, organizing new shops like I loved doing in Nashville. I mean, I spent four years driving a total of four hours a day from Jersey and back to do humdrum work for a local in New York City. I learned a lot, but it wasn't what I wanted to do. I was making good on a pledge I made a long time ago to do whatever it takes to make Laura happy. I'm one of the good guys.

I love my work. It's who I'm meant to be. I would probably do it for free if I didn't have a family to support. I hate that the travel keeps me away from the kids. I hate that it's harder to take care of chores and manage the household. I miss my wife. I'm always rushing home to help out. That means I drive a lot of miles. But it's all worth it. I get to change people's lives if they let me. Not just their jobs, but their lives. And that means a lot. I love the people I work with. I'm part of a movement that can transform the country, not just the workplace.

I haven't told Laura this, but I'm building a better future in the organization for myself too. By working in the trenches and expanding the membership, I'm creating a power base within the union that will protect me from being screwed like I was over the Pittsburgh job. I don't like to go into too much detail with her or she'll start trying to give advice about things she doesn't understand. Somehow, she's turned the fact that I'm happy into some kind of betrayal. She's forgotten that I'm only here because she chose it. I'm one of the good guys.

Cornell is the best thing that ever happened to me. My mother Miriam applied for me because she wanted a lawyer in the family, the kind of job with the right amount of prestige and income. The cheap way to get there was a Regents scholarship at a state school. I wanted to stay on Long Island, live at home, and keep working to help out my family. Miriam almost always gets what she wants.

Politics on campus changed everything. I started out a gung-ho frat boy and ended up a socialist anti-war activist. A lot of my new friends were children of former socialists and communists in the '50s. I didn't get it then, but now I know what it's like to be a revolutionary when the rest of the country likes the way things are. We were a core group in the campus chapter of SDS (Students for a Democratic Society). They turned me on to reading, something I didn't do in high school. I never met a *Cliff Notes* I didn't use. I made good grades, good enough to get into Cornell, but I didn't learn very much that I ever had to think about. I was too busy having a good time, running track, and working.

We were debating issues in economics and questioning political systems, and I didn't know anything about anything. I wanted to become a leader in the debates about solving the problems in the world. So I had a lot of catching up to do. For the first time in my life, I couldn't read enough.

Cornell is also where I met Laura. She was friends with another Black girl named Laura who had just been dumped by my roommate. One night, a group of us, stoned, ended up at my apartment for our weekly *Star Trek* party. We couldn't keep our hands off each other.

It seems crazy that we would get together. She was a big Black Power advocate with an outrageous Afro. I fell hard for her, not like any girl I met before. I loved the feel of her body. I loved kissing her; she's a great kisser. It was amazing to make love to her. I walked around in a cloud. I don't know how it happened, but I'm forever grateful that she loved me back.

The assassination of Martin Luther King Jr. changed everything. Laura went underground with the Afro-American Society (AAS). I was frantic. She didn't come home, and I couldn't find her.

I don't know a lot about what they did, just that they were revolutionary acts. Look, I get it. They were angry. You talk about a police state that's out to get Black people. But MLK's assassination was there for everyone to see on the TV. Shot dead while standing on a balcony! Not that any of the group supported King's politics. Nobody in the AAS believed nonviolence was the answer. They took their rage against society into the streets. They wanted to strike back at a country that cut down Black people like weeds. They were fed up with racism and discrimination. King wasn't the first Black leader to be murdered; he was the latest in a long line—Medgar Evers and Malcolm X, for two—that only kept growing. But this time, a whole lot of white people saw it too.

I supported the group's action, but I was scared out of my mind that she'd get hurt. I called everybody I could think of, but I got warned off. "Don't call her; she'll let you know if she wants to get in touch," they told me. I was terrified that she would stop loving me. I can't change my skin color.

After that, the campus changed completely. Black students on campus were no longer friendly. None of them would talk to Laura, at least not in public. A couple of women like the other Laura would in private, but her other close friends, the ones who had been inseparable a week before, turned their backs. "We can't afford to have white friends anymore," the other Laura told her. Interracial dating became a crime.

I'm so, so thankful that Laura chose me. She made me whole. I still think she's beautiful. She's my arm candy—not the bony kid I first met, but still thin. We're almost forty, but she looks young enough to get carded in bars. I look a lot older. I've been going gray and losing my hair since high school. Now that I'm practically bald on top, it's become an asset. People trust that I know what I'm doing when I'm organizing. Managers know I'm no pushover.

But losing all of her Black friends tore Laura apart. I know it hurt her deeply. Because I torpedoed her social life, I feel like I'll owe her for the rest of my life. I vowed then that I would make it up to her. I would wrap my arms around her and take care of her. My friends would be her friends. I would do whatever it took to make her happy. And I will do almost anything to keep that promise. It's the two of us against the world. I'm one of the good guys.

Miriam was unhappy about Laura as soon as word hit the Long Island grapevine. In my family, nobody holds back. We're a typical extended Jewish family. Our feelings are as naked as butts in the shower. My aunts, uncles, and cousins would gather every weekend to take potshots at each other. It was open season on my dad, Isaac, with Miriam leading the pack. For as long as he lived, Daddy took shit from the whole family. He made the mistake of going bankrupt and losing our house, so we had to move in with my grandparents. I confess the experience has left emotional scars. Not even a psychologist could help me with that.

Miriam tried to bribe me to dump Laura. The last thing was a new car. They couldn't afford it. I had to work through high school to buy the one I had. Only my grandfather could have paid for it. She tried to convince me that Laura's not being Jewish was the problem. She would say that Laura and I would have a tough life together. It could hurt my career prospects. What would happen with our children? On and on.

She'd never say she was racist, and deep down she isn't. Mostly, she worries about what other people think about her. Her neighbors are her moral compass. She can't be proud of her children unless the neighbors admire what they do. She's weak. She can't help it. She doesn't know any other way to act.

Laura made me happier than I've ever been, and my mother should have been happy for me. My family is important to me, but not more important than Laura. When Miriam played her trump card—"If you marry her, we're not coming to the wedding"—I drew a line in the sand. If she didn't come, I would never speak to her again. What else was I supposed to do? It wasn't an idle threat. I don't think she could stand the thought that she wouldn't be able to keep nagging her eldest son the same way she did her husband, so she gave in. I'm one of the good guys.

I never actually asked Laura to marry me. We didn't believe in engagements and rings. We were just trying to protect our living arrangements against a fight with her parents. We'd been living together for over two years without her parents knowing. Laura said they would hit the roof if we wanted to continue after she graduated. Now that I know them, she was right. They're pretty conservative and don't believe in premarital sex. She would have had to cut them off. I was always planning to get married someday, and I love kids. I wanted to have kids with Laura. It just seemed natural. She is and will always be the one for me. We stand together, the two of us against the outside world. I'm a pretty romantic guy.

The draft was hanging over my head after I graduated. There was no way I was going to fight in a racist capitalist war against a Vietnamese nationalist movement for independence begun by Ho Chi Minh at the turn of the century. I wasn't going to Canada like some other guys I knew. I wasn't about to go to jail either. But once I drew a high lottery number, I didn't have to worry anymore. I got a master's in education and a job. By the time of the wedding, I had scooped up a rent-controlled apartment in Washington Heights. I got the place through dogged persistence, one of my best qualities. I'm very organized and thorough too. I don't quit 'til I get it done.

There's one thing I haven't mentioned. I'm the guy who gets angry easily and blows up, any time, any place—at work, at home, at play. I get ugly and loud. I don't want to; I just lose control. But when it's over, it's over. I'm always sorry, and I try to make up for it afterwards. A lot of the time, I'm frustrated about stuff that has nothing to do with the person in front of me. Laura's always accepted that about me, even though she's not happy about it. She hoped therapy would help. It didn't. It's just my nature. But it doesn't keep me from being one of the good guys.

After we married, we were banned from all family gatherings by order of my grandfather. Our first invitation came after Daddy dropped dead in a bowling alley. I swear. He bowled a strike, jumped in the air to celebrate, and fell down dead of a massive heart attack. *Poof*, gone.

Daddy's death hit me hard. I cried, sometimes just out of the blue. Until I got angry. My father had been stolen from me when he was only forty-two. I still mourn the last two years I lost with him. He will never meet my children. They won't ever know him. I hated the whole family. I'm convinced to this day that the unrelenting barrage of insults from Miriam and the rest of them broke his heart long before that heart attack. Daddy took it all, laughed it off, and just swallowed it. Never once did he fight back. I loved him, but I couldn't respect him. That was the hardest part. You're supposed to have a father who can teach you how to be a man. Mine was the perfect example of what not to be. He was a nice guy who let people walk all over him. I fight every day not to be that guy, the failure that my father was.

The family invited me and Laura to sit shiva, a Jewish funeral ritual, with them. I'm grateful that I didn't have to choose between delivering Daddy's eulogy and my wife. I know she would have understood if I had gone without her. She would probably have joked that she never wants to be anywhere people don't want her. But I'm not sure what that would have meant for the two of us. Our united front against the world would have cracked.

Nobody apologized. The family acted like none of that crap ever happened. It was just another family gathering—crazy, in a family that throws their emotions around like basketballs at a hoop. I have to give credit to my grandfather especially and Miriam for being cordial then and since. Now she brags about my kids, to strangers even.

Maybe I let them off too easy, but the past is the past. They are my elders, and I was raised to respect my elders. I don't have to like them. But family is family. And family is important. You don't get to choose who they are.

I want to live my life differently from the rest of my relatives. But I will always regret the time I lost with Daddy, and I don't want that for my kids. I want them to get to know their cousins.

Besides, I want to show off their accomplishments and my own. I want Miriam to know that she was wrong about my career prospects and my life with Laura. I want her to be proud of what I do. So I'm obligated to participate.

Mostly, we interact at weddings and bar mitzvahs. We chitchat the way you do on special occasions. I let it go in one ear and out the other. I can only hear so much drivel about who did what and how much they spent on this or that. I try to switch the conversation to sports, whatever is in season, or I go play with the kids, just like Daddy used to.

Mostly Laura and I survive these ordeals through humor. We sit back and laugh at how ridiculous they are as we watch the competition between the various branches to outdo each other's shindigs. She makes the best sarcastic zingers. At the same time, Laura is always uncomfortable. Even though they've accepted her as part of the family, she thinks they're looking to catch her in a mistake. I can't convince her that they do that with everyone, including each other. Really, we're all pretty judgmental; it's just that our standards are different from theirs. Family gatherings present a lot of contradictions.

For me, those weekends are a lot like trying to walk through a field of landmines. Laura jokes that we were better off when they didn't invite us. There's a lot of truth in that. It's a good thing these parties have lots of liquor. But, inevitably, I have to ask Laura not to do something or other because she's making me anxious. She'll complain that I'm never on her side, that I never stand up for her. Then comes my inevitable explosion at her or the kids. Why can't she just blend in and do what they want? What I want?

Time with my family is always more unpleasant than fun. But you gotta do what you gotta do. I'm being a good guy here.

My family drama has made me an exceptional keeper of household finances. I was the kid sent to tell the bill collector knocking on the door that my mother wasn't home when she was. Who can blame me for being a compulsive saver? It's fun for me to strategize about our investments. Keeping a close eye on them is solid reinforcement that I'm making good decisions. Laura and I don't waste money on extras we don't need. We search for bargains. We don't replace things until they can't be fixed, no matter how old they are. Laura doesn't have to give any of it a second thought. I'm an outstanding money manager.

When the potential for revolutionary change evaporated as people came to believe the Great Society was the answer to the civil rights movement, and the anti-war movement dissolved into love-ins and communes as the Vietnam War ended, I mellowed into teaching at a junior high in Harlem. I loved my job. I was happy to help my students discover a different way to think about the world and themselves.

I was devoted to my students, like all my close friends, fellow teachers. Laura was included in everything we did. But when the New York City school system fell apart in the late '70s, so did I. I got laid off. My friends transferred or quit. A bunch of my closest friends left New York. My self-confidence took a big dive. I know I took it out on Laura, who only wanted to make me feel better. I'm the one who's supposed to make her feel good, not the other way around, so her efforts made me feel like I was a failure. I probably should have gone back to the psychologist, but I didn't think we could afford it. I desperately needed a way out.

So I found a job with a union. It was only a couple of weeks before they dropped the bombshell that the union headquarters was moving to Nashville. They never mentioned it when I was hired; I swear. But I was ready for a change. Without my friends, New York was a lot less fun. Laura, though, hit the ceiling. She said she'd leave me rather than move to the South. Of course she was overreacting, probably pregnancy hormones. We had just had Abbie.

I told her the region wasn't what she imagined, even though I didn't know that; I'd never been anywhere outside the Northeast. But I was confident that it couldn't be as terrible as she thought. Hell, it was 1980. Obviously, she came around when she understood that it would be a new start for the both of us. And we had a new baby. Seriously, where did she think she would go?

I was right. She decided on this medical career. Unfortunately, it's taken over her life, but I won't let it take over mine. I want to be clear. My mission is bigger than her or my family or even me.

I bend as much as I can to accommodate her, but she doesn't give me any credit for the sacrifices I've made for her. How many men would follow a wife around when she is always moving somewhere else? I concede that I got blindsided by the shit that went down with that job in Pittsburgh. Laura says I'm too trusting, and she could be right. She doesn't even know half of what happened, but I like to give people the benefit of the doubt. I believe you have to trust the people you work with. Losing that job meant that Laura couldn't take the fellowship that she'd worked so hard to set up. She got pretty depressed. I feel like I failed in my vow to keep her happy. Weavers Crossing is the best I could manage. It's a happy accident that has worked out so well for me. Laura seems to resent that, as if it was intentional, when I'm only here because this is where she chose to be. I'm one of the good guys.

𝕴 recognize that Laura's a big reason why I'm able to commit to my mission. She's my Coretta Scott King. She is a fantastic mother. I never worry about the kids. I'm showing my love and appreciation when I put this big effort into helping as much as I can. There are so many things that she doesn't have to do because I take care of them. I shop for groceries. I handle the chores around the house even when I'm not always around. I even wash the dishes. I'm involved in my kids' lives. I take care of the kids when she isn't here. I'm a great father.

At this late date, I shouldn't have to tell her all the time how I feel. She should know that from all the things I do. I give her little gifts for no reason: a box of her favorite chocolates, a nice bottle of wine, little trinkets. She should see my love in the effort I put into picking the perfect gift for every occasion. Even when she tells me not to do something for her, I go ahead and do it anyway. I'm one of the good guys.

Chapter 12

EASY WORK, EASY PLAY

A S TEMPERATURES BEGIN TO RISE in advance of another hot, sticky summer, I think the kids have settled in pretty well with this third move. I wonder if they will tell people when they're grown that they're somehow scarred by moving around like Army brats. And we've got a couple more moves to go.

I'm less settled than them, feeling a little envious of the fuller lives that my two best friends are leading. Elise, in Palm Beach, is dating in search of a new husband, and Adrienne is climbing the administrative ladder she's destined to top in California. Here I've shown my new kitchen with its backsplash of multicolored patterned tiles to no one. It's a big space with a central island flooded with sunlight from the French doors that no one except the family has enjoyed. The gray floor tiles, interrupted by black and white ones, blend the breakfast nook into a space meant for gathering people to entertain, not only for our kids.

You take for granted that friendships will evolve from the new people at work or your children's schools or at play. Weavers Crossing, though, has presented the challenge of very distinctly defined social circles based on color and class. The small East Asian community is folded in on itself, leaving two spheres— Black and white. I see the two groups intermingle within the Antioch group, but whether those friendships extend beyond the workplace I can't say. Outside of the staff, the only other people I meet are my patients from whom I feel it's important to maintain a professional distance; my personal life is mine to keep.

I do know that the two groups don't see each other in church on Sunday. Here, the churches seem to be the queens in the town's various social hives. Friendships radiate around close-knit family units that congregate within their chosen house of worship. The town has few other gathering places, outside maybe school sports, which are also separated by skin color. There's very little to do beyond visiting with other people.

Church, for me, is the one place that I cannot go. Unlike Joyce Fowler, there will be no fish fries or Sunday sermons or choirs for me. Karl Marx captured exactly what I was thinking when I read it: Religion is "the opiate of the masses." It's a drug that suppresses the fire to fight for change in the here and now for a promise of a better life in the hereafter. The audacity of Christians to assert that their mythology, unlike the Egyptians, Vikings, Greeks, Romans, and Jews before them, contains the one and only truth. The whole lot were created to quell fear of the unknowable; to bake the questions *Where did we come from?* and *Where are we going?* into an easily digestible pie.

Then there's the con that comes with it. Not far from our New York apartment, Reverend Ike, a radio preacher, used his blessing plans to bilk quite a few of our neighbors, like thousands of others, out of a ton of money. He was straight up exchanging prayers for cash subscriptions. But he's not different from the traditional institutional churches, be it Catholic, Protestant, or Pentecostal. They all siphon financial resources from their members like blood sucked through vampire fangs, one drop at a time. They don't spread the love they profess for others within their own walls, let alone extend it to those not occupying their pews. Instead, they center their mission on collecting coins to build gaudy worship palaces, while the hungry outside the gates go without food. It's a familiar pattern of power and greed.

My journey began in adolescence as I observed the discordance between the words flowing from the pulpit and the behaviors around me in the pews. When I informed my mother that I would no longer be spending my Sundays in the church so central in their lives, an angry slap collided with my cheek—hard. That slap, the first and only one ever, in response to my logical arguments, rocked my world. Her action was so unimaginable, I thought she'd lost her mind. Maybe she thought it was the hand of God.

Her deed stung with betrayal, a pang so deep that an errant word or gesture occasionally triggers it even now. In that second, the idea that my parents blessed exploring every nook and cranny of knowledge withered and died. In its place was the reality that they meant only those paths that led back to their own repertory of approved ideas. My world shattered. Mom's golden girl became a miscreant.

They forced me to attend church each week, but I was never really there. I sang from the choir loft but then checked into a tangled web of my own thoughts when the music stopped. I bullshitted in adolescent angst in rooms with my friends. Through it all, I clung to the thought that college was taxiing on the runway to fly me to parts unknown. That slap threw my young mind into the tailspin from which I emerged valuing distance as my most important defense against parental interference. *Never live less than five hours away* became my motto, and double that was even better. They can't meddle in what they don't know, and my lips were sealed. Shattered trust leaves a permanent scar. It can be camouflaged, but more often it blossoms into a bulbous keloid.

Aaron is equally dismissive of religion but indifferent to Protestant and Catholic institutions. He often meets with organizing groups in church halls where he has no problem delivering a speech sandwiched in between an opening prayer and a farewell benediction. For him, pews are alternative seating, and the pulpit is simply a convenient dais. For me, facing an altar and massive cross has a physical effect; I'm drenched in a sense of my own hypocrisy, sweating like a chain gang on a humid summer afternoon.

Consequently, I'm effectively blocked from the organizing hub of community life unlike anywhere else I've been. In an urban area, there's a broad range of people with similar interests to meet in other activities. And yet, I haven't met a single Black professional outside the medical community since we arrived— not a lawyer or a businessman, except Jonathan Whitehead, Phyllis's husband. I'm not saying they aren't here, just that I don't know a way to meet them.

If patients are the only people I meet, then maybe it's not possible in a small town to maintain professional distance from them. Joyce, married to a local boy, wants to be another Marcus Welby, the friendly family doctor of TV fame, who is just another neighbor. No thanks; I prefer the anonymity of large urban spaces. Friendships may have to wait.

We used to play racquetball, tennis, and squash, but if they exist at the country club, they're off limits, my choice and theirs. Having shed my intense interest in photography during medical school, I now use automatic cameras to take snapshots of kids and family, not cityscapes and skylines. I've gotten out of the habit of doing anything outside complete immersion in medicine.

Our grueling pace during residency, about which I complained so bitterly, was a double-edged sword. On the one hand, the volume of cases provided the opportunity for exposure to the broadest panorama of disease. On the other, it sucked going through it, a blessing only in retrospect. Ironically, the slowing of that breakneck rhythm to the tempo of a ballad has exposed a gaping hole.

At McCune, we were constantly in motion tending to women across all the ob-gyn subspecialties for twenty-four hours a day. There were nights, like on any L&D, when laboring women were few but almost none when sleep wasn't interrupted by nurses' calls to report a fever or unexpected complaints. I was happy with three or four hours of sleep, but I would settle for at least a two-hour nap by four a.m.—what I call my Wall, when without sleep, my brain goes on vacation. My motto was, *Grab a nap in the slow moments just in case a stormy night lies ahead.*

Some nights, L&D triage looked like Grand Central Station. The steady stream of women most often complained of false labor or suspected rupture of membranes that proved to be a leaky bladder. Sometimes it was a first prenatal visit because, as one adolescent told me, she knew she wouldn't have to wait as long as she had to in the clinic. We got drug addicts with needle marks in the distended veins streaking across their breasts looking for a bed to spend the night and get breakfast before signing out against medical advice the next day to get their fix. As crack cocaine swept through the city during my internship, we got a big bump in the number of women in premature labor whom we tried desperately to stop, some more successfully than others.

Outside L&D, we were responsible for all in-house ob-gyn patients, private and clinic. They included antepartum, postpartum, gyn cancers on chemo, and postoperative gyn surgeries scattered across various wards. We drew blood and did cultures for fever workups to rule out sepsis as well as blood gases to assess oxygenation in patients with respiratory complaints. We were called to the ER for rape cases and consults on women with suspected STDs and early pregnancy losses. Even though we had three levels of residents in the hospital on any one night, it was still a lot of work.

The nurses controlled the rhythm of pages, generally handling minor complaints with standing written orders. Traditionally, they sent a barrage of pages to new interns at the start of their year to demonstrate a nurse's power over our sleep and that their fund of knowledge was nothing to be ignored by newly minted interns. Sometimes, they used night pages as payback for some dispute with a resident.

In the early morning at the end of call, we rounded on and discharged our service patients and tackled the circumcisions before our morning report at seven a.m., an educational session where we handed off overnight L&D patients to the day team. Afterwards, everyone fanned out to their day assignments in the OR or L&D or the clinic before leaving work around six p.m. In between, we were dictating operative reports and discharge summaries, signing verbal orders, completing various other pieces of paperwork, and maybe catching a meal or two.

Periodically, we were assigned to one-month rotations at associated community hospitals, where typically there was only one resident on night call for L&D and triage, but that could still be overwhelming at times. One memorable night, I was busy with five deliveries during a single hour when the nurses failed to call me for a sick patient with an abnormal fetal monitor strip whose baby ultimately died. There's nothing like watching the unsuccessful forty-minute resuscitation of a baby you've just delivered to sear a birth into your mind forever.

In Weavers Crossing, we have about twenty deliveries a month covered by two doctors, compared with over three hundred a month in Philly. Pregnant drug users are practically nonexistent, and premature labor cases are infrequent. There are many nights when we have no calls at all. Most of our surgeries are simple outpatient procedures that don't require hospitalization because our nonpregnant patients can't afford major surgery. Many mornings, I rise well rested and get my kids ready for school before I head into the hospital or office ten minutes away. Most afternoons, I can be home in time to make dinner. Sounds like an ideal job, but I'm in a place I don't want to be, not doing what I want to do.

My beautifully renovated home is quietly empty of adult companions engaged in conversation and the laughter of people just hanging out. I'm not lonely, exactly, because I don't mind spending time alone. I do wish Aaron were more open to socializing with couples like Kelly and Dave or Joyce and her husband. Just casual weekend stuff. Instead, he's usually recovering from yard work and talking on the phone with people from the union. I don't quite understand his hesitation, but I do sometimes wonder: What use is a husband if you have to do everything by yourself?

Still, the phone calls with my best friends from residency are great emotional support. If they can't visualize my predicaments, at least they're empathetic listeners like sisters usually are. We often wander into ob-gyn cases, theirs and mine, like we always have, breathing fresh air into this otherwise bleak landscape. Phyllis is probably my best friend in town, not solely because of Abbie and Geena's friendship but also the hours we've spent together responding to maternal and neonatal emergencies. We've commiserated and cried and advised and cheered each other. She, as the more even keeled, has hauled my spirits out of the cellar on numerous occasions. Nevertheless, even with her, I feel too vulnerable to start navigating the emotional watershed around the epidural debacle, fearful that she may think it was too presumptuous or egotistical or self-indulgent or something else she'd find less than admirable.

Sometimes I wonder if Aaron and I invested more time in building friendships, there wouldn't be so much pressure for the two of us to wholly meet each other's emotional needs. He doesn't seem to need much from me. I guess he gets what he needs from his work. If he's less needy than I, I must be the problem.

I've started calling my situation "semi-single parenting"—the effort to manage the kids, work, and do various projects on my own. Actually, we're more relaxed at home when Aaron's not around, relieved that there's no taskmaster ordering us to get something for him at the drop of a hat. We're thankful that there are no predictably unpredictable temper flares around the corner.

The other night when the phone rang during dinner, Aaron sent Abbie into the kitchen to get the phone with the extra-long extension cord on the receiver. The kids and I looked at one another as Aaron's voice boomed into the mouthpiece as if the caller was almost deaf.

"We're playing the Pikesville team on Thursday and—" Damian began.

"Quiet while I'm on the phone," Aaron rasped as he covered the mouthpiece.

And that was that. We all knew that an avalanche of "shop talk" would overwhelm the dinner table, blotting out our usual routine. We finished eating quickly and dribbled away from the table, Damian to play video games, Abbie and Kyle and I to play Candy Land. I don't think Aaron even noticed until he found himself at an empty table when the call ended. It's never clear to me why he isn't the one to leave the table; he's not eating, and we are. But then again, whatever he's doing is always more important than what anyone else is doing.

Beyond the lack of a broader social circle, I miss the medical collegiality around interesting cases and challenging diagnoses and new research findings. With little else to turn to, the workaholic in me compels me to fill my leisure time with something medical, a comfortable and familiar default. Even with all its ups and downs, medicine is my refuge.

Chapter 13

A RIDE IN THE COUNTRYSIDE

G ATHERING SLATE GRAY CLOUDS ARE threatening rain when I stop for the flashing red light. I linger to catch a glimpse of a camouflaged sun, vainly poking at crevices to break through. I'm heading out of town on a seldom used two-lane road that leads to our Hackenberry clinic thirty miles away. On that road, travel time depends on an occasional tractor inching along from one field to another or an eighteen-wheeler carrying a load of hogs struggling up an incline. I'm looking forward to the thrill of riding that double yellow line, searching beyond a curve for it to turn white and then shifting into gear to pass with a jolt in my pulse as I accelerate. I'll slide into the oncoming lane and then quickly back in front of the slower vehicle. Satisfied, I'll watch it recede in my rearview as the weight of my foot sets my speed to whatever I want it to be. Or maybe, when the cat-and-mouse game takes more concentration than I want to expend, I'll bide my time until the slow mover turns off or there's a long straightaway with unobstructed vision.

Sometimes I'll let the music streaming out of my speakers dictate the rhythm of the open road.

This is my first trip to Hackenberry where I'm going to fill in for one of the PAs. As the asphalt snakes past a few occupied houses, I have to keep checking the directions, written on a piece of paper unfolded on the passenger seat. Swaths of kudzu that overwhelm and devour abandoned shacks creep through doorways toward the pavement, an occasional stalk daring to breach the edge. In the quiet morning, the skies seem to be clearing.

A couple of little brown-skinned boys appear on the right side of the road. They play in the puddles around a pump in front of a row of wooden cabins as drops plop in the red clay. No indoor plumbing then. No electrical wires running from the road to the eaves. On a whim, I pull over to indulge my curiosity. I'd seen a news piece about a dubious honor Stephens County has earned, the 1989 title for the "county with the most nineteenth-century plumbing," even as we're approaching the end of the twentieth. I doubt that there's a county in the country that aspires to that crown, although there's no indication that they're ashamed of it. This group is one of the numerous old slave cabins scattered around the state. Over a century and a half old, the cabins' repatched wooden plank walls are still holding together.

The two boys look up momentarily, then jump into the puddle, splashing red mud up their shins. Behind them, the middle of worn wooden steps sag from the weight of a million footfalls. Stilts lift the floors above the ground, a shield against the moisture seeping up from the clay layers below. Do these floorboards hold the tears of mothers grieving the loss of children sold away? Did the joy for a child's birth bounce off the wooden planks? Do the walls hold the wails of children stripped away from their mothers? Are the rafters filled with the cries of wives whose husbands had been beaten or castrated, burned, and lynched? Did gospel rhythms reverberate from the door jambs?

The ghosts of generations past seem to rustle through the trees at the back of the bare ground. On the far end of the complex, an outhouse stands abuzz with flies in the heat. A long wooden table stands near a big stone grill on the opposite side of the lot. No doubt in the best of times, it's been the site of many a festive gathering, piled high with bowls of potato salad and slaw, roasted ears of corn, and plates of beans. Pies set at one end, burst with peaches or berries or sweet potatoes. My people are from Kentucky, but I wonder if some of my ancestors might have passed through this very area as cotton-growing expanded westward.

It occurs to me that the majority of the time these cabins have stood, their occupants wanted freedom from bondage and safety from violence from neighbors. Not until the year 2111 will the descendants of slaves have been free for as long as they were held enslaved. No one alive today will celebrate that milestone.

The rapid splatter of raindrops from a sudden cloudburst startles me out of my reverie. I pull back onto the roadway as the two little boys twirl with their arms extended to celebrate the cooling rain. A little further down the road, the downpour just as quickly vanishes, as if the heavens have dumped a bucket on us and moved on for a refill. The sun manages to peek out of the clouds by the time I pull into the far edge of the clinic's parking lot.

I grab my white coat from the back seat, unusual for me, but I'm not sure what's at this location. I need pockets to carry my driver's license, credit cards, and a few bills so I can leave my purse locked in the trunk. I'm not sure what I thought I would use them for. A quick look around reveals not a single other building in sight. If a potential purchase isn't in the clinic, there's no real point.

I keep going because the coat is not simply a substitute for my purse; it's useful to identify me at a glance as a provider in a clinic where I've not worked before. A wall of hot, moist air hits my face as I step out of my air-conditioned car. It's obvious that the rain hasn't dropped the temperature or humidity one bit. A rainbow emerges over distant clearing skies, an ephemeral announcement of possibility.

If I'd known that Phyllis would be here, I might have tried to carpool for a little girl talk to start the day. She greets me with a cup of coffee and a broad grin plastered on her face, the color of maple syrup. Unlike me, she always looks impeccably put together—perfect makeup and hair beautifully coiffed. I can only admire from afar. I'm the first to concede her look is nothing I can even aspire to.

Now that I think about it, it's dangerous for two doctors to depend on each other for transportation. Phyllis could easily be called to the hospital for some emergency, leaving me stranded. However, pairing pediatric and OB visits is a great idea. Moms tend to bring an infant for a checkup when they won't take the time to see a doctor for themselves. Mothers usually bring their children with them anyway, so we could kill two birds with one stone. This kind of scheduling might go a long way toward boosting the number of postpartum visits we do. I file the idea away for later consideration.

Eunice Jefferson flashes a big toothy smile, short one front tooth, deepening her chocolate dimples. She's pretty gregarious, and laughingly admits that she needs to shed some pounds. Still giggling, she volunteers that each of her three boys and two girls brought five more pounds, a massive increase on a five-foot-four frame. She had planned to have a postpartum tubal ligation after her daughter was born, but the baby had come early, before the Medicaid sterilization consent papers were valid, or what we call "mature," as if a sheet of paper ripens like a peach. Eunice was delivered for preeclampsia at UNC where they referred her back to us to schedule the surgery. Now we're racing to squeeze it in before her Medicaid coverage ends at six weeks postpartum.

Eunice met two of the Medicaid consent requirements. She's twenty-six, so older than the necessary twenty-one years, and she's completely on board with the procedure being permanent and irreversible. Her problem at UNC was the four-week waiting period. That four weeks turns out to be a major sticking point for many women who end up missing the window to obtain a tubal ligation, primarily for financial reasons.

The document, the consummate informed consent, sounds like uncharacteristically strong protection for poor women—a stark contrast to our dark history. The advent of written consent followed legal challenges to the politically popular policies of forced sterilizations done well into the 1960s, an outgrowth of the eugenics movement of the 1920s. State government programs performed involuntary sterilization on "undesirable women," a grab bag of the disabled, mentally handicapped, "hysterics," unwed, imprisoned, morally lax, poor, and of course "the Colored," usually without their knowledge. I had a white friend who had been a victim at fifteen when, as an unwed mother, she gave her baby up for adoption. She and her boyfriend only discovered the reality of her infertility after a doctor asked her about her scar. Ah, to be female and "immoral," "deficient," or young in the USA!

This war on women continued invisibly for almost five decades, primarily because the victims had no public voice.

But like most regulations, the consents can't get out of their own way. As part of a chain-link fence around tubal ligation, one of the most popular forms of contraception in the country, current policies leave many poor women having more children than they want and Medicaid paying for more prenatal care, births, and children than it otherwise needs to. This is yet another case of state officials spending our tax dollars to the detriment of poor women. The least they could do is allow individual exceptions.

The age limit of twenty-one may sound reasonable, but it's arbitrary. Countless times I've seen age work against a woman's contraceptive choices. In Philly, we petitioned Medicaid to make an exception for a nineteen-year-old having her fifth C-section. She had wanted a tubal during her third surgery, when it can be done in only a few minutes while we're holding the tubes in our hands. But she was only seventeen, and they refused. Before her fifth cesarean, where she faced serious maternal complications, it was denied again. Obviously, she hadn't hit upon an effective alternative, given the back-to-back pregnancies we were delivering. Somehow, though, it felt like a mother of four, even at nineteen, was mature enough to make a decision about her reproductive future.

And what is magical about a four-week decision time? For bureaucratic purposes, why not twenty-four hours or seven days? It seems like a woman can decide in a couple of hours. Why shouldn't we be able to ask a woman on the day of delivery whether she wants to have a tubal ligation and do it the next day? As a matter of fact, if she has private insurance, we do.

I've long been passionately opposed to the idea that physicians should be making contraceptive decisions for women who are best placed to know their own needs. They have to raise the kids— we don't. But I do what I was taught and tell women younger than twenty-one that we're protecting them from themselves, saving them from potential regret later in their long reproductive lives. This is another way of infantilizing women as inept decision makers. In any case, life doesn't come with a guarantee that the decisions we make today will be the right ones tomorrow. Who among us hasn't regretted some past choice?

Personally, I'm aggressive about getting tubal papers signed, counseling patients that if they're even considering a tubal, they should sign a consent just to create the opportunity. They can change their mind even when they're lying on the OR table. On the other hand, if they don't sign a consent antepartum, they're shit out of luck. It's not going to be an option as a gyn patient.

We should be thinking contraception is less like a poncho and more like a business suit that needs to be individually tailored to fit. I wish we had more options that didn't come with so many disadvantages, but women don't control that agenda. If men carried babies, contraceptive research would have been elevated to a higher priority. Unfortunately, we've got what we've got, and we have to make do until circumstances change.

I feel a little responsible for Eunice's current predicament, mostly because I haven't given much thought to when the consents should be signed. We're still using the same parameters that I came with, but it's within my power to taper what we do for a better fit, both when we sign the consents and our availability for performing the tubals postpartum. I'll give it some thought on the drive home.

Throughout the day, I'd hoped the weather would keep some people away so I could head home before too late. Thankfully, we're at the beginning of the month when government checks arrive in mailboxes and people wait for them so they won't be stolen. This afternoon, unsettled by the prospect of unlit roads in a stormy dimness, I'll leave culling through abnormal lab reports to someone else.

Once I leave the parking lot, I'm cut off from the world. If my pager goes off, there's no way to respond until I reach home. If the kids have an emergency, I won't know. If a tire blows out, changing it means I'll be swallowed up by the blacktop, shrunken into a near invisible lump wedged against the wheel well, unseen by an approaching vehicle on this unlit road. If my car breaks down, I'll have to walk on the road to find a house with a phone. Would that house belong to a friendly face or a son of the Confederacy? A flag across a pickup's back window might serve as a warning, but if one isn't there, how will I know? If not that house, then it's a longer walk in the pitch black and possibly pouring rain to find a different one. If I can catch a ride with a passing car, how will I know I'm safe? From rape? From murder?

More rain brings a shroud of tire mist and fog. Droplets fracture the headlight high beams. The darkness interlaces with columns of blowing water drops, creating a sealed tunnel. The edges of oncoming headlights dissolve into a scattered fringe in my increasingly blurry night vision.

Eerie curtains of leafy kudzu loom along the roadside, as the vines cling to telephone wires. The encroaching gloom invokes images of hooded white riders in sheets, phantoms from my parents' family vault blended with my own sightings from our first year in Nashville. Raindrops flung against the windshield draw out apparitions like dogs panting for water. Is that an animal in the road? Leaning forward in an effort to improve my sight line, cold sweat beads on my brow. I ease off the accelerator momentarily to get my bearings and collect myself. I don't want to stop completely.

There's nothing there. A drumbeat of raindrops hammers on the car roof. The windows are getting increasingly fogged. I have to remind myself that the car is purring like a kitten, fine-tuned to maximum performance. The tires are fine. The distance from home is shrinking with each mile.

The rain slows as my car nears the junction with the main road into town. Soon the lights of the hospital, then Fast Food Alley come into view as I arrive in familiar territory. I exhale in grateful relief. Unnerved by the ferocity of my anxiety, I try to crawl back off the edge of that cliff into the reality of the present. Maybe it's a KFC night.

Chapter 14

A NEW GAME IN TOWN

T HE HOSPITAL MAY HAVE CLOBBERED me over epidurals, but I, like the plank of a boat smashed against the rocks and haphazardly pitched up onto shore, refuse to sink into the deep. I stagger on with little things. For instance, yesterday, we used our new portable fetal monitor on the way to the OR. With a device about the size of a transistor radio, we could hear the fetal heartbeat until just before the mother was draped for surgery. It was just a test run, but now we're more familiar with the glitzes. This innovation is at least a field goal that deserves a victory dance. Last night, I toasted myself out loud with a single glass of a lovely Pinot.

The prohibition against bringing a fetal monitor into the OR steadfastly resisted my rational arguments. I suspect the presence of only one monitor on L&D was the original reason for the ban. Somehow, that evolved into a misconception that the monitor was banned because it wasn't sterile—a preposterous confection. The only sterile fields in an OR are the top of the instrument stand covered in a sterile drape and the area on and above the patient. Even the drapes below the surgeon's waist are considered contaminated. Anyway, aren't ORs disinfected in between patients?

Sometimes fetal monitoring is crucial until just before the start of a surgery, especially in view of the distance we have to travel. I'm not paranoid; it's my job to anticipate the worst-case scenario. I've been in multiple situations in the past where we poured betadine solution over a belly and started cutting because the fetal heart rate was low. I guess I've seen more bad stuff than people here, or maybe they haven't seen that unfortunate outcomes didn't have to go the way they did. If Antioch is the only group that uses the little device, that's okay. They may not understand the potential until something has gone wrong. For that, I have the breadth of my experience to thank.

If I can't make a big difference at the hospital, I can score some key goals within Antioch Associates. Today, we're making a huge step forward for the practice, a celebration that calls for fireworks. We have to settle for balloons and banners and a cake at the close of the day. Our brand new office ultrasound machine is slotted into my patient schedule. The service rep has been here since its arrival bringing me up to speed. She's assisting for the next couple of days to make sure I'm over any bumps, and then I'm on my own. We're taking back control of our obstetrics and gynecology ultrasound while I satisfy an ever-present itch to hold an ultrasound probe in my hand; to catch a fetus hiccupping on the screen; to watch some thumb sucking. The rep will spring for the cake and party snacks because that's what reps do; she'll fold it into her expense account.

I'm so excited I could barely sleep last night. Fate intervenes in surprising ways. A few months into my tenure here, the prospect of living without capturing the ultrasound images I love hit me like a ton of bricks. Ultrasound is what propelled me toward the subspecialty of perinatology where fetal sonograms will ultimately replace pelvic exams as the mainstay of my practice. Spending four years away from it threatened to dissipate the skills I had worked so hard to acquire. It was like being stranded on a raft in rolling seas under looming storm clouds. My survival unscathed seemed doubtful.

Beyond mourning my loss, the less than stellar performance of the hospital radiologists was a constant irritant. They clearly didn't have extensive training in obstetric ultrasound. It's probably nothing nefarious; some radiologists aren't interested in prenatal diagnosis, and in-depth study isn't available across all radiology programs. Obstetric ultrasound remains a small sliver of the department's business.

Here again, like with epidurals, I come overly prepared. I was thoroughly captivated, at first glance, by 2D ultrasound as a third-year medical student. I'm still amazed that a collection of black and white dots on a screen can create the same recognizable images every time. The first machines produced static images, but the advent of 2D real-time technology gave us a window into the womb's inner sanctum. It requires a special vision to take the pixels from two dimensions to three, and not everyone has it. The challenge in interpreting the implications of the images comes in deciding what's normal and what isn't and, further, what an abnormality means for a baby when it's born and for the parents who will raise it. The radiologists have no real training in prognoses, the special province of obstetricians and perinatologists.

1986

$\mathfrak{M}$y eyes are glued to the screen, tracking a bright line which advances haltingly across the ultrasound screen. The image is the tip of a small-bore needle trying to penetrate the lumen of a fetal umbilical artery. If only I could will it along the right path. Carla, the second-year maternal fetal medicine fellow, is attempting an intrauterine blood transfusion. The fetus suffers from Rh negative isoimmunization, a condition caused by a mismatch between the mother's blood type and the fetus's. The mother's antibodies destroy fetal red blood cells, causing the baby to suffer a life-threatening fetal anemia.

It's warm under the OR lights, causing the plastic shield on Carla's mask to periodically fog with her breath. She's trying to hit a target the diameter of a toothpick inside an umbilical cord that she can't touch or see. There's only the image on the screen to guide her. She has already given the fetus an intramuscular sedative to minimize its movement. Because the cord floats in amniotic fluid, the trick to getting the needle in place is to trap a loop of cord against something stable, like a body part.

The mom, invisible under the surgical drapes, is fidgety. She's complaining that her back aches. I try to reassure her that we'll be done soon even as my eyes remain focused on the needle's progress across the screen. I warn her that she can't move; if she does, she could cause the cord to shift positions and scuttle the whole thing.

Carla makes a decisive stab with the needle, anchoring it in the Wharton's jelly surrounding the blood vessels as she advances. I breathe a sigh of relief; there, she's almost in. But when she draws back on the syringe, there's no blood return. She replaces the stylet inside the needle to advance further into the vessel, but it doesn't help—another dry pull. Carla looks to her right at Dr. Wegman, the faculty attending, pleading for help.

"Just pull it. You're not in, and you can't correct the angle. We'll have to start over with a new needle," Wegman states unsympathetically.

That was her second attempt. Her shoulders sag; you can see her face droop despite the face mask covering it. They step back from the OR table; the ultrasound tech relaxes as a nurse slips under the drapes to slide a pillow under the mom's back, hoping to relieve some of the strain. It's been at least ninety minutes. They'll have to find a new site for the next attempt, so the mom can wiggle around a bit. She can't sit up because we need to keep the drapes in place and the field sterile.

"I think you should take over, Dr. Wegman. I'm not sure I can do it," Carla concedes, obviously discouraged.

"No. There will come a day when there won't be anyone else but you. You need to develop the frame of mind that enables you to seize control."

I want to catch Carla's eye to reassure her, but I'm a lowly second-year resident, there to run the blood sample to the lab. She won't care. She takes a deep breath while the tech scans for a suitable place to try again. Dr. Wegman and Carla confer quietly before she picks up a ten-inch-long needle. It's long because it has to traverse the mom's abdomen, the uterine wall, and a pocket of amniotic fluid.

"Don't be timid. Once you've plotted the right approach, trust your calculated angle to move forward, adjusting as you need, to maintain the image on the screen," Dr. Wegman coaches quietly. "Slow is not always better. Moving more quickly helps solidify the image in your mind's eyes. It's hard to explain, but you'll feel it."

I'm riveted, glancing back and forth between the screen and the movement of her gloved hand around the hub of the needle. The loop of cord and needle tip converge; I cross my fingers. When Carla draws back on the syringe, there is a flash of maroon blood. It's time for me to hightail it to the lab to have the fetal hemoglobin measured. From there, I call into the OR to report the value, so they can calculate the volume of densely packed red blood cells to transfuse, maybe two or three milliliters.

By the time I return, they've injected the blood and withdrawn the needle. They're watching the screen for the blood spurting out of the cord until it clots. The tension in the room has been replaced by an almost jubilant group exhale. Masks are off, and Dr. Wegman is talking with the mom to reassure her that the procedure went well. She'll be going back to L&D for fetal monitoring.

Carla asks me to write the orders for the patient's transfer to L&D. "That was amazing," I tell her, unable to conceal my enthusiasm. She had stayed with it, and I admired that.

Damn, I want to do this.

And so my career plans fell into place. Prenatal diagnosis combined with basic lab research would be my one-two punch to advance into academic medicine. Lately, I have felt far away from that, like a bear in hibernation. But a spring thaw is coming.

Our office ultrasound is the beginning of my reawakening. I will be generating my own real-time images, no longer having to make do with the static X-ray films the radiologists use. This is how ultrasound is meant to be done. Reading films means that if the tech hasn't seen and captured it, the radiologists won't either.

I will no longer have to depend on the radiologists' dictated reports with scatter-shot information instead of the preformatted ones I was used to. What's omitted varies with each radiologist or even the time of day. I found myself chasing down the numbers in order to calculate variables that were important for my assessments.

Until today, I tried to maintain my expertise at evaluating images, albeit static, by reviewing the films in hospital radiology. I'm confident enough in my skills to think that I might even find something the radiologists had overlooked, especially when I ordered an ultrasound with a certain diagnosis in mind. After all, I had trained with some of the authors of the leading textbooks in the field. Particularly important are evaluations for fetuses who seem to be growing too slowly, a finding that could trigger a consultation or referral to another institution to prevent a complicated patient from delivering here.

My insistence made me a thorn in the radiologists' sides. Well, maybe a gnat they could swat and ignore. They felt no need to respond, given that they're the only game in town, literally daring me to find somewhere else to go. I did find that snacks, candy, and a friendly smile have cemented solid relationships with the techs who are the key to getting access to the films I need to review. I try to do a little teaching too—a formula that has bonded us women together in mutual respect. Sometimes, they let me watch while my patient is being scanned.

No more of that. Starting today, that "somewhere else" is right in our office. Beyond the usual scans to establish due dates, we'll take a look at fetal anatomy if they're far enough along, and we'll be offering biophysical profiles (BPPs), an alternative test of fetal well-being to the nonstress test (NST). Our patients will be able to skip the wait on L&D where the NSTs are done. These tests, in complications like diabetes and hypertension, are done once, sometimes twice a week—certainly a burden for patients. Best of all, everyone will receive an immediate interpretation of the findings rather than waiting for a follow-up visit.

Our journey to newly found independence came from a serendipitous encounter I had at an annual ACOG meeting. Annual meetings are a lot like an old-fashioned carnival where thousands of practicing physicians flock to locations chosen to scream "vacation destination" for physicians and their families. Their stated purpose is continuing medical education, but the presentations from which many attendees play hooky are sandwiched between a mixture of leisure, food, and entertainment. The meetings are always laid out so attendees must pass through an enormous pavilion where merchandisers of all things associated with obstetrics and gynecology exhibit their products. The booths overflow with trinkets emblazoned with trademark brands, handy reminders of a company when we take out a pen or notepad or calculate a due date on our wheels. Conference materials come in a handy tote bag, brought to us by one of the major corporate sponsors. Physicians strut like peacocks between coffee machines where the drinks come in trademark decorated mugs while they munch on trays of croissants and Danish pastries. They gobble up invitations to evening receptions with copious hors d'oeuvres or dinner consumed during a lecture by a so-called expert. Obviously, the way to ob-gyns' wallets is through their stomachs. All of this comes with the added bonus of travel paid for by the physician's practice and/or a tax write-off as a business expense for professional education.

The outrageousness of the setting struck me as patently absurd, especially after I watched a disgusting display of attendees stripping fruit from a decorative sculpture to carry back to their rooms. Looking like a piranha feeding frenzy devouring bananas and apples, these were people with high six-figure incomes sneaking food in a luxury hotel. It would make great comedy movie fare if it weren't for the reality of people's lives right outside the doors. Thinking about the whole extravaganza, I felt downright righteous that I haven't succumbed to the mantle of privilege that many in this profession carry.

I had come to the gathering in search of a professional portal to the discussions I miss so dearly in Weavers Crossing. I ache for the intellectual interplay that creates opportunities to learn from the experiences of others and for them to learn from mine. But now that I find myself in a rural outpost, unvisited by pharmaceuticals, let alone equipment reps, this circus has presented a magical mystery tour of the new technology. Besides, I welcome travel to cities like New Orleans as much as the next guy.

Walking by a hands-on demonstration of the latest portable ultrasound equipment, I was dumbstruck by the quality of the visual images, almost as good as the larger ultrasound equipment in radiology suites where I'd trained and sometimes better than the older equipment at Stephens. I happened to overhear a rep talking to another attendee about leasing, and *boom*, an idea to marry my desire to perform ultrasounds with better service to our patients struck me like a lightning bolt.

Beyond the accuracy, to have a machine in the office would mean that I could not only hone my skills but also receive feedback on what I diagnosed as abnormal from referrals to other facilities. In doing so, I'd expand my interaction with the consulting academic centers. Rather than no scans, I could do one every day. The ultrasound truism—the more scans you do, the better you get—was ringing in my ears.

To sweeten the pot, ultrasound in the office represented a new potential revenue stream, a hook to pitch a leasing plan to Antioch administration, always anxious to improve our financial status. And ultrasounds, a natural draw for women who love to watch their fetuses, may attract new prenatal patients once the word spreads. This is a win-win. There are so many advantages to this plan that it's practically a no-brainer. I'm dreaming big again.

The fact that it means more work for me hardly matters. The opportunity to scan is too thrilling to pass up. I'm happy to shift some prenatal and routine gyn visits to other midlevel providers to free up time to perform the scans. The time I'll spend at home reading to link images to diagnoses and prognoses is fun for me. That prospect will help fill the hours, certainly a better use of my energies than the simmering disputes that keep popping up across multiple fronts. No question it beats housework. It probably sounds a little crazy, this elevation of a simple ultrasound machine into a building block for better care integrated into my career growth. I don't know; it's kinda what I do. So starting my scheduled scans today represents a mile marker on a long road, and I'm trying not to let it go to my head.

.

Chapter 15

NOT KNOWING

KELLY, NOW EARLY PREGNANT, CAN'T resist the idea that she can follow her pregnancy with unofficial scans done after hours. Her friendship with fellow PA David Burton eventually flamed into passion and marriage in South Carolina. They returned to a cozy new home strategically placed between the various Antioch clinic sites. The couple are in their thirties and anxious to start a family before her fertility clock winds down.

Kelly has been infected with the ultrasound bug too. Bones, kidneys, hearts, and lungs blossom from the scatter of black and white pixels before her eyes. Since the more scans you see, the more you know, I'm happy to supervise as she starts taking some courses.

As she hops up on the exam table at the end of the day, she lowers the waist of her pants. I run hot water over the bottle of ultrasound gel to warm it, a maneuver to avoid one of my pet peeves, the shock of cold gel on the belly.

When I spread the glob of gel over the pink skin just below her hip bones, the amniotic cavity, a large black area nestled inside the stippled gray endometrium within the uterus, comes into view as I adjust the focus. A small circle, the yolk sac, peeks out of the dark background. Just like the yolk in our breakfast eggs, it provides nourishment for the developing embryo. A tiny peanut-shaped splotch, the fetal pole, sits perched on the rim. The circle is too big, the peanut too small.

I hadn't entered any demographic data into the machine because this was supposed to be a magical mystery tour, not a clinical encounter. As I quiet momentarily, Kelly can see the problem unfolding with her own eyes. We both know that dating errors are one of the most common things we see, but the writing on the wall is leading to a place neither one of us wants to go. The fetus has not continued to develop; she has what we call a missed abortion.

We remain silent for what seems like an eternity. I wipe the gel off her belly and put my arms around her when she sits up, her tears wetting my blouse.

"I'm so sorry," I whisper during our long embrace. "I'll give you a few minutes."

I pick up the box of tissues by the door and put them beside her on the exam table. I leave the lights off on my way out.

When I peek my head back in through the door, she says, "I need to call Dave," staring into the darkness without turning to face me, her head bowed, her back hunched over as if she has given in to the weightiness of the loss. Suddenly, as if someone has flipped a switch, she gets up and walks into one of the offices and closes the door.

When I knock on the door some minutes later, she has stopped crying.

"Is he coming here?" I ask, thinking it might be better if she doesn't drive home right now.

"No, I'll meet him at home."

We both know the clinical options. Kelly has probably given the talk a hundred times to her own patients who have miscarried, a natural consequence of a developmental process so complicated that it can and does go wrong in thousands of different ways. Humans aren't very efficient reproducers; only about 25 percent of fertilized eggs end in a live birth. For many women, it's a closely held secret, not even shared with their families. But if you ask, like we do, you'll see how common they are.

"I just need to sit with this, to have Dave hold me and cry some more. We'll mourn with our families. I don't know how long that will take, but there's no reason to rush."

Kelly has just opted out of a D&C, the standard treatment; she'll wait for spontaneous resolution in a process where the fetal tissue is naturally reabsorbed, often making the next period heavier than usual. Ultrasound has allowed us to detect pregnancies earlier, and with that more miscarriages. In olden days, many of these pregnancies would have remained unknown, chalked up to menstrual irregularities. It may be that our technological advances have caused more sorrow and grief, and they often do.

I hug her again, a long embrace filled with regret for the couple—and for the vagaries of life. I hightail it to my office to work on finishing my notes and reviewing lab results so I don't disturb her any further. After she leaves, I turn out the lights and lock the back door behind me.

An ultrasound machine reveals the unseen in ways that can shatter dreams. There can be jubilation or outright grief or somewhere between not quite sorrow and devastation. Sometimes there are only questions. That's true for both the operator and the examinee. Not in the case of a loss. There, there is only sadness. But sometimes there can be relief in explanation. For me, though, there can also be the exhilaration of a correct diagnosis, an inevitable boost to my self-confidence, confirming that maybe, just maybe, I'm going to excel at my chosen subspecialty. Therein lies an inherent contradiction that on the surface may seem a bit ghoulish. But I'm energized when I diagnose some variant just because it can enlighten the parents. Although we have almost no tools to alter inborn modifications in fetal development, we hope through prenatal diagnosis to enable families to examine the limited options that exist and prepare for the future.

Unfortunately, the implications of our findings are shrouded in the decidedly murky landscape of individual variability. Except for a few fatal conditions, we can't say what any one condition means for any single individual neonate, only a range of consequences. For me, it's a continuing source of frustration. Hopefully we will expand the possibilities in the future, but congenital diseases, because they are uncommon, are not at the top of any research agendas. At this point, my job is to detect what I can, give a bare-bones description of implications, and pass them on to UNC to fill in the rest. I can't wait until I'm the one with the fuller picture my referrals now need.

Kelly seems sad in quiet moments despite the sparkle sprinkled across her face, now back from two weeks of sick leave. I notice I'm more handsy in our interactions, and sometimes I want to hug her and do. Like today, when she brought in that chocolate chess pie, baking being a common antidote to sadness. A warm oven feels inherently nurturing. Who says pie can't substitute for a morning muffin?

Monica Jackson is here to date her third pregnancy. She's excessively thin, an advantage that yields crisper images. Abdominal fat cells, which trap the sonic bursts emitted from the probe, decrease the quantity of sound waves reflected back. Since an image is formed by variations in wave intensity reflected from different types of tissue, interfering adipose tissue results in fuzzier pictures. Monica's belly bulge looks like a size-date discrepancy, where the pregnancy is further along than the last menstrual period indicates.

As anticipated, the top of Monica's uterus sits above her belly button as I spread the warmed gel more evenly over her chocolate skin. Not one but two fetuses appear within the blackness of the amniotic cavity, which sets Monica giggling.

"Is that twins?"

"Yeah, which means I need to concentrate on scanning. We'll talk about everything when I'm finished."

I can't locate an amniotic membrane between the two fetuses, so they're in a single sac, unusual and more complicating. But something else isn't quite right. The appropriate visual planes seem beyond my grasp no matter how much I struggle. Is it my ineptness? No, it's them; I think these twins are joined together in the abdominal area.

Meanwhile, my schedule is stuck on hold. Twins usually take longer than a singleton, but this exam is dragging on and on. Since I have to refer Monica anyway, I should stop, but I want to put my best foot forward for fear I'll look like a rookie. There's always a moment when I'm afraid that I'll embarrass myself with a stupid suggestion, even though it's equally as good to know when you're wrong as when you're right.

Monica and I talk in my office about conjoined twins, how it occurs, what it means, and that the prospects for separation will depend on a detailed analysis of their organs after they're born. Monica cries intermittently. Still I have to push on with my quick summary, even though I realize that many patients may not be able to hear most of what I've said after "conjoined." I only have the time I have.

I need to get to the part where Monica must transfer her care to UNC if they confirm my findings. It's critical for her to become familiar with the multiple different neonatologists and surgeons who will be involved in the babies' care along with the perinatologist who will do her scheduled cesarean. She says getting to Chapel Hill for her visits won't be a problem, but if it gets to be too much of a burden, I offer to work out a co-management scheme where she has some prenatal visits in our office and others at UNC. I ask Allison to start making the arrangements for the consult.

It was a lot. I tried to limit the information and leave space for her to ask questions, but she was too stunned to say much. She began the visit being excited about having twins, and here she was hearing about a devastating abnormality. Overall, it would probably be better to have a patient come back for more details and maybe write down questions as they think of them before they return. That doesn't feel quite right either, kind of like leaving your laundry in the washing machine for a few days without drying it. My sense of urgency to reassure is too acute.

Thankfully, Kelly has already seen quite a few of my scheduled patients when Monica heads toward Allison's office. My lifesaver. She likes doing postpartum and gyn visits because she can generally handle their needs on her own, without consultation with the docs. She's built relationships over time with many of these women and knows their children, who often play in the office as they wait to see her. And while the prenatal visits will end with a birth in which she has no part, she's happy not to be included and to see the mothers back with flattened bellies and another kid in tow.

I jump in to plow rapid-fire through the routine prenatal visits left, each taking ten minutes as I gather what has happened since the last visit, what we call "history of present illness," and simultaneously measure the belly to assess growth and listen to the fetal heartbeat. I'm trying not to be distracted by my recent ultrasound diagnosis, my first conjoined twins. Luckily, Kelly has taken the new OB patient, which includes a full medical history and physical exam including a pelvic.

Allison Murray's addition to our multispecialty group has been a godsend for our concept of "total care." It's ambitious, Antioch's idea that a range of services to improve health can be delivered through our small medical group. Allison often brings women with complicated pregnancies to their more frequent visits, sometimes coaxing them, sometimes locating them when they forget, sometimes providing a ride. She helps them pick up their medications at the drugstore or stop by the grocery store while they're in town. That's only a fraction of the duties she performs across the full spectrum, family practice to pediatrics. Her strawberry-blonde hair can often be seen bobbing in laughter with a couple of women in the parking lot outside our offices.

At home, a family dinner doesn't seem to be in the cards. Abbie's going to eat at the Whiteheads'. Damian is heading off to the movies with some friends. I wonder if there's some dating involved but don't ask. He'll tell me later if it's important. The only movie theater in town is a short walk away behind the mall. Its owner feels that his Christian duty demands that he safeguard the community from material he deems undesirable. Family films play on the weekends; slightly more risqué fare like *The Fabulous Baker Boys* is shown on a Wednesday or Thursday and then they're gone. The boys will eat in the mall or on Fast Food Alley before heading to the cinema.

What a relief. That leaves Kyle and eventually Aaron. I change into a T-shirt and shorts, slowly unwinding. Even though I'm still pretty excited about the conjoined twins, I'm hungry enough to want something quick. Kraft Mac & Cheese, the only macaroni and cheese Kyle will eat, is the solution. I long ago surrendered the prospect of a tasty dish for a quiet meal. Why go through the trouble of making a béchamel sauce only to suffer the inevitable grumbling, always hard to stomach at the end of a long day. Kyle will be happy no matter what else I put on his plate. Because he's one of the most finicky eaters on the planet, he probably wouldn't eat anything else anyway.

Giving in is the inevitable result of an eight-year spread between your oldest and youngest. Ours is the age-old story of older parents too tired to fight over the things that seemed so important with the first child. Alongside the Mac & Cheese, I fry pork chops and steam frozen peas and carrots, both quick and easy. We'll probably eat before Aaron gets home anyway; he can microwave the leftovers. I add tomato slices, creating a rainbow of color on my plate. I'll play some games with Kyle and then wander downstairs to work on Monica's chart notes after his story time. I never bring clinic charts home, but I've made this exception because I want to be as detailed as I can about my findings before we send a copy of her records on.

Aaron comes home in time to get Kyle ready for bed. After a cursory check-in, I head downstairs, slip on my headphones, and turn on my Walkman to cancel the penetration of Aaron's deep voice as it resonates through the house when he's on the phone. His volume tends to rise when he gets mad, an unpredictable yet predictable occurrence. I don't want to get distracted by the natural impulse to eavesdrop. I wander upstairs around eleven thirty to the murmur of a TV voice as he sleeps in front of it. I quietly slip into bed.

Chapter 16

MORE TO THE STORY

LULA HUBBARD CAME IN TODAY. Same complaint, same result: normal pelvic exam, no pap, no HIV test. We agree that she will return as needed.

Allison pulls me aside during a birthday party for one of our nurse's aides to update me on the work she's been doing with Lula. She lives out in the county in a trailer on a dirt road forked off another dirt road. A small store with a pay phone and a gasoline pump sit at the intersection, the only visible light during the night except the moon. Lula and her four neighbors are right now grumbling about getting repairs to their common septic system that fills the summer air with swarming flies drawn to the stench. This is only the most urgent problem. They have periodic issues with their plumbing, water that sputters abruptly or runs brown or red and then mysteriously clears up.

"It's in bad shape," Allison says. "It must be almost unbearable when it gets cold. But it's cheap enough that it's hard to find something elsewhere. I'm trying to convince her to move closer toward town, but it'll be more expensive."

Lula isn't sure she wants to move. The lady next door loves Lula's daughters like her own, and she's always happy to babysit. The girls know they can go next door whenever, and Lula too can talk with her about anything. She drives them to church some Sundays, and Lula can sometimes catch a ride to town if she needs it.

Housing isn't Lula's biggest problem. Occasionally, the night brings an unwelcome two-legged predator. Big Jonah would bust in, smelling of sweat and stale cigarettes, breathing whiskey in her face when he jerked her toward him. "You know you're mine," he'd insist. The first time, she had pulled away, only to fall backward over a chair. That act of resistance had awakened her daughter Naomi, but he let Lula settle her back in bed. Her reward had been a slap across the face. He's bigger and stronger. Her terror is real. She can't win this fight. Superman will not be coming to her rescue. So she simply went limp and let him get on with his business, roughly humping as she shut her eyes tightly, singing "Just a Closer Walk With Thee" in her head.

She prefers him taking her from behind so her face doesn't have to be near his. She doesn't have to close her eyes then, but she always does. Usually, he's mercifully quick, staggering out the door still zipping up his fly. Afterwards, Lula takes a lukewarm bath, the best her hot water heater can manage. Then she sits with a glass of sweet tea.

All this information had come to Allison in dribs and drabs over a glass of iced tea or two during a number of visits. The last time, she fixed the front screen door hinge so it wouldn't fall off on one of the girls if she slammed it too hard. Allison had also repaired one of the front steps.

Once, the clerk in the store at the fork in the road told Lula he'd seen Big Jonah around and warned her not to go home. Not that he knew for sure what happened, but Big Jonah likes to brag. The clerk may have seen a black eye before, and he kind of liked Lula. She sent the girls to the neighbor and called her sister to pick her up. Isolated as she is with her three girls, she's decided that her best defense is to ensure that she doesn't catch any diseases from him.

Lula and Allison haven't talked about reporting the rapes because they both know that would change nothing. Even if moving could protect her, Lula is still on the fence. If Big Jonah is a temporary hazard, the next visit could be his last. Then, she fears she will lose more than she will have gained.

For a minute, I want to put my fist through a wall. No woman should have to live like that. It makes me furious, this casual acceptability of rape and physical abuse in our society. They're hardly even considered to be crimes. First, people assume the victim is lying. Even if it did happen, it's always her fault. She's too provocative. She shouldn't have been there if she didn't want it. She asked for it. She provoked the violence by resisting a demand. Or a man has a right to touch a woman however he chooses. A man has a right to have sex when and where and how he wants. Maybe at one point, the two were in a relationship; maybe they're strangers. Should it matter? Have we advanced at all since caveman days? Lula Hubbard, intermittently raped in her own home by a man she knows, is simply a statistic, or she would be if she ever reported it.

Lula's isolation on a back road doesn't distinguish her plight from women packed into urban housing projects or quiet suburbs. My work on a domestic violence/rape hotline in Nashville made clear that freedom from any consequences and silent neighbors with blind eyes ensure the violence will continue. Many people think what happens behind closed doors is none of their business; that's how they want it to be in their own homes. Besides, any neighbor who wants to help would be at a loss for who to call. The police? The incident will likely be over by the time they arrive, and the best they would offer is a trip to the ER for medical attention. For the cops, there's nothing to see here. If you're Black, they probably won't show at all. If they do, they're just as likely to grab somebody else on some bogus unrelated charge. There are so many tentacles to these problems—the police, the judiciary, societal apathy, cultural and political attitudes—that it feels utterly hopeless.

Lula's situation is simply preposterous; she's been reduced to building a house of straw to withstand a hurricane. When he comes again, she can avoid a black eye and bodily harm by submitting. But she believes, because he's only committed to shooting craps and drinking, that he'll move on to someone else eventually. She's thankful she doesn't have to worry about having more babies. She can protect or at least shield her girls as much as possible. She will wait.

"Sometimes I think many of the women here are truly brave. I don't know how I'd react in a similar situation," I admit to Allison.

"We think we'd never be in one," Allison whispers, as if deep in thought. "But relationships are complicated."

"Yeah, the rape crisis hotline showed me that. It's an honor to care for these women, but it's painful sometimes."

"I know you know that we can't fill in all the holes. We don't have enough . . ." Allison sighs. "We do our best and can take comfort in that. Sometimes we make mistakes, but most of the time, shit just happens. Even if we can see it coming, it's still gonna happen. All of us are doing what women have always done. We put one foot in front of the other, and do what we have to do to keep going." For a moment, she seems drained of her usual optimism.

"There's just nowhere for women to go around here. In Nashville, we at least had one women's shelter. It takes a dedicated group of women to get them going." I'm making an obvious point that doesn't need to be said.

"Nobody here has the resources," Allison answers, shaking her head. "It takes guts first, and then some money. There are a few women working on it, but it's hard going. A lot of women just can't leave the area, and it's tough to hide inside it."

"Dr. Hampton, you got a call from L&D." One of the aides pokes her head in the door after a soft knock.

"Duty calls," I say, saving us from descending into near suicidal despair.

It's Ginny calling about Theresa Jackson who's three centimeters dilated, contractions every five to six minutes with her second baby. She has a healthy baby boy weighing eight and a half pounds around seven p.m., and both are doing well when I park in my driveway. Still, after the kids go to bed, I keep thinking about Lula Hubbard's plight. Stupidly, we in the women's movement thought we were going to change the world after abortion became legal. Yes, women can now get a credit card without a male cosignatory, although not many of my patients can take advantage of that. Women are still not safe in their homes, not to mention on the streets. We are still less than citizens in so many ways.

I was almost included among the one in three women in the US who will be sexually assaulted during her lifetime. That's an astonishing 20 percent of the total population. My passion about violence against women is fueled in part by a narrow escape from an attempted rape during college by someone I thought was a friend. Women are not safe, not because of our actions but because, through the tacit consent of society, we're prey for any man. For my first medical school research project, I chose a study to create a forensic rape kit that would hopefully make possible the apprehension of assailants. I collected similar rape kits in the ER at McCune. I haven't gotten any calls to do them here. I'm skeptical that many women come in and, when they do, that the ER docs are using them, but maybe.

One thing I know is that women are being sexually assaulted here because violence against women is a fact of life. Lula Hubbard's only crime is to sit in her home minding her own business. Despite my passion, as long as we live in a patriarchal society, I've accepted that I'm powerless to do much of anything about it, but that doesn't make it any less appalling.

Chapter 17

THE GRAND OPENING

THE DAY THE WALMART CAME to town, the humidity crinkled straightened hair at its roots and flared it out in frizzy unruliness at the ends. The condensed moisture pressed heavily on our shoulders, slowing our pace to a near crawl. Cars were stacking up at the flashing red light in a once in a lifetime rush-hour-like snarl. Despite the thermometer, Weavers Crossing bristled with a festive air. Right next to the Piggly Wiggly, alternating red, white, and blue flags crisscrossed the expansive new parking lot catty-corner from the mall.

My plans for a family outing to check out the store crumpled. Aaron refuses to patronize an aggressively anti-union establishment that exploits workers. Instead, he's planning to clean the pool with Kyle's help. Damian's going with Abbie and Geena and some of his friends. Deserted herself, Phyllis is going to rescue me. We head first to the barbeque joint on the other side of the interstate where, outside our dry county, we can relax with a beer or two.

I marvel at how put together she looks, even now in a pale blue sleeveless top with khaki Bermuda shorts. Despite the humidity, every strand of her hair is neatly in place. Mine is a haphazard afterthought pulled back near the base of my neck. Her makeup is flawless; mine is nonexistent. In the air-conditioned room, we laugh through renditions of encounters with the reliably fatuous physicians at the hospital, captured in their native accents. Phyllis is especially good at Dr. Patel's lilting New Delhi cadence.

As we search for an open parking spot, we watch heavily laden shopping carts snake through the lot as kids joyfully skitter along with new toys and smiling parents pat each other on the back. Go in for one item, leave with five. The carts roll over torn flyers blown around by the movement of the cars in and out.

The Walmart doesn't disappoint. It's a wonderland of eye-popping bargains; one-stop discount shopping has arrived! Aisles filled with toiletries, electronics, gardening supplies, and hardware sit under one roof. The Sears catalog will fast become an afterthought. Calloway and Sons hardware store will be fighting for its life. The thrift shop will be supplanted by rows and rows of inexpensive shirts and skirts and shorts that are brand new. Hundreds of earrings sparkle from a sea of paper cards, ready to brighten up new outfits freshly plucked from stacks and racks.

We find aisle after aisle of cheap plastic stuff. I have felt the lack of shopping opportunities deeply, occasionally venturing to a large outlet mall outside Washington, DC, a little over three hours away. Discount shopping on Manhattan's Lower East Side had been a staple for Aaron and I when we first started out. This isn't Lower East Side kind of merchandise, but some bargains are irresistible, like an array of discounted lotions, shampoos, and laundry detergents that jump off the shelves into our carts. I added some Mason jars for canning tomatoes in the fall. As we leave, the Piggly Wiggly in the adjacent parking lot beckons with sales on milk, eggs, chicken, and a few more minutes of air conditioning. Sucking up the chill, we meander past the freezer cases and wait to check out with one of the few Black cashiers, Melissa Spurling, whose baby, Faith, is now Phyllis's patient. I had delivered her last year.

When we reach Melissa, we tease her about some of the free samples and prizes she might want to check out in the Walmart during her break. We gab about how Faith is doing as the line stacks up behind us, but people here don't mind that much. The pace of life is so leisurely that people expect to chat at length with their cashier.

Melissa, the pride of the Spurling family, is the youngest of five generations of women who have lived in the county for as long as anyone can remember. Her grandmother, Big Mabel, is a trusted lay midwife in the community, sought out for her knowledge of herbal healing for all maladies. Rumor has it that she's still delivering babies in area homes. Melissa is the first in the family to go to college, joining her boyfriend at UNC Wilmington. He's a local fast-talker who means to make his way in the world by selling his toothy smile. He had been her only sexual partner since hooking up in high school.

And then it all fell apart. When Melissa finally admitted to her mother that she was pregnant, she had come home alone. The boyfriend had stayed at school, severing himself from the destiny of the family he had created. Melissa, ashamed to have fallen from the heroine who had entered a freshman college class, tried to delay disappointing her mother and Big Mabel as long as she could. Now, she wasn't any different from her older sister, a teen mom high school dropout working at Wendy's. She felt that she had betrayed her family's investment in their future, one surrounding a college-educated professional. But Big Mabel had simply whispered, "Every child is a blessing from God" as she hugged her. And that was that.

I saw Melissa for her first prenatal visit when she was five weeks from the due date she hadn't known until then. The results of her prenatal labs contained a bombshell. She had a host of STDs except, mercifully, HIV. She might have been monogamous, but her partner had apparently been sampling a smorgasbord of coeds and probably campus workers as well. The gonorrhea, chlamydia, and trichomonas were easily treated with antibiotics. But syphilis, which has been around since Roman times, is more complicated for both mom and baby.

Syphilis can cause a host of inborn anomalies, some that end in perinatal death. Surprisingly, penicillin, the drug withheld in the US Public Health Service study at Tuskegee, has remained the drug of choice for treatment since it was first discovered. After decades, it remains 99 percent effective, unlike other sexually transmitted organisms that are beginning to develop resistance to commonly used antibiotics. For me, this was a lock; we could cure both Melissa and her baby.

Just as the disease occurs in a progression of several stages, Melissa's treatment was more complex than a few pills. At her stage, an injection of penicillin in each butt cheek for three consecutive weeks was required. The critical target of the medication is the fetus, who can still be prevented from being born with congenital syphilis.

No doubt, the Spurling women were disappointed that Melissa had lost her chance at potential prosperity, but they were excited to welcome a new baby. For her part, Melissa brought a quiet intelligence to her questions as well as complete compliance. As required by law, we reported her case to the public health department that would track down her boyfriend and his other partners and their partners, leaving both the clinic and patient outside the usual blowback that follows contact tracing. The health department can send out the sheriff to bring people in for treatment if necessary.

The Spurling women gathered with Melissa throughout her labor, and when Faith came into the world, they hugged and cried in loud celebration. Two days later, Phyllis brought devastating news. Although physical examination showed no signs of trouble in Faith, her test for syphilis came back positive. Faith's discharge from the hospital was delayed for a few days for immediate treatment. Still, because Faith had shown no physical symptoms, her prognosis remained promising. We had to watch and wait.

I was no less rocked by the diagnosis than Melissa. This was unlike my extensive experience with drug addicts and the HIV infected. I had never before seen the treatment fail, even in the third trimester. Obviously, no treatment is 100 percent, but I just couldn't take it in—that Melissa, of all people, would be in the 1 or 2 percent that fail. How ironic that an innocent young girl with great promise should be ambushed, unlike women struggling with addiction whose behaviors risked infection every day. Now Faith will have to be monitored for seizures, defects in her bones, and a normal rate of growth, as well as be tested for deafness and, by school age, normal intelligence.

These days, Melissa still struggles with guilt over waiting so long to tell her family. In her mind, it's all her fault, getting syphilis in the first place and worse, not getting timely prenatal care. Despite her efforts to appear otherwise, she's often depressed. It's not simply the guilt; she's mourning her future that is forever changed as she watches it sliding by on the conveyor belt next to the milk and eggs. In agonizing over Faith's future, she feels she's paying mandated penance for her sins. Even if her daughter proves to be unscarred by the disease, Melissa sees her child as an innocent victim of her own sinful transgressions.

We don't have much to offer in terms of mental health treatment around here, so I try to coax Melissa to see the broader context. The boyfriend, a cesspool of noxious organisms, is the sole villain here. She believed he was monogamous. And she did all the right things during her prenatal care, even if it came later than for others. More than that, the past is unchangeable, but the future is not. She has no idea what time will bring. Faith might have no ill effects or only minor ones that are easily managed.

Melissa is only nineteen. I tell her not to lose confidence in the abilities that took her to college in the first place. If she retains that drive, she can return to school just like I went to medical school after I already had two kids. She has tremendous family support that is ready and willing to help her accomplish her goals. She should stay ready to take advantage of any opportunity. Phyllis and I assured her that we're willing to help in any way we can.

I repeat these narratives as much for me as for her. Intellectually, I know that Faith's infection was neither Melissa's fault nor mine, but somehow, I'm left with this deep ache that I failed her. This is a new experience for me. I had never faced my patients in a store or on the street in Philadelphia. I lived across the river in a comfortable suburb in New Jersey. Most of my time in Philly was spent in the hospital or at surrounding eateries, not in the neighborhoods where our patients lived. I might know about a bad outcome, but I hadn't watched those children grow up. Anyway, I was only one of a whole team of providers.

In Weavers Crossing, an Antioch patient can be around any corner. Strictly speaking, it breaks patient confidentiality to acknowledge that someone is our patient outside of the office. But in this small world, everyone seems to know everyone else's business, and nobody cares, except maybe about HIV status. But that's a death sentence that people, in their ignorance, think says lots of other things about a person.

Sometimes I run into a woman, whose baby we delivered only months before, getting prenatal care from one of the other ob-gyns in town. I can't help but wonder if she wants to be pregnant so soon. Had I failed to provide the best contraceptive care? Certainly, there are some women who want to have their children close together, like my college roommate who wanted to "get it all out of the way, have her three kids, and be done with it" after her husband's vasectomy. Similarly, many of my patients don't care about birth intervals "if that's how the Lord sees fit." But some are surprised and desperately disappointed that "it's happened again." I want every baby to be planned and desired, a goal I think most of us share. I keep thinking if I'd made a better connection or had given better instructions for effective birth control pill use or provided more free samples or something, these women wouldn't find themselves pregnant when they didn't want to be. The problem continues to haunt me.

As much as I enjoyed seeing Melissa, she triggered a cycle of blame that's sapping some of the fun out of the day. It's almost too much, layered into the muggy air. If Phyllis notices, she doesn't mention it on the two-minute drive home before the air conditioning has time to cool the car. By the time we're at the house, Aaron is overseeing a pool party with Abbie and Geena who had wandered back and decided to swim. Damian came later with Alonzo and Trey. Aaron says he'll fire up the grill. Phyllis calls her husband to join us with her bathing suit. There isn't a better day than this one to spend floating in a pool.

Chapter 18

CHANGE IS IN THE AIR

E UNICE JEFFERSON AND TUBAL CONSENTS have been on my mind since her visit. It's just wrong for physicians to dictate decisions on reproduction that rightfully belong with partners or within a family. For me to start the pill while in college, I was forced to enter a clandestine underground of off-campus ob-gyns willing to write prescriptions for teenagers and single women. Those prohibitions had nothing to do with scientific evidence; they were conjured out of puritanical misbeliefs. That wasn't a complete surprise, given the inherently sexist nature of obstetrics and gynecology, the specialty *for* women dominated *by* men. I have to follow the rules, so I, too, am now part of the madness. It's bad enough that we control access to the most effective contraceptive methods through the power of a prescription pad. But tubal consents go a stratosphere beyond, expanding proscriptions to age.

Mindful of my own difficulties wrestling with contraceptive issues through the years, I have long argued that if a woman comes to me and says, "I don't want to have any more children," isn't she in the best position to know how many children she wants, whether that's one or twelve and she's eighteen years old or thirty? I know three children is more than enough for me, and I was over thirty at the time. If she says that she can't effectively use other forms of birth control, shouldn't I honor her choice rather than sentence her to unwanted pregnancies until the government decides it's okay? Why do men refuse to accept that women know what they need?

Worse still, should the leading light of democracy be dictating personal reproductive choices? That sounds more like the one-child policy under the brutal autocratic Chinese regime. Should a government be dictating different choices for different groups of people? But then again, throughout our history, the glow of equal treatment has shone feebly or completely evaded the descendants of slaves, Native Americans, Puerto Ricans, Asians, and anyone else considered nonwhite. Somehow, the fact that we're talking about individual human beings has been forgotten.

My frustration about women's impotence continues to feed my anger. Obviously, no matter how much I bloviate about it, the issue is on nobody's agenda, not in obstetrics, not at Medicaid, not in state or federal government. However, if nothing else, I can make one tiny contribution for the women in Antioch Associates' practices.

Eunice Jefferson is one of the many Black women who give birth four weeks or more before term, at least twice as often as white ones and more than any other group in the US. Individual practice groups make their own decision about the best time to sign consents, usually late second trimester. I've continued to use what I learned, somewhere between twenty-seven and thirty-two weeks. But thinking back on my experiences here and elsewhere, Eunice is only the latest in scores of women where the paperwork was completed too close to a birth before thirty-six weeks. Over time, this is no small number in practices like ours when the national rate of preterm delivery among Black women is around 15 percent. It's probably more important for us to change since we transfer our preterm laboring patients to other institutions where, if consents are valid, the tubals can be performed there.

I'm thinking that if you're the woman who finds herself pregnant when her efforts to avoid it went awry through little fault of her own, a small change can matter a lot. Not that I'm discounting the fact that she did the deed that led to conception, but she's already admitted that she isn't so great with other methods of birth control and selected permanent sterilization as the most appropriate for her.

Since statistically the color of our patients' skin makes them twice as likely to deliver prematurely, the obvious solution is to move the time when consents are signed earlier in the pregnancy. Many women know at their first visit that they want a tubal, so making the change should be easily implementable. And they can always change their minds right up until the time we make the incision. So I've started with the patients I see as I create the written protocols for the other Antioch providers to follow. While Joyce isn't involved in performing the surgeries, she's happy to facilitate in any way she can. It's as simple as one, two, three. We do not have to keep doing what we've always done.

The season when graduates move into new practices has come and gone without any candidates to join us. The clinic administrator, Robert Pierson's, call about an interested applicant came out of the blue. Robert is the lynchpin that holds the group together, ensuring that we survive our bumpy up-and-down finances. The opposite of a hard driver, he exudes an air of tranquility like the kind of guy who might say "go in peace" when he leaves a room. But his mild manner doesn't interfere with his ability to get things done.

I'm hugging my fourth cup of coffee when Joyce Fowler joins us in Robert's office, her eyes sagging into pillows of skin underneath, probably because she had an uncomplicated vaginal delivery around two a.m. When she speaks, her mind seems to be one step behind her mouth, an uncharacteristic slow clip to her usual rapid fire. I jump up to get her the cup of coffee she needs more than I.

The good news is an inquiry; the bad news is the candidate's background. Dr. Otis James got caught up in the crack epidemic. His marriage and career disintegrated before he found his way to rehab and a prolonged recovery. Crack is probably the most difficult addiction to kick, harder than heroin, which at least has substitutes like methadone. A crack addict will chase that never-to-be-duplicated first high through increasingly desperate repeated bumps to the ends of the Earth as their life shatters around them. Abstinence is the only treatment for crack abuse, a daunting task when the addict's environment is chocked full of sources and friends who are still using. The hospital, where cocaine is available in vials for use in anesthesia and some medical procedures, is an even more challenging setting for addicted physicians. While I was on duty one night during my residency, an anesthesia resident overdosed, a quiet mild-mannered guy in rimless glasses whom no one would have suspected. I'd been talking to the guy a couple of hours before they found him dead in a call room.

It seems likely that Dr. James cycles through waves of shame each time he repeats his narrative in every interview. People have trouble accepting that addiction is a disease, not a personal failure. But he has persevered, returning to his medical school alma mater to chart a course for reeducation. It probably speaks volumes that they've been willing to help, a buoy to keep my hopes from sinking into an abyss. Otis has carved out a mentorship with a private group and a provisional license under the state medical board's program for recovering addicts. The weekly drug testing is meant to enforce compliance.

Within a week, I'm extending a hand to meet a larger, slightly darker one as we stand outside the Rest Stop Buffet next to the interstate. Dr. Otis James is tall, over six feet, with slumped shoulders that camouflage his height. His broad smile reveals strikingly white teeth, perhaps not his own. Inside, as we sit at our table giving drink orders, my thought is Otis doesn't look like a crack addict. But of course he wouldn't look like the many patients I'd seen in Philadelphia, their frazzled neediness excreted from every pore. Suddenly, I'm flooded with sadness for this man who has lost so much—his marriage, his middle-class life, and the role of caregiver he'd trained long and hard to become. All this through no fault of his own. Addiction is, after all, a disease.

Neither, not the instant stereotype nor the pity, is appropriate. If I weren't in public, I would slap myself for the distraction. As Otis pushes his horn-rimmed glasses back up onto the bridge of his nose, I focus on his face, so openly friendly that it invites you to confide in him. After the server arrives with our drinks, I begin our conversation with a little about my background as we head for the buffet. Mid-sentence I reflect that my remarks are a typically male way to begin—a dodge to avoid the elephant in the room; I mean his current level of expertise, not his sobriety. That discussion is for later. I don't want him to think that drug use is my primary concern. I figure I have enough experience to deal with that.

This is my first attempt at interviewing a potential practice partner. I don't think these things are intuitive. I should have thought more beforehand about what type of assessments I should be making. There's probably some training that needs to happen that I've not had anywhere along the way. I'm not sure how to verbally discover desirable characteristics for an ob-gyn to mesh into our group.

When we sit again, Otis jumps right into the progress he's making in his mentorship, telling a story about a laparoscopic tubal ligation, a procedure done through small abdominal incisions. I laugh, startling him a bit.

"There is no laparoscopic equipment at Stephens Memorial." I chuckle, leaning back in my chair.

Otis laughs too. "Maybe we should get some," he says as he winks.

Is the "we" presumptuous or simply a slip of the tongue? Is it meant to indicate his eagerness to join us?

Thankfully, he's gotten the ball rolling about both addiction and competence. We wander through his training and his desire to get back on track. I allow him to give as much detail about his personal journey as he wants, but I don't want to wallow in the lows. He's trying to repair his relationship with his two kids, which I guess must involve some renewed interactions with his ex-wife. Our next stop will be a hospital tour, and afterwards, he'll visit our various office sites with Joyce. She's already covered our structure and patient load, but I throw in my two cents about our idea of patient-centered care and how we hope to expand it. I'm trying to assert how dynamic I want the ob-gyn practice to be. I talk about my career goals, proud of my ambitions. He reassures me that he's itching to get back to work.

Standing by my car in the Rest Stop parking lot, Otis leans in closer in a moment of shared intimacy to talk about his drug testing after three years of sobriety.

"I see this as an ongoing day-to-day struggle. Most days, it's somewhere in the background, but I have resources to turn to if I feel the slightest sign of trouble. Once I get started, I'm looking forward to a long career in stamping out disease." He laughs again, flashing those teeth. "Wait, let's get some ice cream from that HoJo's." He points with a devilish look in his eyes. "I'm in the mood for something sweet. They got all those flavors. There must be one for you."

"Sorry, I don't do HoJo's, but if you didn't get enough to eat, go ahead and I'll wait here." I'm teasing him about his intake at the buffet.

"You boycotting something?"

"I guess you can call it that," I answer in an attempt to brush it off.

"There's got to be a good story behind that. So shoot."

"Maybe another time. We should probably get going."

"Now you've piqued my curiosity." He smiles sweetly as if pleading, *Aw, come on.*

"Oh alright. It's not that big a deal. I'll make it quick. I was maybe ten or eleven when my parents were bringing us kids back home from a trip to Frankfort, the state capital of Kentucky. We always took these day trips around the tri-state region. Kinda my mom's version of living history lessons. Inveterate travelers, my folks knew the roads in their home state like the backs of their hands. But we kids were yammering about being hungry, so my dad stopped at a Howard Johnson's. It was late afternoon, so they thought it wouldn't be very crowded. After we sat down at a table, they acted as if we weren't there. Not a single waitress would even look in our direction.

"After what seemed like hours from a kid's perspective, the sheriff walked in the dining room and right up to our table. He pulled my dad up from his chair and said something like, 'Boy, you know you can't be in here. You wanna eat, you go order 'round the back and eat in your car. You the one with that Ohio license plate?'

"My dad is a soft-spoken but stern man who doesn't smile much. He'd kept us hungry, rowdy kids in check with the intensity of a steely stare. And yet, that idiot sheriff pulled his hands behind his back like he was a rag doll as he bulldozed him toward the door. The sheriff wore this stupid grin on his face, looking around at the other patrons and nodding. My dad knew the drill. His eyes focused on his feet, his shoulders slouched to shrink his slight build to less than his erect five-foot-seven-inch height."

I hadn't meant to get this much into the weeds, but the tale kept unraveling as I searched for a way to get out of it.

"'You too, gal. Git on up and git out of here!' the sheriff screeched in an upper register, just as my mom was hurriedly gathering us up, her eyes fixed on her toes. Never look a white person in the eye. This was the Kentucky they'd grown up in; their reactions were automatic. We kids were just scared. The sheriff had a gun on his hip.

"My mom took us to the car and got behind the wheel while the sheriff marched my dad around to the back window to order some food. We thought he was taking our dad to jail. She kept reassuring us it'd be fine, we'd be eating soon. I'm not so sure she believed that, but she had her brave face on. I'd lost my appetite anyway. By the time my dad returned to the car, the sheriff had moved on to take in the applause of some white folks in the parking lot.

"My dad was the respected director of an Ohio state government agency. He's so much better educated than that stupid-ass cracker. And yet, that fool had put the fear of God in him. In all of us. I saw my dad in a posture I had never seen before. It was pure agony to witness his utter humiliation, such a proud man. I couldn't understand it. I understood that the police are powerful, that he had to give in, but I was disappointed too. I hated that goddamn sheriff more than anyone I had ever seen.

"Stuff like that is why my family moved to Cincy in the first place. That's where I grew up. They didn't want us to learn the colored man's shuffle. Looking back, I think my dad was brave in that he was willing to do whatever it took to live to drive his family home. He's a proud man who always stands tall despite his short stature. The pain of his downcast eyes, his degradation, still lacerates my gut.

"I was just a kid, but we put my dad in that position. They took a chance because we were hungry. To this day, I don't know why we stopped there. Did he just forget where we were? Was it an act of civil disobedience? Not with us kids there, I wouldn't think. I don't know why they didn't pick some fried chicken take-out joint."

I didn't mean for my emotions to spill out all over what started out to be a short summary.

"It's crazy that I've just told you, a perfect stranger, that tale. I almost never talk about that day." I'm trying to corral my hate for that f*@king sheriff to keep from breaking down in tears.

"Yeah, that sounds like a good enough reason to pass on the ice cream." Otis tries to lighten the mood by putting his hand on my shoulder. "And I'm not a complete stranger. We've been getting to know each other for a couple of hours now." He bends to open the car door for me to get in behind the wheel.

"We can try the Dairy Queen if you need some ice cream."

"Naw, I'm good for now unless you need a treat."

What was there to say? He grew up in this state when segregation was still legal. Serious now, Otis distracts from my sordid tale by saying that he thinks our practice will provide a low-stress, unhurried setting, the kind that can support his continuing recovery. He would have no problem dealing with an occasional catastrophe, but an unending string of perilous situations might represent a challenge to his sobriety. He doesn't sense that in our practice.

Dr. James's amiability washes over the nurses on the postpartum ward and L&D. He's a pretty smooth storyteller himself. He listens intently as I pour out venom over my fight over epidurals, patting my hand as I exhaust the narrative as if to say, *That's the way the cookie crumbles.* Although he's used epidurals before, he has no training or interest in administering them himself. After we cram ourselves into our tiny OR elevator, we emerge to don foot covers and caps as we talk about cesareans and the constraints on a timely emergency response.

I'm torn between giving a more sanitized version and telling the whole truth and nothing but—the stuff nobody told me on my tour. The desire to make the warts plain so a newcomer wouldn't feel sucker punched and leave quickly won out. I want another ob-gyn who will stay at least as long as I will, as if I have a right to demand that. Otis's reaction leaks out of his eyes, smudging his toothy grin. His previous practice was in a level-two hospital in a city, so these level-one hospital restrictions are new to him. Now he understands about the laparoscopic equipment.

Maintaining a facade for three or four hours is no great feat. What can anyone know about another in that amount of time? Even though Dr. James is certainly easy to get along with, I have no clear picture that our work styles will mesh. I hadn't wanted to grill him on how he would handle different clinical scenarios, even though that's the heart of the matter—his level of clinical competence and decision making. There are a number of different ways to achieve the same ends; it might even be fun to debate them as long as his are based on the best clinical practices. None of this "my third-year resident always said blah, blah, blah." At least superficially, he sounds as if he's stayed up-to-date.

In all honesty, Otis has limited options for practice. He's astute enough to understand that there will be few job offers for an African American physician with an extended period away from clinical practice now undergoing weekly drug testing for a history of crack addiction. He's a walking Black trope. Only places like Stephens Memorial would consider granting him privileges.

Are Robert and Joyce asking me to look for red flags? The weight of my opinion isn't clear. Do I have veto power? I doubt it. Why should I, a fleeting presence, eliminate a potential long-termer? Who am I to deny him an opportunity anyway?

By the time Otis is probably leaving Weavers Crossing, I've decided to simply go with the flow. I don't know what I don't know. I can envision a welcome division of labor where he handles the majority of gyn patients; he's very interested in them and I'm not. Moreover, he can bring the kind of collegial and consultative relationship I've been craving. The rest will have to sort itself out. If worse comes to worst and Otis proves to be an overbearing, unresponsive prick, say like Nwachukwu, I should be able to hold my own for another couple of years. He's not a man without weaknesses.

Chapter 19

OUR CELEBRATION

THE SATURDAY SUN IS SETTING as our car coasts along the two-lane road, the warmth of the summer day slowly dissipates as the landscape grows darker. We sit closer to the doors than to each other. A noisy, cooling column of air whooshes through Aaron's window, rolled down halfway. As we pass, a crowd's whoops from a game of horseshoes are swallowed up like the beer in their bottles. Our conversation is sporadic, words periodically squelched by the wind. Aaron says something about the wine in the back, our mandatory dinner BYOB in this dry county. Something about one of the union's organizing campaigns drifts in my ear and out, just as news of Kelly's new pregnancy probably drifts through his. Then quiet, as often happens during a drive.

In the dimming light, Aaron's rim of hair seems more salt than pepper. I watch him drive, dressed in his subtle pinstripe suit from his stint with the union local of salesmen at Barney's and Brooks Brothers in New York. He looks good.

Who could have guessed in 1969 that we would ever have a twentieth anniversary celebration? Tonight, ours is in a restaurant we haven't tried before. We're not looking for haute cuisine; our favorites from Little Italy will do. And importantly, the crunch of a bread crust around a chewy center, unlike the Wonder Bread soft and squishy ones around here.

My gored skirt with floral print mirrors the colors in Aaron's tie, but he's not attuned to the subtleties of color, so only I can see that. Outside our destination, my skirt swirls when I step out of the car, which draws his attention, enough for a quick "you look good" and a nuzzle of my neck, exposed by my upswept hair. We're looking our best as we scan the parking lot for other customers who may want to defend their idea of exclusive dining. We find only empty cars. Adrenaline surges to our already tense muscles when we near the restaurant door. Reservations over the phone give no hint of the guests' appearance. Our antennae have been tripped automatically and unbidden—habitual unconscious adaptation to a lifetime of exposures.

Confederate flags are a crude indicator of hostility, but less salient signals can't be read from a distance. I assume a white stranger is unfriendly until they have established themselves otherwise. It isn't fair, but a mistake can prove painful, if not physically, then emotionally. Even then it's not clear that a friendly facade won't turn hostile behind our backs or in the privacy of a home. An interracial couple is like a wounded water buffalo inviting lions to tear it apart.

The maître d' approaches us with a smile, potentially a positive sign. Should we let out our breath? The dimly lit indoor seating area is small, maybe ten tables set fairly close together. As we follow him, heads swivel, momentarily interrupting conversations. We're accustomed to the eyes at the other tables that consider us a diversion between entree and dessert. In one sense, we bask in the attention, a disruption to the norm that we've internalized as an act of defiance. And yet, we are a provocation that can elicit a dangerous backlash. In this instance, it could follow us on the ride home. We're in a hostile jungle.

He seats us in the back, the restaurant laid out before us. Seemingly, we're in a crowd of observers, not activists. We can relax a bit more and shift our attention to the menu, eager to gauge the fare. Should we order the same entree? Or sample each other's plates? Our waiter, a soft-spoken blonde in a black jacket, pours our water, then confidently recites the specials. The aroma of garlic makes Aaron eager to taste the rolls. The thought of veal scallopini rolls over my tongue; the memory feels distant in time and place. The thrill of treating ourselves for our lasting union is making us giddy. Osso buco, bruschetta, caesar salad.

No red flags yet; we can relax our guard still more. Our conversation sparkles like the wine in our glasses. I spy an older woman, too blonde for her saggy cheeks, looking in our direction. What is she thinking? I laugh as I look knowingly in Aaron's gray-green eyes, colluding in a joke we have long ago grown accustomed to. I like it best when we're with the kids, watching quizzical looks trying to untangle the nature of our relationships. Mother, babysitter, father? The one-drop rule holds that we're a family of four Black people and a white man. But sometimes, people see four white people and a Black woman. Whatever we are, it's "race mixing," and for some folks, that's just plain wrong.

Aaron slides his hand across the table to squeeze mine. We're excited about Damian starting at the new school. Our conversation is interrupted by piquant marinara sauce over al dente spaghetti. Perfecto. He's got his fork in my scallopini before I can ask to taste his. Tasting better with each sip of wine, the food is good, more flavorful than we had hoped. The panna cotta with blueberries and a cheesecake slice are the perfect finish. I glance at the upturned wine bottle floating in the bucket and suggest coffee before we drive home, but Aaron declines. Unlike me, coffee at such a late hour will disrupt his sleep. Inhaling the aroma, I drink in the warm black liquid, the perfect accompaniment for dessert.

Our senses dulled by full bellies and wine, a cool breeze blows across the nearly empty parking lot and brings a gentle wake-up. There are no headlights in view as we pull out onto the road. The car fills with the scents of dinner, fondly wafting from our doggy bags. Our tongues are still peppered with residual spices. We settle into a quiet review of our dishes, which completely distracts me from the unlit ebony road, except for a couple of bright headlights approaching us.

Aaron sees only pitch black in the rearview. There are no flashing lights like the night the sheriff stopped us coming home from Hendersonville. Terrorized, I had turned around when I heard the siren. Aaron, putting his hand on mine, had smiled in a way that ensured he would take care of it. Confident in the wiggle room he used to imply that he was my employer taking his maid home from serving a party, his pale complexion and wry smile allowed the two men to bond over the implied pleasures of a brown woman's body. In order to drive away in one piece, I had quietly choked on the implication of Aaron's mastery over his servant. Perhaps it had been I who had saved us both. Tonight, sputtering lights that turn into a driveway near where it entered the road is the only car we see behind us.

For me, deserted country roads and darkness reflexively trigger images of unruly white men, a deeply inculcated apprehension of white retribution. Spun tales of bygone events and personal observations had fired my resistance to moving south; too many unnamed Emmett Tills over the years. Aaron, however, thrives on the knowledge that he will always get the benefit of doubt and that will be enough to keep us safe.

The house is quiet when we get home. Damian and Abbie are not asleep but have settled in their separate rooms. Only Kyle is quietly nestled in his sheets. A small gift box sits on our bed. It holds a beautiful David Yurman sterling silver ring, studded with small turquoise and quartz stones across twisted oxidized bands. It's so perfectly me. As Aaron begins to explain how his mother had gotten her discount from Neiman Marcus, I put my hands on his cheeks and pull his lips to mine. A long, passionate kiss. He's still a great kisser.

About halfway through my day, Monica Jackson is grinning back at me from her perch on an exam table—a pleasant surprise. A quick look in her chart shows that she hasn't been back since her initial diagnosis of conjoined twins eight weeks ago.

"Sorry for the wait. How've you been?" I keep apologizing even though a wait is more standard than not.

"I'm good, ma'am. The babies have been moving a lot, almost more than I can stand."

I flinch slightly at the "ma'am," feeling as if it plops me squarely into middle age when I feel more like her contemporary. Nothing more than a traditional term of respect, it triggers a moment of mourning for my passage beyond young adulthood to middle age. That milestone feels like it's arrived as we send our oldest away for school. Silly really, but there it is. Batting that back, I'm anxious to hear what the perinatologists at UNC said.

"How did your consults go? They haven't sent us any records."

"Oh, I didn't go," Monica answers matter-of-factly, without embarrassment. "I went to Dr. N, and he sent me to the hospital for an ultrasound just to figure out how far along I was."

"Did you tell him you'd been here and wanted a second opinion? We don't mind that, you know. That's your right."

She smiles as she answers. "No, ma'am. I didn't bother with that."

Dr. Nwachukwu is the only ob-gyn in town who hadn't been recruited through Antioch Associates. Maybe he thought he was going to have the town to himself after Dr. Jenkins retired and resented the intrusion of first one and then another practice in a town where the population isn't growing much.

"They said it could be, you know, that twin thing you said, but they weren't sure. Dr. N wanted me to go to Chapel Hill, but he wasn't gonna call them to make an appointment like you, so I came back."

Great, she's recognized that we provide a better service at Antioch. "Well, I'm happy to see you. Feeling good overall? Twins usually deliver as early as six weeks before their due date, so we need to get those appointments as soon as possible. As I explained, you'll need to have a C-section there. We should probably do the test for diabetes where you drink that really sweet stuff. Women with twins are more likely to develop gestational diabetes earlier in the pregnancy. We can send those results to Chapel Hill when we send your records. When did you eat last?"

"Last night."

"We can go ahead today. It takes an hour. But you know, eating breakfast is even more important for twins. Your body uses up all of your stored energy overnight. You should really be eating three meals a day, and a couple of snacks can't hurt. You need the extra calories for twins, especially since your weight was on the low side when you started. Do you have enough food at home?"

"We're good."

I couldn't resist a quick look with ultrasound; conjoined is not something you see even once a year. The intervening weeks had complicated the picture. The two larger fetuses were more crowded together into what looked almost like an eight-legged insect. It was really fascinating, but knowing I don't have the time, I force myself to quit after recording the two heart rates and a couple of measurements. I need to leave the details to the experts.

"While you're getting your test, Allison can start working on your appointments, and she can look to see if you qualify for food supplements."

When faced with a complicated pregnancy, I inevitably flash back to the chaos around Maude Henderson and her baby with arthrogryposis. But Liddie Braithwaite, who surprised us all with twins, was equally unnerving. Without prenatal care, she thought she was "about due," but when I felt the baby's head as it came through the cervix, it was swallowed up by the palm of my hand; maybe twenty-five weeks, I thought. When we paged Phyllis STAT, we had no idea a second baby was coming. There was nothing anyone could do. The babies were too early. They both died. We were befuddled by the problem of two preterm babies and one pediatrician. Thank goodness for the respiratory therapist. Can Joyce Fowler serve as another pediatrician if we find ourselves in a pickle? That's a question we don't want to have to answer.

Chapter 20

NO. 1 TAKES FLIGHT

AS AARON ARRANGES THE LAST of the bags and boxes in the car's trunk, I watch from the side door, trying to catch the vague chatter behind me. Abbie's scolding Kyle for something. She continues to assume a parenting role that she appropriated as five years his senior. I've tried to dissuade her from this pseudo-mothering, but the simple truth is that the cracks in our childcare between Aaron's goings and my comings mean that her monitoring has proven useful. It's hard to press the case that her babysitting when needed doesn't grant her special privileges at other times. Actually, Kyle frequently goes to her on his own for help. These occurrences will become even more frequent because today Damian is leaving for NCSSM, the North Carolina School of Science and Math.

Since the kids seem to have worked it out, I let sleeping dogs lie. I'm somewhat preoccupied by flickering images of Damian's childhood—his day-care center, seesaw rides at a nearby playground, the time he fell asleep in his highchair chewing a peanut butter sandwich. I allow the memories to unfold, a maternal prerogative at this sentinel moment. Damian's leaving is a good thing, I hope, full of possibilities that many other students in the state would kill for. After all, you raise your kids to launch them into the world. You instill the basics, encourage them to think freely, and they're ready to take on whatever is ahead. You've built trust, so they seek your advice and share their lives with you. Sophomore year is just too soon.

Aaron's deep in the details of packing, maybe to avoid his feelings, still a mystery to me. He's not big on emoting, at least to me. Instead, his intricate positioning of packages represents his insistence that only he knows how to properly load a car. There's no point in trying to help; it only annoys him—a potential trigger in stressful moments.

As the car backs out of the driveway, the kids are settling in to play in the back seat. Abbie and Damian are bandying some gossip back and forth across Kyle, strategically placed over the middle hump. He's short enough not to care, sometimes slipping down there to roll his matchbox cars across the seat while his siblings sleep. Damian picks up a toy, grabs Kyle, and starts tickling him. Then, they all collapse in laughter.

The atmosphere in the front seat is more tense. We ride in silence, Aaron's lips pressed tightly together. I reflect that his expression may expose his sorrow as I watch from the corner of my eye. I wish we could share it, and maybe we will later. Or, he could be thinking through some work problem. Who knows? I lean my head against the window and put my headphones on.

"Wake up. You need to wake up and get the directions." Aaron is shaking my arm. The car had rocked me into a welcomed nap.

"Where are we?" I venture, struggling to shift my brain into gear.

"Somewhere outside town. Don't you have the map?" he snaps.

"I just need to find it. I need a minute to focus."

"We don't have a minute!" he roars.

"Oh, wait. I think we just passed the exit."

"Goddammit." Aaron is fuming. He hates to get lost, and yet his sense of direction is practically nonexistent. He's going to blow.

"Figure it out!" he yells, loud enough to wake the dead.

How is it that I can decisively handle an obstetric emergency with laser-focused precision, but I am now unnerved into a muddle? In the first, I'm very sure of my footing, but now, I'm in unknown territory. Maybe the volume? The closed space? I used to walk away mid-stomp from a boss who had tantrums, but there's nowhere to escape from this traveling box.

"Just pull over. Give me time to figure it out." A reasonable request delivered in a whiny tone I didn't intend.

"I'm not stopping! It can't be that hard!"

Shit, I can get this done, I think. When I suggest a right turn, he's determined it's a left. I have to suppress a smile when we pass an outlet store we'd just seen on the other side of the road.

"Looks like we just went in a circle," I point out, maybe a little too smugly. I mean, why ask for advice you refuse to follow? Livid now, he slams on the brakes so hard that it launches everything off the seats onto the floor, and then he peels into a U-turn. I check the kids in the back and scan the landscape for nearby cops. But we've finally gotten back on the right track.

Turning my head toward the window, I quietly smile. He's going to have to admit I was right. No "thanks" or "sorry" ever comes my way. He never apologizes for his outbursts anymore. By the time we pull into the unloading area near the dorm, there's only silence in the car. The storm has blown over.

The kids tumble out of the back doors like someone hollered "Fire!" Aaron hops from the driver's seat, barking orders about which items each of us should carry as he opens the trunk. I head towards the student guide standing in the doorway to get directions to Damian's room. My oldest is trying not to look overawed as we mount the stairwell up to the third floor. This is our first time on the campus. It never mattered how it looks because the promise is so much bigger than the alternative. His selection is an honor, one of two kids from each county. Bringing up the rear of our caravan, I step behind Kyle, just to keep him moving in the right direction. I'm creating some distance, bracing against another tempest, but this time in public.

The dorm room is small. There are two desks, two beds, two dressers, two small closets, and one window. Damian's roommate hasn't yet arrived, or at least he hasn't left anything in the room.

"You get first dibs on a bed." I laugh, turning to Damian.

"I think you should take that one," Abbie pipes up, pointing to the one furthest from the door. Kyle immediately plops on the mattress.

"Get up, Kyle. Not on the bare mattress. We need to put some sheets on it. Let's go back and get more stuff from the car."

"Maybe I should wait to talk to my roommate," Damian adds hesitantly, thinking such a move is too presumptuous.

"It's an unwritten dorm rule. You snooze, you lose," Aaron adds quickly, no doubt thinking about his own roommate experiences.

Abbie seems to be sagging under the weight of the impending separation. She's going to feel like she's lost an arm. Suddenly she'll be without her confidant and protector.

Some last-minute shopping sucks the wind out of our sails. Abbie is clinging more closely to Damian as if suddenly aware that their closeness will become a casualty of distance. Damian, in the meantime, is making an effort to share some individual one-on-one moments with Kyle. I love that he's so kind and considerate.

Damian seems to be itching to spread his wings, unafraid of what lies ahead, when he gently herds us out of his room to decorate it on his own. I leave a stack of loose quarters on the way out, having made sure he knew how to do laundry before we left home. It's a small gesture, wrapped in my love.

Aaron adds some coins of his own, seemingly unhappy that I seized the initiative. Dragging the farewell out isn't going to make it sweeter. He's only two hours away. He'll be home for holidays and maybe some weekends, probably bringing his laundry to save those quarters.

Retracing our footsteps back through the hallways, we pass three kids talking about orbital calculations for a flight to Mars as if it were odds for a UNC NCAA basketball title. That's the essence of this experience—lots of smart kids bouncing off each other without boundaries. The universe is their playground. NCSSM students have aspirations to broader horizons beyond state schools, maybe Stanford or MIT. To my surprise, many kids in Weavers Crossing had never heard of them. The state's large corporations underwrite the labs and facilities at the school in an effort to rescue the best and brightest from lackluster schools like Stephens County's. Their strategy is to keep the state's best prepared students within it. To that end, they make it very easy to interact on University of North Carolina campuses, but for those who escape out of state, it's a good bet that some will return to their home workforce near family and friends.

NCSSM is a great bargain, an elite school without an elite price. It's a tuition-free public school with the earmarks of an institution that offers early connections to the people who will become the movers and shakers in government and business. It's a bell ringer for college admissions committees. Alumni status can be the ticket through a door that is otherwise closed. I know all too well that people with brown skin can work twice as hard as everyone else and their work go unnoticed and unpromoted without those valuable connections. Brown skin amid a flood of white comes with double A (affirmative action) scarlet letters that label us less qualified. But not at NCSSM where admission criteria use county of residence, PSAT scores, and GPA. I'm sure, like anywhere, there's some behind-the-scenes maneuvering, but because they're the least likely to have extra influence, the African Americans in the student body earned their place on as equal a playing field as can be found.

I want a future for my children where they can achieve their best selves, whatever they decide that will be. In that, I'm like every white parent I know. It's also a desire shared with every Black parent I've ever met, although they often lack access to the same toolbox available to well-connected folks who aren't descended from slaves. In Stephens County, the dream fades when people look around and find that the chances are slim to none. They quietly accept that and do the best they can.

Our journey was bittersweet. On the one hand, NCSSM may be the single best thing that has happened during this rural sojourn, at least for our son's future. On the other, I've lost my portal into Damian's daily life. I won't know his friends. He won't write. He may call, but only when he isn't caught up in his own stuff. There's a chance that as the firstborn who still craves parental approval, he'll concede to Aaron's demand for a ritual Sunday chat, an echo of his own weekly calls to Miriam. He's also a teenager, which means he'll skip a few times, and even so, those clipped phone conversations will not contain the kind of juicy details that we used to share face to face in our quiet moments together. I'm jealous that Aaron can visit him on the way to or from some work destination, a luxury beyond my reach. Deep down I sense that my eldest is leaving home for good, a thought that has jettisoned me into a weekend sprinkled with reminiscences both distant and near.

As I sit at my basement desk tonight, I already miss the chance to wander over to his room a few feet away and check in. I've released my eldest into the wide world like an owlet soaring from its nest for the first time. I'm confident he's ready, but that doesn't fill the hole left in the nest. Our family life has changed.

Damian's departure and the anticipated arrival of Dr. James make this the perfect time to jump into the process to become officially board certified as an obstetrician gynecologist. This stamp of approval is a huge deal, the goal of every man or woman who starts a residency. Stupidly, I had deferred application when I first became eligible in order to tilt at windmills in the hospital. I lacked the bandwidth to gather the information for the application, let alone study for the exam. My friends Adrienne and Elise plowed straight ahead to sit for the test last year and continue to nag me to woman up. We figure the monstrous long-distance phone bills are well worth the fun we have during them. My mother always calls after the rates go down, but we don't care anything about that.

Board certification is an ob-gyn's Mount Everest, an arduous ascent through oxygen-starved air that threatens to annihilate the climber. The most intimidating element is an oral exam, a complete departure from the routine multiple choice tests that we've come to know and hate over the years.

One year of unsupervised general ob-gyn practice is the first requirement. Having already ticked that box off, what's ahead is the preparation of a case list—a detailed listing of the circumstances which surround all the hospitalized, surgical, and complicated patients treated over the previous year. The board defines competence by the breadth of the applicant's experience; a record that lacks the desired diversity will bounce the applicant into another year of collecting cases.

My list will include women like Fanny Hoskins, prenatal patients admitted to the hospital and discharged before they're delivered, and inpatients with postpartum, surgical, and neonatal complications, like Faith Spurling and Isaiah Henderson, as well as any gynecologic admissions and all surgeries including cesareans and tubal ligations. Details like blood loss, lab results, and length of hospitalization as well as neonatal outcomes can only be culled from individual medical records. Luckily, we have a certain amount of wiggle room since our submissions are on the honor system; ACOG doesn't have access to any resources that could verify our data.

Once a completed case list is approved, examinations are scheduled during a few weeks in November and December in one Chicago hotel. One section of the oral exam covers clinical decision-making in patients from our lists. The other involves more generalized questions across the spectrum of ob-gyn. I've decided that my peace of mind is worth the cost of staying overnight at their pricey hotel. The inevitability of winter snowstorms makes flying into O'Hare a nail biter in and of itself, but added to the anxiety surrounding the four-hour exam, I would be apoplectic.

The oral administration isn't the only element that will be different from Part I. Back then, the monumental importance of passing the boards had been used to stir a cauldron of terror more intense than the ubiquitous fear central to medical education. Taken at the end of residency, our faculty petrified us into thinking failure was an actual possibility, even though most of us had never failed a test in our lives. Granted, our test-taking aptitude had slipped after the first couple years of medical school, when written tests were replaced by faculty observation and daily grilling during surgeries, rounds, and conferences. Those sessions were forums of intimidation where ridicule and humiliation in front of peers and nurses hung over any wrong answer.

The fact that many program directors provided review lectures during their program's designated educational hours signaled the extraordinary importance of passing the exam to our programs. This investment in dedicated time, exclusively for learning, was an exception to the normal rhythm of our training where clinical duties superseded everything else. A 100 percent pass rate was important to a program's reputation. Anything less would leave a black mark that would reverberate across all 120 US medical schools.

Fed by this dark cloud of calamity, an industry of board review test courses sprang up to guide us to victory, each charging a hefty fee. Or maybe it was the other way around; the courses came before they generated the fear. I merged my desire for international travel with my program's required fourth-year educational conference to attend a five-day board study course at a luxurious hotel in Acapulco. Attendees brought their families and relaxed by sun-drenched swimming pools for the latter part of each day. That experience was at the high end of the spectrum. There are cheaper bare bones courses in airport hotels where participants sit in lectures from seven thirty a.m. to six p.m. with lunch and dinner breaks before resuming evening sessions until nine p.m.

Ironically, outside the brouhaha, the test is graded pass/fail, using a threshold set by the board for each individual year. The faculty's insistence that both Parts I and II are make-or-break career moments turns out to be part of the hype. If someone fails, they have two additional chances to retake the exam, although for the rest of their career, every privilege and license application will ask if the applicant has ever failed. Beyond the embarrassment, the only answer that counts is that the person passed at some point despite the continuing shame associated with "publicly" admitting ad infinitum that they failed to meet a significant moment.

This time around, there's no faculty pressure, no scheduled lectures or study sessions, just me, slogging along in my basement office entering my information in the ACOG-created computer program, poring over it to ensure its accurate and free of typos.

Then, I'll send it by certified mail and wait. Confident in its acceptance, my study plan is to review the standard textbook in each subspecialty. They say the questions will be exclusively clinical, nothing about basic science or etiology or even risk factors like on Part 1.

I'm certainly going to miss the joint study sessions with my fellow residents where we'd pore over our "bootlegged" questions, a list of questions from previous years that were remembered and regurgitated immediately after the exams by those who had preceded us. We knew that many of the questions repeated year after year, and although we didn't have the verified answers, we worked through our best approximations. Following our exam, we too gathered to add our own contribution for residents who would follow us. After all, we are type A personalities, and as veteran test takers, we know how to position ourselves to succeed.

Shamefully, I too had been suckered into the failure mania around the written exam. But by the time I received the results, I was knee-deep in moving and settling in at Antioch, assuming that I'd passed. I want to say the board letter was anticlimactic, but actually, it was a huge relief that put to rest a nagging bit of uncertainty. Now I'll have to ride that roller coaster again for the oral exam, hopefully in a more stable mood. Fear can be contagious.

Aaron seems blissfully unaware of the whole ordeal. I mentioned something about a trip to Chicago and the ridiculously expensive application fees several times, but he hasn't retained it. My career timelines and milestones seem to slip through his fingers. Certification is an in-group ritual for sure, but somehow, I imagine that other physicians' spouses know enough to support their partners. In my funk, I often forget what stuff Aaron does or doesn't remember.

In his defense, he fell in love with his college sweetheart. This whole medical thing didn't come along until ten years into our marriage. If I'm being honest, I didn't understand the full course of training when I started either. That the length of a residency varied by specialty from two to five years, came as we rotated on their services, as did information that further specialization would add even more. So I can hardly blame him for not knowing initially, but this far into the game, he should have caught up, at least the outlines.

What's important now is to put this oral exam behind me while I still have gynecologic patients here in Weavers Crossing. Once I enter fellowship, it'll be strictly obstetric patients from then on. Those two more years where others will determine my destiny is the price I must pay to eliminate routine annual exams and frequent on-call nights from my life. Even though Aaron jokes that I'll be fifty, only a few years from retirement before I'm on a tenure track, my late start hasn't dulled my intentions.

Aaron has always said that he supports my career choice because he wants me to feel fulfilled. He watched me be overwhelmed with a new baby on top of the exhaustion of residency and took on new responsibilities, like grocery shopping, in response. It's no surprise that he threw himself into poring through circulars for the best bargains, obsessively collecting coupons, and stopping at different stores to take advantage of the specials he'd found. That's his modus operandi, all to our benefit. And of course, he's been willing to move around as my training dictated, something that most husbands are reluctant or unable to do. Emotional support is the thing that he can't seem to wrap his head around. His indifference in that area is forever frustrating when it isn't infuriating.

I was in the dark too about how a career in medicine could upend my family life. It's no accident that ob-gyns have high divorce and suicide rates, but nobody told me that when I was choosing specialties. Not that the information would have made a difference; we all imagine we'll be the exception to the rule.

I'm pretty sure that those gaps in information can be laid at the feet of our mostly male trainers. Men of their generation felt little of the consequences for raising kids in their virtual absence. They believed in the natural order where men were the breadwinners, and physicians were wholly dedicated to their practices. Some specialties didn't allow resident physicians to marry until well into the 1970s. Their wives probably believed in the breadwinner-absent husband as well. It will take a reasonable number of women entering the subspecialty, as it happens around me now, before trainee mentoring includes particular difficulties female practitioners face.

Embarking on this undertaking, I worry the additional year that I've waited has allowed that post-residency Part I fund of knowledge to quietly dribble away like cash surreptitiously embezzled from a bank account. This endless cycling through a limited number of diagnoses has further curtailed what should automatically emerge from the medical ether. I can't remember the last time I treated a patient with thyroid disease, either overactive or underactive. I know the medications, but I'm rusty on the dosing. I feel like my medical treasure trove has been shrouded in a fog, rolling in off frigid mountain tops. Oh how I miss my little study clique of fellow residents united in shared panic that kept our knowledge base palpably fresh by pumping up any sagging enthusiasm. Here, I must go it alone.

Chapter 21

ANOTHER CHANGE
IN PROTOCOL

THE WEATHER HAS FORGOTTEN TO warm up. Usually the sun brings the thermometer up during a winter day, but we've been in the twenties for a week. Yesterday, a tincture of snow flurries periodically blew around, nothing that would leave a coating to cover the brown lawns though. These days have been a cruel reminder that North Carolina has seasonal weather that includes winter cold. When I think about how hard it has been to keep our poorly insulated house warm, I worry that some of our patients could freeze to death.

I'm happy to be in the office where our space heaters are cranked up so women stripped down for their pelvics don't shiver. During a prenatal visit, we signed tubal papers under my initiative to shift to an earlier date. The idea is to discover any unintended consequences before we enshrine it into standard protocol. It's comforting to consider having to solicit Otis's thoughts, but even if he's not personally on board, patients rotating through the providers should catch everyone. I can't imagine why he would object.

Although Florence Bivens is here for a routine prenatal visit, she's not a routine patient. She's one of our candidates for a trial of labor after a previous cesarean, VBAC for short. Given her history, it's a small miracle that Florence has had no complaints so far. People say that it's her "high-yella" freckled complexion and curly reddish-brown hair that has cursed her, or at least, that's what the staff have told me.

Now at twenty-eight weeks, a normal uncomplicated pregnancy feels even more important for Florence whose first two were anything but. Her first daughter remains in a NICU stepdown unit at UNC, not yet home some two years after her birth twelve weeks early. The placenta previa that had covered Florence's cervix had started bleeding. Even mild contractions can cause a piece of the placenta to pull away from the uterine wall, causing a hemorrhage. This sets up a vicious cycle where blood accumulates and forms clots behind the placenta, causing more of it to pull away and bleed. A trickle of blood can become a waterfall that threatens both the fetus and mother.

The standard treatment plan is to delay delivery to allow time for the fetus to mature. Two things are needed: a twenty-four-hour blood bank and a NICU. Stephens has neither. But things didn't go as planned. Soon after her transfer to Chapel Hill, Florence had an emergency cesarean after which her baby had a number of complications associated with prematurity over the ensuing months.

Florence, without a means of transportation, was unable to visit her tiny daughter enmeshed in an explosion of tubes and machines. While she talked with the social workers and nurses who called, except when her phone was turned off for nonpayment, her daughter outgrew the pictures they sent, and her memory receded into a distant haze, almost as if the whole thing had been a dream. The mother-baby bond became a casualty of Florence's struggle to eke out a living two hours away.

Florence's second pregnancy took a different wrong turn. That baby's cranium failed to form, a condition known as anencephaly. Without a skull to protect it, the brain is exposed to the outside world where it will be overwhelmed by infection. Typically, the cerebral hemispheres, the thinking part of the brain, don't develop either. The condition is fatal, most often within a couple days of birth.

With fingers crossed to reach term, Florence has chosen to go into labor this time like her friends, using the newer alternative to "once a cesarean, always a cesarean," the standard in our specialty. Known as VBAC, vaginal birth after cesarean, the protocols were among the earliest changes I made after Dr. Edwards left. To offer our mothers a chance to avoid the attendant complications of an operative delivery seems important as long as it can be done safely.

On exam, I note Florence's scar, widening and darkening in the midline as her skin stretches to accommodate her growing belly. I can feel the baby moving as I check for fetal heart tones. Her blood pressure is normal; she has no complaints. I ask about her daughter and if she'll be coming home soon. Florence doesn't know. She gets off the exam table and hurries out to the lab to have her blood drawn, tossing a "Thanks, ma'am" over her shoulder. That's a couple more weeks under her belt, all reassuringly normal. We'll see her back in three more weeks.

It feels good to be on the forefront of a trend rather than decades behind. So far, none of our patients has resisted the idea. In fact, with the help of the grapevine, some women have come to the practice specifically because they wanted to escape the scheduled repeat cesarean they could expect at the other ob-gyn offices. It's not a ton of women, but it's a start. And true to expectation, we haven't had a major complication yet.

I still think that a surgical delivery should remain a rescue procedure when vaginal delivery isn't possible or is potentially harmful to the baby or the mother. However, many women have been seduced by the possibility to pick their baby's birthday and, of course, avoid the pain of labor. So as more and more of their friends have C-sections, the operation's commonness has made it seem benign even though it's major abdominal surgery with a list of potential complications that are substantial. Doctors should be using our medical expertise to discourage this rush to the operating room.

Fortunately, other far more prominent ob-gyns agree. We're joining a rising trend, spearheaded by ACOG itself. Unlike the organization's gradual, staid approach, it has launched a campaign to coax more physicians to hop on the VBAC bandwagon. There have been a flurry of publications in the specialty's journals and thematic educational conferences and highlighted research at their annual meetings to hype recommendations around allowing women with previous cesareans to have a trial of labor, even though some will not ultimately be able to deliver vaginally.

ACOG has taken these extraordinary steps because a confluence of rich and powerful entities have applied significant pressure. Insurance companies were grumbling loudly about paying the cost of cesareans, several times more than that of vaginal deliveries. In turn, employers, particularly those with lots of child-bearing aged employees, were groaning about rising health insurance premiums. Under the "once a cesarean" rule, the projected number of surgeries was going to skyrocket as the number of first-time cesareans continued to rise. ACOG itself had become increasingly concerned about surging cesarean rates and the associated risks and complications.

In the meantime, a mountain of scientific evidence was accumulating that demonstrated that VBACs are safe, and the most dreaded complication, uterine rupture, is rare. And so, ACOG changed its recommendations, and here we are.

I didn't need the encouragement because I've been following the literature closely to confirm that VBACs remain safe. Beyond that, I'm relying on my experience.

McCune's OB department was an early adopter of the change, which presented opportunities for me to have numerous experiences with both successful and failed VBACs. Even more importantly, I'd had a part in the diagnosis and treatment of a couple of uterine ruptures. For every physician, negotiating a serious complication successfully implants an indelible impression in our minds that we have met and conquered the beast. And that we can do it again. We can respond more quickly when presented with similar symptoms because the diagnosis has moved up in our differential lists, faster than if we've only read about something in a textbook. If I close my eyes, I can still see that baby floating in the abdomen, up under the liver, after a uterine rupture. It comes with the feeling that we saved two lives in a matter of moments. It's beyond amazing!

McCune was ahead of the curve; many private practitioners and hospitals have been reluctant to give up the convenience of scheduled cesareans, the number and timing of which can be easily controlled unlike vaginal deliveries and cesareans during labor. Their lawyers worry that malpractice suits will proliferate, and just that prospect would drive insurance rates up. In fact, complications from VBACs have already become a leading basis for legal action.

Happily, I don't have to worry about interference from the hospital. The administration and their lawyers are not very aggressive about prevention of future complications. They're content with the assumption that our population will remain non-litigious, without the activity of urban area ambulance-chasing lawyers waiting around every hospital to drum up a lawsuit. They're pretty comfortable as well that Southern juries notoriously favor defendants over plaintiffs. Most citizens in rural areas are afraid that a judgment against their doctor will chase them away. So small pretrial settlements are the norm.

I'm proud to have flipped the script in our office so that rather than automatically being scheduled for a repeat C-section, a trial of labor is the default for women like Florence who meet the recommended criteria.

Needless to say, we're hoping this time that Florence's bad luck streak will come to an end. In the meantime, she seems completely unaware of the pitfalls. Our goal is for her to have a normal vaginal delivery at Stephens Memorial around the time of her due date, and the baby's father can take them both home after a couple of days. And Florence is certain it will happen that way.

Chapter 22

NOTHING I DO IS RIGHT

I 'M STOKED ABOUT OUR RECENT organizing efforts. I've got a couple of victories under my belt. The shops are small, but the wins are important. I wish Laura could see it; how these people feel the power of unity. They're winning. Now they understand that skin color doesn't matter. I feel like I used to during the City College strike in 1970. The students were unified in huge rallies and marches that led to victory. Obviously, the situation is different. These are men and women fighting for a decent wage to house and feed their families, not students wanting more freedom to pick different courses. Times have changed, but the issue is the same: power for regular men and women to control the institutions that rule their lives. These workers will no longer be dictated to by bosses, because their union will speak up for them. Trust me—they've dealt with lots of bullies.

When I get folks rocking and shouting at meetings, there's electricity in the air. It's not a feeling you can duplicate anywhere other than in a movement. It makes me feel like I'm saving the world. When I go into homes to recruit supporters, going house to house, getting up close and personal, there's nothing like good talk over a drink. People trust me—trust me to tell them the truth. Man, it's the best.

That's the part Laura doesn't get. She doesn't give me credit for making a difference in people's lives. I'm really good at what I do. I need her to be proud of what I accomplish. I need her to recognize my abilities. At best, her response is nonplus; at worst, she thinks what I do is simply disruptive to her life.

Don't get me wrong—I'm glad she found medicine. It's something she jumped into with both feet. The road has been hard, but Laura's good at what she does. I don't know anything about medicine, but she must be good because she's good at whatever she does. She says she can't think of anything else she'd rather do.

It looks to me like she's sitting pretty now. She hardly ever spends a night in the hospital anymore. Some nights, she doesn't get any calls at all. Most days, she goes to the office and then goes home, simple as that. When she does have to go in at night, she's usually back before morning. I can't see how she wouldn't be overjoyed. She does seem to have some disagreements with other doctors in the hospital, and again, I'm unfamiliar with the details. But that's nothing in comparison to how much better our lives are.

It's too bad that the job she has now isn't what she wants. She says she wants to transform the way medicine is practiced. It's an admirable goal, but it's not like she's part of a growing movement with power. A solo act, by a lone Black woman no less, seems pretty unrealistic. I don't have the sense she's making much progress. Again, I don't know about this medical environment, but it sounds like, at this rate, she'll be old and gray before she's in any position to make a difference, if ever.

I guess her plan is admirable, but I signed on to something much simpler in the beginning. If I'd known it was going to be ten years and counting, I probably would have been less enthusiastic. Not that I would want to stand in her way. I would never do that. I guess she changed what she wanted the further she got into it. I have to worry though. Is there another curve ball coming? Some other opportunity that I don't know about yet?

$\mathfrak{I}$ always look forward to walking through my door at Oakdale Court. I'll yell "I'm home!" and the kids will come running, excited to see me. I love those moments. Unfortunately, I'm often disappointed, almost like they didn't notice I was gone. They don't even stop what they're doing. I want Laura to look glad to see me and give me a hug and kiss. That usually doesn't happen either. It's like I'm not important. I miss them when I'm gone. Don't they miss me?

No sooner than I've changed my clothes, Laura is coming at me right out of the gate with some complaint. Doesn't she know I'm doing my best? Doesn't she see how much I lighten her load? I call home every night no matter what else I'm doing. I think about her all the time. That's why I remind her to put out the garbage cans, so she'll know she's on my mind. She's always got some snarky reply, like, "You know the garbage men will be back in a few days" or "Oh, you think I don't know that?" I'm doing it to show I care, but she's always offended that I'm calling her inadequate.

Or she's got some complaint about work. It makes me want to nod off almost as soon as she starts talking. These people sound like assholes, even though I don't know any of them. I don't have the time to sort it out. Usually, I change the subject so she'll take the hint. I know she's capable, and I'm sure she can handle it.

My quiet night with the family falls apart a little at a time. Why does she come at me until we end up fighting? It's not what I want. My nights are never what I imagine before I get home. Maybe it doesn't start until dinner. If I'm not at the table as soon as Laura calls, she's pissed. If I have to take a phone call, she's pissed. She has this way of nagging, a lot like Miriam. It's like an electric drill driving into my side in short bursts. *BZZZZZZ. BZZZZZZ.* By the end of the night, you'd think I can't do anything right. Too often, I'm on the verge of exploding and not completely without reason. *BZZZZZZ. BZZZZZZ.* I don't understand why she can't just appreciate that I'm here. I'm one of the good guys.

Do I bitch when she gets calls after hours? No, they're part of her job just like they're part of mine. I need to hear from people on the ground to know what's breaking. They call me about violations and employee disciplinary actions. It's the only way I have some control over what's happening. I need to build trust. I have to put out small fires before they become infernos. I have to be able to assign the best person to a job. I need to mediate arguments within the staff and between the members. These are issues of personnel management. And that's on top of issues with plant management. These are small businessmen who think nothing of their workers and think they need to cut corners to survive. Or they need to cut corners to make more profit. It's always a war with management, but over time, I'll get to know them, and they'll get to know me. I can make them more cooperative. They respect me for driving hard bargains, but more than that, being fair and honest. They know I know my stuff.

I don't know what else I can do at home. We've had trouble before, like any marriage. At one point, Laura wasn't happy that I wouldn't spend more time with her friends, even though they were mostly lab techs, and almost all of them were single. Basically, Laura thought I wasn't giving her enough time and attention, even though I included her with my students, and my friends were her friends. A change in circumstances made all the difference. In Nashville, we made friends as a couple, and then she had all her girlfriends and people from medical school. And we were both doing what we really wanted to be doing. Laura doesn't have many friends in Weavers Crossing, but I can't help her with that.

I do a lot, but even with all that, I don't seem to be enough. Laura's unhappy with me no matter what. I don't get any credit from her for moving around the country. How many men would do that? I take charge of so many things she never has to think about. How many other guys take on so many responsibilities around the house or with their kids? Why can't she see that I'm one of the good guys?

Chapter 23

D DAY ARRIVES

DECEMBER FIFTH IS THE DATE of my scheduled showdown with an ABOG (The American Board of Obstetrics and Gynecology) tribunal. While we all know the scope of topics to be covered, what topics are going to be fished out of that vast ocean on our specific day are unknowable. Is there a path to improve the odds? Elise and Adrienne keep telling me that my concerns are overblown, and if I just describe what I do every day, I'll be fine. After all, hundreds of applicants simply show up without studying at all.

But at the last minute, I couldn't escape my faith in classroom preparation, so I took one of those airport motel review courses. They place special emphasis on the areas the examiners most frequently cover every year. Some of them are obvious, like obstetric hemorrhage, which is considered an emergency that every ob-gyn must know how to handle rapidly and efficiently, and our unique disease, hypertension in pregnancy, which is one of the major causes of maternal and fetal death worldwide. It's the less obvious choices that worry me, especially cancer and gynecologic surgery complications. I wanted to believe that the course, a chance at an intense total immersion frame of mind, would be a worthwhile although costly substitute for communal study.

Of course, Adrienne and Elise didn't approve. We joked that the money would have been better spent on more long-distance phone sessions with potential test questions, and far more fun. Through it all, their advice was simple—you know more about these cases than anybody else in the room, so sound confident. A particular hemoglobin or bilirubin doesn't matter; it's the principles of practice they're testing. My girls have been there for me the whole way.

Despite their reassurances, the specter of failure has continued to quietly lurk in the background. If Dr. Nwachukwu, who is delaying his third attempt at passing until the clock runs out, is an example of what happens in these outer reaches, I may be doomed. That's ridiculous; his results reflect his relative incompetence. Logically, if over 80 percent of the examinees pass, then certainly I should be among them. But, when the psyche is in, logic isn't part of the equation.

I ooze anxiety like an oil spill seeping into a waterway, slowly but surely enveloping the entire biome. Waiting on hold on the phone sends me into a quiet fury, usually unfortunate for the person who finally answers to my ire. I watch myself transform into Cruella Deville when my kids send me off the deep end for no good reason; I am powerless to control it. I manage to calm down after a night of study, but the anxiety creeps back the next morning with my first cup of coffee.

The Sunday before the exam, Aaron detonates a bomb. This is a pattern he has repeated before every major career marker. Why do I keep expecting his behavior to diverge from its past? After I casually ask him about his schedule for the week, he reels off a couple things for Tuesday that immediately rattle me.

"You remember I'm going to Chicago on Tuesday and Wednesday?"

"No, what are you talking about?" His volume is already on the rise.

"I have my oral boards on Wednesday. I told you weeks ago and have reminded you several times since. I get that you don't care about what I do, but Jesus, this is ridiculous."

And we're off! His dagger thrust into my heart has it pumping in anxious agitation, disappointment, rage, and sadness all wrapped into one.

"You'll have to arrange for a sitter," he says matter-of-factly, like he's reading the newspaper.

This is something we never do; we always tag team overnight absences.

"What the f$@k!" I've slipped off the deep end, with smoke belching from my ears. I'm so livid that I can barely get the words out. I grip my hands tightly behind my back, fearful that I may slug him.

"These are your kids, are they not?" I squeeze out in a strangely formal cadence I don't recognize as my own. "I informed you that I would be out of town, leaving you with the responsibility to take care of *your* children while I am gone. I take care of them during *your* extensive absences. I am always f$@king here. You could at least schedule a couple of nights to be home with *your* offspring or arrange for someone else to be."

"Laura, Laura. Don't go ballistic. Calm down. We can sort this out." Aaron raises his hands, responding in an uncharacteristically low register as if in surrender. In a strange reversal of roles, he's actually trying to calm me down. He usually rolls full speed ahead as if unable to downshift gears, but there must be something about my speech pattern that alarms him.

"Don't I? I am just doing what you always do. How does it feel? I will be leaving early Tuesday and back on Thursday during the day. The rest is up to you. This conversation is over—something else you do." I'm so furious that my skin is screaming like a second-degree burn, excruciatingly hot and red.

I storm out of the kitchen and down to my office. Anger is easier to cope with than the sting of invisibility. His actions directly parallel the invisibility of Black women I face in the rest of the white world, overlooked and undervalued. How has it happened that my marriage looks exactly like the hostile environment outside? I'm pacing in my little office, running through the dialogue I didn't say. "You like the meals, the laundry, and the childcare I provide because that allows you to do whatever the hell you choose and still have a family. Why do you make our children my problem?" Our "two of us against the world" shield looks like Humpty Dumpty after the great fall.

"I can't get no satisfaction. I can't get no . . . satisfaction" bursts from Mick Jagger's pouty lips into my headphones, prompting me to swivel my hips and roll my shoulders and twirl my arms as I step into a different realm.

"Can't you see I'm on a losing streak?"

Rhythm pulsing through my body makes everything better. At this moment, it drowns out the replays of those alternative argument scripts that always plague me, sometimes for days. My wrath cools as the beat reverberates. Is Aaron rebelling against the idea that me and my stuff are equally as important as him and his stuff? Naw. He wants me to succeed.

Enough! The board exam must take priority. I can use the time to keep studying. He's not going to sabotage my efforts. Anxiety is a great cure for anger. I don't have the bandwidth for all this crap.

As Raleigh recedes in the plane's window, the childcare arrangements are whatever they are. I refused to discuss it again; didn't even say goodbye. I cannot, much as I want, shield our children from their father's behavior, even though that puts them in the midst of raised, combative voices. My parents never fought in front of us; they deferred their civilly discussed disagreements until after our bedtime, or at least I assume that they must have. On the other hand, Aaron's family is always going at it as part of their usual social discourse. He says his father merely observed the fray like a rabbit hiding in the brush. I have no firsthand observations of the man I met only once, at the wedding, precluded by the family's ban on my presence until he would never utter another word. So I have only Aaron's version of his domestic unrest. Certainly, he uses his family as the template for his hyper-reactivity, meant, I believe, to atone for his dad's passivity. The problem is, none of those people live in this house. It's just me and our kids. And I'm not Miriam.

In the end, we're not responsible for the actions of others, only our own reactions to them. I admit, I was the hyper-reactor this last go-round, what with tension over the exam and feeling so very alone. I'm beginning to believe that it's fruitless to engage, that it's wiser to retreat into the trenches where stalemate rules the day.

I have planned to follow my Wednesday morning test with a trip to a museum or shopping and then relax over a nice dinner with a glass of wine—things I can't do at home. Normally a journey to a big metropolitan area would send me singing and dancing through the streets, a darker duplicate of Maria in *West Side Story*, but this is the dead of winter in the Windy City, and I hate the cold. Approaching sidewalk intersections where the wind swirls in frigid eddies isn't something to be overjoyed about. But tonight, my only concern is reviewing my notes and taking a final look at my case list. My one indulgence is a Chicago deep dish pizza, my first, delivered from a place nearby. I'm able to get to sleep by one a.m., a good night's sleep for me.

I didn't get up early to study before my shower or flip through notes while getting dressed. I'm not an until-they-start-the-test type of examinee, flipping through my notes in the test room until the proctor calls for people to clear their desks. I've watched that sort of behavior since junior high, but last-minute cramming only muddles my thinking. I leave behind my copy of the case list scribbled with notes, bringing only the unmarked copy we're required to have in the hotel room. Before I head down to registration, I check my red suit in the full-length mirror on the closet door. Not bad; a serious, competent professional stares back at me. I grab a donut and a cup of coffee at the continental breakfast downstairs and, armed with an additional donut, take the elevator up to the assigned floor.

In the room, I sit on a chair across from what feels like a panel of three appellate court judges without the black robes. Chosen from a group of well-connected academics and their protégées, they've made this annual pilgrimage for years. No examiner will have served at the same time in the same departments as the test taker, out of a concern for fairness.

I'm immediately starstruck by one of them, a legendary pioneer in preeclampsia, my chosen research interest, and another who's a noted academic leader in the specialty. I'm feeling additional pressure not to sound like an idiot in front of people I hope to encounter later in my academic career. Academic ob-gyns are a tiny fraction of our small club, so you want to be known by someone with a national reputation as a competent if not learned colleague, not as a bumbling bonehead. Once again, I don the armor of a Black warrior battling the perception that I am one of those lesser-thans. I must represent the best of my people and triumph here. The metamorphosis is as automatic as breathing.

After the examiners deliver their reassurances that they truly want every physician to pass, their cordial smiles fade into poker-faced neutrality. They toss out a few easy questions before they get serious. I've been warned not to sound like I'm "teaching" them with explanations of causation or disease mechanisms, so I keep my responses basic and short. Anyway, they just cut you off, so you can't talk yourself out of a full complement of inquiries.

Most of the questions are pretty straightforward, nothing exotic or obscure. And yet, the deadpan unresponsiveness of the examiners is disarming, causing me to search for some hidden meaning. This is completely outside our customary educational interactions where often an instructor's expression provides an inkling to a student that they're on the right track. Helpful hints are acceptable on ward rounds. In this room, there are only sphinxes whose thoughts are as impenetrable as a desert sandstorm. Despite earlier warnings, this indifferent facade is perturbing and unnerving. If my answer is completely off base, not that I think any of them are, I'll be totally in the dark.

The breast lesion in a new question intersects with my realization that I've omitted a critical side effect in the previous one. A wave of terror grips me. That drive to always be right rears its grotesque head. Keep going? Ask to go back and correct the answer? My internal narrative skitters across the question being asked.

"I'm sorry, can you repeat the question?" I interrupt. The desperate stab to regain my composure forces me to refocus on the breast in the question, not my own where my heart is pounding. Thankfully, it's the final probe before a bathroom break, taken within the hotel room itself, a security measure to prevent a candidate from ducking out to cheat by checking notes.

I grab a lukewarm cup of coffee from a carafe sitting on the counter and carry it over to face a window. Eyes closed, I tilt my head back, soaking in the sunlight streaming through. The first part is behind me; it's immutable however it turns out. Forward and onward. I take my seat, recovered and almost confident.

Door after door along the hallway opens as I file out of the room with the other examinees. Some were busy comparing notes on which topics were covered and the best answers. We form a small cadre who share an experience that people outside the profession can't understand. In that spirit, we're like GI's in basic training, helping each other over the hurdles. Today's examinees will spread out and share their recollections with the colleagues who will follow them, just as my friends have shared theirs with me.

The smell of fear mixed with sweat hangs in the hallway as I fall into conversation with a couple of people, mostly sharing their overwhelming sense of devastation, another ritual. Most people are unsure about their performance, some of it for show, of course, but doubt is as contagious as syphilis. In contrast, there are always one or two ego-involved individuals who extoll their performance, positive that they're in the ninetieth percentile. That, too, is part of every post-examination script.

During the elevator ride back to my room, I'm slowly filling with anger, just as my friends had predicted. All told, the exam was much easier than I had thought, despite those few moments of terror. I was in total command as I cruised through the interrogation of my case list. The whole thing was unworthy of the hours of mental anguish. I'm pissed at myself for falling for the hype; for succumbing to the assault on my self-confidence. I've reached the boiling point when I fling open the closet and yank out my suitcase. That goddamned motel conference! I had to get the hell out of here. I begin throwing my clothes into my suitcase.

A long, jagged run slices through one leg of my pantyhose when I take them off. I toss them in the wastebasket on the way to the shower, as if I can wash the whole experience away. The hot water jets are tranquilizing, which allows me to neatly fold my suit on top of the other clothes already packed. I climb into my navy corduroy pants and throw on a gray sweater. I've only been able to get standby status on the plane, but I don't care. I'll wait at O'Hare and grab some lunch there. I'm not really hungry.

In my desperation to flee the scene, I wouldn't have waited for the elevators if it weren't so many flights down. The elevator means overhearing people coming from or going to the exam, but there's no alternative. No shopping, no museum, no dinner. As I trudge through O'Hare's sprawling terminal, I'm suddenly hungry as the thought sinks in that my getaway is practically secure. The ticket agent believes that there's a good shot at the second flight but not the first.

During the four-hour wait, I meander through the food court looking for something I can't get in Weavers Crossing, my fantasy of a fabulous shopping spree along the Magnificent Mile reduced to a tour of airport food stalls. A Philly cheesesteak and fries catches my fancy, a fitting tribute to the education that had gotten me here. During my first year of residency, all my on-call night dinners were a cheesesteak and fries, an amount completely covered by the department-issued meal ticket that provided nourishment for those of us trapped in the hospital overnight. The airport sandwich would only be an approximation of a real Philly steak, but the memories are good enough—a little pink pill for the trauma of the day.

I sigh deeply as the plane taxies into a line of jets waiting to take off. The whole nightmarish ordeal has come to an end. The experience will live on in tales for future residents and fellows, but this raw emotional version will evolve into humorous cautionary tales. The nearly setting sun portends a flight through black sky, perfectly matching my mood.

My thoughts drift to Miss Bessie as my head plops back on the head rest, now reclined for the nap that will overtake me. Bessie Metcalf was on my case list as an eighty-three-year-old Black female diagnosed with tubal carcinoma. The examiners hadn't asked about her; the diagnosis is too rare—a total of about two hundred cases ever reported in the scientific literature worldwide—but I had boned up on the cancer just in case.

Miss Bessie's care represents my Achilles heel, or at least one of them. She had not seen a gynecologist since the birth of her last daughter in her twenties, not an uncommon circumstance. Her generation was particularly reticent about pelvic exams from male physicians, unchristian behavior for a woman to expose her genitals to some strange white man. Not to mention the unavailability of medical care outside emergencies and sometimes not even then. But she had been feeling bloated all the time, so her daughter had brought her to our exam room. Her ultrasound had shown an ovarian mass, a red flag for women so long after menopause. Still, ovarian cancer is unusual in an eighty-year-old. I had wanted to refer Miss Bessie to the gyn oncologists at Chapel Hill for additional imaging, diagnosis, and treatment, and she said she would think about it. After a couple of weeks, Miss Bessie decided she wouldn't go, and her family agreed.

At the time, I didn't really understand their reluctance, but people don't like to leave Stephens County, period. It wasn't just the cost of the gas and the parking. Their county wrapped them in a security blanket of the known. They were familiar with the people and the pitfalls to navigate around. They knew who to call for help. Outside was as dark and mysterious as a swamp under a new moon.

The parking lots at UNC felt bigger than Weavers Crossing itself. Multiple different buildings connected with hospital corridors filled with signs and variously colored arrows mapped out on the floor, each color charted a path to a different department. The array was confusing, often difficult to interpret for people educated in a school system that frequently left students barely able to read after graduation. Many of my patients hadn't finished high school, particularly those in Bessie's generation, when almost no schools for colored kids existed after eighth grade. Where schools did exist, they operated to accommodate planting and harvest season. Even so, many children of sharecroppers had to work in the fields full time.

In addition, it was quietly embarrassing not knowing who to ask. The generational scars of Jim Crow that enforced meekness in the face of powerful racial animus remained an invisible force. Many older people still approached whites with downcast eyes, a habit ingrained in childhood not easily shed, even by old age. They spoke only when spoken to. They would rather ask a janitor, invariably Black, than any of the white staff who were often unhelpful, dripping with a disdain for backward nigras that was even more intense than the way they treated their counterparts in town.

Furthermore, Weavers Crossing residents were fearful of being sick away from the people they knew—their family, their ministers, and church congregations. The distance made it hard for family and friends to visit. Although they knew they needed their support network to get through it, they didn't want to be a burden to their neighbors.

I knew the clock was ticking for Miss Bessie. I couldn't provide the kind of imaging or specialty radiologists to diagnose what would turn out to be tubal carcinoma, not high on my differential list. Still, it was more complicated than that. The hospital didn't have the nursing knowledge or facilities to support complicated postoperative care. Beyond that, I was torn. I knew that some women who were referred would get no care if I didn't do it. Once again, was some care, even if it turned out to be suboptimal, better than no care?

In retrospect, the audacity of my ego played more of a role than I could have admitted. I thought my credentials allowed me to circumvent the basic truism that physicians can be no more skilled than the facility in which they work, even when they possess the latest medical knowledge. Plain and simple, if there's no oncologist there, surgery should not be performed on a potentially malignant tumor. If there's no twenty-four-hour well-stocked blood bank, no surgery where excessive hemorrhage is likely should be performed. If there's no NICU, it's no place to deliver a premature baby. If the nursing staff has no experience with or education in potential complications of serious conditions, the signs of a problem will go unnoticed. The bedside presence of nurses 24/7 makes them the first alert system for parameters outside the norm, unlike a physician who drops by once a day. If the nurses miss it, so does the doc.

When those critical elements are absent, the best care is delivered in a tertiary hospital. Physicians can do their best, but bad things happen when patients are transferred after their emergency rather than before. Unfortunately, when you train in a tertiary center, that's not immediately apparent. These truths were as clear as sunrise to me when it came to obstetrics, but somehow, with my first potential cancer case, daylight never broke.

My experience here in gynecology had been mostly limited to routine procedures, so I wanted to rise to the challenge, even though I hadn't done a complicated gyn surgery since my arrival. Conceding the primacy of patient transfer was another blow to my professional development. I have the expertise to do so much more, to diagnose and care for very complicated problems. So even when I had an inkling of the limits of a hospital facility, I still clung to the idea that I could somehow wriggle a way around them. Infused with this cocktail of hubris, I was blinded by a crusader's light.

In the end, it was all at Miss Bessie's expense. I compromised her chances of survival because I hadn't anticipated what I would find and so did not, could not, stage the spread of the carcinoma present in both ovarian tubes. Although I did a hysterectomy and bilateral salpingo-oophorectomy (both tubes and ovaries), it wasn't nearly enough for her diagnosis. Because of that, Miss Bessie would need a second surgery for staging and treatment after the first.

Miss Bessie had said, "It's alright, child. I've lived a long life."

I still feel guilty as hell.

Why hadn't I listened to her concerns and let her forgo treatment initially? Why had I charged in like a knight in shining armor only to find that the sheen had rusted into a facade pockmarked with holes? Not hearing her concerns was the same thing I accuse Aaron of doing to me. In the end, her instincts to make the best of her remaining time had been right; her disease was too advanced, her prognosis poor. I had not made her life better, only more enfeebled.

I saw her on daily hospital rounds once she was admitted to Stephens for what amounted to comfort care. I dropped in at various times, more a social call than a clinical one, sometimes sitting in the room with her two daughters to work on a jigsaw puzzle. Patting my hand as I sat on her bed, she told me that her long life had been a good one. Soon, Stephens Memorial became Bessie's place to die. The central dilemma remained: Was my shoddy care better than no care at all?

I doze off.

By the time my car is barreling toward home, I'm pretty sure I've passed the exam, but I'm not willing to jinx it by saying it out loud. Kyle runs up and excitedly throws his arms around my legs as soon as I cross the threshold. "Mommy, Mommy, you're back." He brings my sanity back. Aah, somebody loves me! The child that I had worried about most had survived my short absence unscathed. I'll get more details in casual conversations over the next couple of days.

In contrast, Abbie simply looks up from the TV, smiles, and whispers a quiet "Happy you're home" without much fanfare. I'm wrapped in my bulwark against the craziness of my chosen profession.

Chapter 24

I DON'T KNOW WHAT I THINK

WHAT'S DONE IS DONE. I'VE filed away my anxiety and anger in a drawer next to my board study notes. In an effort to redirect my restless thoughts, I'm thinking I'll examine the data in my case list to explore some patient outcomes. The data entry, the statistical analysis, the search for potential interactions are links back to my days in the lab. This time though, it's about people, not rabbits or dogs or sheep or pigs. For me, this is fun, like Aaron enjoys following our investments—the perfect diversion when you're in the middle of nowhere crying out for some form of entertainment that challenges your mental faculties. I guess I could write a novel or learn to play a new musical instrument, but dabbling in research ideas intersects with my hunger to rise in my chosen profession. Not that I'm not open to some other avenue if it should surface. But cynical ole me can't even imagine what that would be.

I'm thinking I might review our practice's experience with VBACs, what with the intense national interest and the sparsity of community hospital outcomes reported in the literature. Between housework and playing with the kids, I have time to daydream about the research career I hope to have when I arrive at a destination where significant research is being done. This is my version of knocking on the door.

Dr. James taps on the door as he sticks his head into my office. "Hey, Laura. I can't tell you how glad I am to be here." He beams with a welcoming grin.

"I think you just did." I laugh. "We're equally happy to see you." I walk around my desk for a hug. "Are you settling in okay?"

"Yeah, I'm good."

And so it begins. Otis is here to get familiar with our office environment: patient flow, prenatal record system, billing, charts, etc. We're still waiting on his hospital privileges to be approved, hopefully in a couple of weeks, so he's getting started in the office where he needs no credentialing. I'm thinking we'll do antepartum/postpartum rounds in the hospital together, just to introduce him to some of our patients and navigate the paperwork hoops. I'll sign the notes while overseeing what he's doing. I don't want him to feel like I'm glaring over his shoulder, although I'm sure he's had to endure just that in order to arrive at this point.

Otis heads out for Joyce's office after lunch while Kelly joins me here. I'm spending the afternoon raiding my birth control pill samples, my answer to filling in where Medicaid leaves off. Oral contraceptive pills (OCPs) are not cheap; patients without insurance can find relief in our offices. Unfortunately, the pill requires consistent dosing and timing to be its most effective, a regimen which is more complicated than it seems. At McCune, quite a few women working among us had trouble keeping track of their daily dose across changing overnight call schedules; the result, "contraceptive failure." Even so, no method is 100 percent, except abstinence, which tends to fail when the commitment fades.

Autumn Massey has come in today for irregular vaginal bleeding. When I ask about the first day of her last period, she frowns and seems confused, unable to decide what was her period and what was a day or two of spotting.

"Sometimes I miss a pill," she admits, "and I have to take two the next day. Or I just stop and start all over again after my next period."

Autumn has a new boyfriend and a one-year-old boy playing with her sister in the waiting room. The baby's father is in jail for selling weed.

I smile back. "Yeah, I know it's confusing. But you can call us anytime to help you figure out what to do when you can't remember. After hours, you'll get the doctor on call. Sometimes, that will be me." I motion with my thumb pointing at my smiling face.

Where to start? Talking about missed pills or the need for some other kind of contraception when you do?

"Do you use condoms when you've skipped a pill?" I opt to assess her risk of being pregnant before we get back to the contraceptive regimen. "You know, the pill doesn't work when it's in the pack," I add.

Autumn looks as though she's bracing for a scolding. I had wanted it to sound like an inside joke, but it came out more maliciously than I'd intended.

Sensing a misstep, I cover with, "Just kidding. I was thinking that we probably should do a pregnancy test before we deal with forgotten pills."

I send Autumn to the lab, and while she's gone, I move to the next exam room where Zora Spelman is sitting in the chair near the exam table, her caramel legs crossed. She's twenty-five years old and has had one miscarriage but no other pregnancies. Her history is unusual among our patients where most women her age either have other children or a number of miscarriages. I can't resist asking Zora about her unusual name. Her mother named her after one of her heroines, Zora Neale Hurston, a perfect fit with her last name, Hurston's alma mater. I confirm with her that she's been feeling nauseous but not vomiting much; it's more a feeling she experiences in the mornings since she started a different birth control pill a few weeks ago. When I ask if she's worried about an unplanned pregnancy, she hesitates and then admits that the idea is in the back of her mind. She has none of the other symptoms of early pregnancy, so I debate whether to do a pelvic exam now that she's already undressed or get the pregnancy test first. We would have two exam rooms waiting on lab results, so I opt to proceed with the physical exam while we explore other symptoms that might be associated with gastrointestinal problems. Although pregnancy is the most common diagnosis by leaps and bounds, nausea is such a vague symptom; there are numerous other causes besides a side effect of OCPs. I've been in a contraceptive groove for the afternoon, but now is the time to snap out of thinking like an automaton to a broader range of differentials.

I'm surprised that she's a few inches taller than I when she rises to get on the exam table. My progress down through her various organ systems reveals that she's thin, possibly undernourished. Maybe thyroid dysfunction or some other endocrine dysfunction? As I finish palpating her pelvic organs, I conclude that if she's pregnant, it's early. I will send her for a pregnancy test and have her return to my office to allow the exam room to be turned over for another patient.

When I return to Autumn Murphy, the nurse's assistant has already asked her to take her panties off for a pelvic. Her uterus feels about eight weeks in size. She's still recovering from the news, not visibly upset but not overjoyed either. When I ask how she's feeling, she hesitates, then, "Okay . . . it'll be fine," lurches out as if she was thinking through the ramifications as she was forming the words. We talk about scheduling a new OB appointment or termination, and I send her to see Allison to help with the Medicaid application, a bottle of prenatal vitamins in hand.

Back in my office, Zora Spelman's pregnancy test is negative. Going from OCP-associated nausea to an endocrine or gastrointestinal disorder feels like a stretch. Should I look in the cupboard for at least six packs of the same brand of OCPs? Maybe only one or two and have her return for more if they suit her? Without a clear direction, I don't think I should send her on a wild goose chase, racking up a stack of lab bills along the way. But I don't want to miss anything either.

I ask Zora if she has any concern about her weight since I hadn't thought to cover her recent weight loss. She reports that she's always been thin, but without a bathroom scale at home, she doesn't know her weight. Are her clothes looser than they have been? Zora didn't think so. I give her two packs of pills, review the instructions, remind her, like I've told Autumn, that she can call with questions or problems, and tell her to follow-up in two months. Theoretically, her nausea should improve with the placebo pills in her current pack, so I suggest that she try Dramamine from the drugstore for the nausea. Finally, I admit that I'm not sure if something else might be going on, so we'll schedule an appointment to see Dr. Fowler for a more extensive workup in a couple of weeks. If the nausea resolves with the new pack of pills, she can cancel that appointment.

We agree that we've got a good plan as I reassure her that I don't think there's anything seriously wrong, but it never hurts to check.

"One last question." I chuckle. "What do you do when you miss two pills?"

"Take two one day and two the next." Zora and I both crack up.

I'm not happy that I'd let my frustration hang out, not at Autumn, but at my own inability to create the magic where my patients communicate their difficulties with OCPs and we address them before they fail. All my efforts since medical school to develop a patient-friendly, concise set of instructions haven't done the trick. Maybe there's something in Zora's reply that makes a jingle—*miss one, take two tomorrow; miss two, take two one day and two the next.* I've got to work on the rhythm. Or maybe give out laminated cards to put with the pill packs in the medicine cabinet or a drawer.

Somehow I keep imagining that if I can just deliver the right words, unplanned pregnancies will become a thing of the past and all babies will be wanted at the time they're born. I'm not thinking about the part when the lights are low and desire high. And they definitely aren't thinking about me then. But I'm pretty sure that "every child wanted" is a goal we all share. I try not to be the doctor who "knows best" but the one who lays it out so a patient can decide. This is not to say that I don't have my preferences. I just wish we had a broader range of effective options. Ideally, the patient and I are a team, working together to move closer to our "every child wanted" goal.

"To be honest, you think you're more important than you are," Allison warns me when I grumble to her about this disconnect. "I mean, these women don't know you, and you don't know them. You're not at church on Sunday or the fish fries on Friday night. You're not a member of any club. They see you for less time than they wait to see you, and then you disappear. You're nowhere except in the hospital or this office. I think they find your invisibility suspicious."

She spoke sympathetically, trying to let me down easy. Without a hint of malice, she thought she had pointed out an aspect I didn't see.

The words walloped like a ton of bricks. I let them thud. There's some truth in it. For the most part, my world revolves around the flashing red light, a momentary stop between the office, hospital, and home. There are occasional parent-teacher conferences, family outings, various things with the Whiteheads, but I'm hard pressed to think of much else. My patients and I are seeing each other on our best behavior, confined in the landscape of their medical problems and little else.

Would it be better to have a woman maybe mention she was having breakthrough bleeding while we're on the sidelines of a soccer game and I could encourage her to keep taking her OCPs and come to the office, maybe to switch brands? That hasn't happened, but is that because people see me as unapproachable or because I'm not usually in places where any of my patients go?

The question is, would that make me a better practitioner? Joyce knows her patients pretty well. Is she any better at contraceptive compliance? Is there something about this area that demands a physician be the neighbor next door? Is it the rural or small town or Southern aspect? Does the anonymity of the urban landscape seep into trust between doctor and patient there? My experience so far has been in settings where patients churned through the clinics like a paddle wheel blade dips into a new slice of water. More often than not, seeing the same woman over a couple of years was far outside the norm. I guess I have no way to know if my contraceptive counseling was any more successful there than here. Is my thinking totally off the wall?

I am who I am. I understand myself well enough to know that I'm someone who enjoys the anonymity of urban spaces with no desire to undergo the scrutiny of neighbors' prying eyes, like the suburb where my family moved.

As long as I aspire to take care of women who are poor, our lives will diverge. We'll live in different neighborhoods, entertain ourselves differently, and probably belong to different organizations. I'm a doctor in the office and hospital but just plain Laura with friends. I'm happy to answer questions and give general advice to friends, but the questions that I need to ask to do a competent clinical job feel too probingly personal. Beyond the occasional prescription for something benign, it feels too complicated to provide medical care to my friends who'll have their own private physicians. Without a patient chart in my hand, an off-the-cuff suggestion could cause my friend harm, like an inadvertent drug interaction for instance. I covet keeping the two worlds separate.

Allison is right—I've made myself more important than I am, but perhaps not for the reasons she said. I'm a little cog in an enormous wheel. There are too many factors out in the world that impact contraceptive compliance. It ain't all on me, no matter how perfect my spiel is.

An envelope from ABOG waits for me when I get home. My heart skips a few beats. For a moment, I don't want to know. I leave it unopened while I change my clothes. *Don't be stupid*, I goad myself. *You know you got this.* And I have. The letter brings a surge of profound joy from the tips of my hair to the soles of my feet.

Damn, I am now a board-certified obstetrician and gynecologist! Another milestone done and dusted! Soon, though, the seeming ordinariness of the accomplishment diminishes it. This is what most people do—nothing exceptional, simply the norm. Another line on my CV, a certificate for the office wall; no more. It's a mile marker in a maybe four- or five-year trek beyond this point. In the game of life, a steady march down the field to the end zone is never guaranteed. There are first downs to make, with the threat of an interception or a fumble or a penalty that can erase yardage won. They don't do victory dances outside the end zone.

Chapter 25

TOO EARLY TO TAKE A BOW

SURVEYING THE YARDAGE DOWNFIELD TOWARD the end zone, fellowship in maternal fetal medicine is the next first down. In the best-case scenario, I'll submit several programs in a ranked list to the Match. Yes, after almost a decade, the national platform that assigns medical students to residency programs is back in my life. In the intervening years, the Match has added ob-gyn subspecialty fellowship programs. After submitting applications, individual programs invite candidates to interview. The ranked lists of interviewees are thrown into a computer algorithm with those of the programs, and *voilà*, on a designated day each March, the applicant discovers their fate tucked into an envelope handed out during a medical school celebration. And for some, it could be no match.

Yet again, my future lies in the mysterious recesses of a computer. To be a wife and mother at almost forty years old dependent on mathematical assignment after so much work, really hard work, seems both ridiculous and outrageous. But, even if I had known the full extent of this long and winding road, I can think of no other avenue I would rather travel.

Aaron surprises me with a certification celebration dinner at a restaurant in Rock Creek. He sensed that the milestone was important to me without completely understanding what it meant. He'd assumed it was a perfunctory exercise with a predictable outcome; I would have been better off if I had too. He asked if it meant a raise in salary, thinking it was sort of like a promotion. Nope. Still, the night out was a relaxing change from our routine.

The dinner was a nice gesture, but dinner at home with relaxed, free-wheeling conversation would have been even better. I confess he's racking up demerits that he can't see. I feel like I tell him what I need, and he ignores it. He insists his travel is the problem, which it isn't. I accept that his work demands travel, and even though it wasn't what we planned when we first arrived, I'm genuinely happy that it's working out well for him. Despite my vigorous denials, he's cast me as the wicked witch who resents his travel, an excuse to resent me in turn. The exact opposite is true; his travel makes it easier for us to create stable routines at home. This semi-single parenting is easier in many respects because I don't have to ask for anybody else's opinion. I would never tell him that; to admit that would devastate his sense of self-worth. He needs to feel needed.

What we haven't done, in between kids and chores and phone calls and the mysterious places his mind goes when he has that blank look, is prioritize some time for the two of us. I'm available, and if he prioritized it, he could be too. I want him to want it without being prompted. If I try to nudge him in that direction, I become the nagging wife. Although he's all for family outings, he seems almost fearful of too much time alone with me. I find that I'm increasingly less generous about gestures like that dinner; they're too little. A meal with a sprinkling of Aaron-centric happenings without regard to my own, deflected and rerouted back on him, is more sedating than invigorating. Maybe after so many years, married couples are not supposed to have thoughtful exchanges. I think they should if they are doing completely different things and they don't see each other all that much; perhaps Aaron disagrees. Changing our situation would have to begin with up-close-and-personal dialogue about what's wrong, the thing missing in between the steady stream of everyday events.

This morning Florence Bivens is having her breakfast on the postpartum ward. She's excited about her new and now only daughter after she signed her parental rights for her other child over to the state. She's free now to focus on the first baby she's ever taken home from the hospital. She's so unimpressed by the vaginal delivery that you would have thought her planning on it had made it happen. With a hug, I happily announce that she will be sleeping in her own bed in one more day. I'm ecstatic and sorry to have missed the birth.

Each of her children has a different father, almost as if Florence has shed partners in search of one that could make a perfect baby.

"Florence, we need to talk about contraception," I begin my usual discharge banter.

"I'm thinking. Duane wants to have more kids," she mutters, her face twisted like she drank spoiled milk.

I caution her, "It's not healthy to get pregnant too soon. It takes longer for a mother's body to build back her stores of iron, calcium, and folate. Really, it's better to wait a couple of years for the best baby outcomes. You should think about using something, even if it's only condoms. They're the least effective, but they're better than nothing. You could try birth control pills as a stopgap until you have a longer-term plan."

Florence shrugs, letting the remarks slide like water off a duck's back.

"Think about it today so we can talk about it tomorrow. Maybe talk with Duane," I suggest, confident that won't happen. I hold out some pamphlets about each contraceptive method. She looks at them blankly without making a move to take them. Knowing full well that she wouldn't read them, I slip them onto the bedside table. The literacy level probably isn't ideal for her anyway, but they're all we have.

I worry that oral contraceptive regimens may be too complicated for her and she'll just quit. I sense she's just as happy to have "an accident," which is far less effort than active decision-making about child spacing. There are people who are satisfied for life to happen to them in order to avoid feeling responsible for a mistake. Decision-making can easily lead to a few wrong turns. No judgment here; a simple observation. Florence is probably betting that crazy medical complications are in her past. She's the one who has to live with the consequences, so who am I to push her one way or the other? I'm trying to present the range of alternatives straightforwardly so a patient can make the best decision for herself, fully aware that how I present the choices can put a thumb on the scale for one over the others.

These last couple of days, the thought of a job well done has brought a smile to my lips when I think of Florence happily at home, cooing to her baby. Idealized for sure, but in the crush of new motherhood, it must happen a few times a day. For me, it was always rocking in our yellow wicker chair nursing Damian, minutes of quiet watchful connection to my new son that might end in a shared catnap.

Joyce's call puts an immediate halt to the delight. Last night, Florence had developed shortness of breath, which ended in admission to the ICU for heart failure. *Bam!* I literally had to sit down. We had been patting ourselves on the back for her good fortune, as if it guaranteed a happy ending. But we'd popped the cork on the champagne too soon. Florence is now facing a life-threatening illness that if she survives, could cripple her for the rest of her life.

Right away, I suspect the diagnosis is postpartum cardiomyopathy, a pregnancy-related disease where the heart muscle is weakened and can't pump an adequate amount of blood throughout the body. We don't understand the cause, but luckily, some women, with treatment, will recover within six months. If not, cardiac function will forever be compromised, leaving the sufferer unable to resume normal activity. And worse, in any subsequent pregnancy, Florence will have a 50 percent chance of dying. Although she is as yet unaware of it, this condition will be an even more devastating blow to her plans for more children.

When I get to the hospital, she's hunched over in her bed, breathing too rapidly despite the nasal cannulas streaming oxygen up her nostrils. It doesn't seem to be helping all that much; the doctors need to increase the percentage of oxygen or better yet, switch to a rebreathing mask that covers her nose and mouth completely.

"Do you know . . . how long . . . I . . ." Florence huffs out.

"You have to stay here?" I finish the sentence as Florence struggles to get it out. "You don't look like you're quite ready now," I try to joke. "You at least have to be breathing without the oxygen."

"Worry 'bout . . . baby."

"Is your mother at home with her?"

"Not sure . . . long she . . ."

"Can stay. Won't she stay as long as you need her? What about Duane?"

"He no . . . good . . . at . . ."

"Is there someone else? A sister or a friend, maybe?"

"Not sure."

"Okay, I don't want you to have to keep talking. It's going to tire you out. We'll get Allison to look into how we can help. It's hard, but try not to worry too much about it."

I put my hand on hers and squeeze. "Try to concentrate on getting better. These doctors are doing everything they can."

I can't do anything to make her better. I'm not sure the doctors are doing everything they can, like the oxygen supplementation for instance. I consider reviewing her chart and talking to the internist about increasing her oxygen, but, painfully aware of other failed interactions, I don't want to fight in an arena where

I'll be butting heads without changing her management. She isn't my patient, this isn't my area of expertise, and I haven't been asked to consult. The treatment is the same regardless of the diagnosis; it's just the prognosis that's different since most affected women are usually young and otherwise healthy. Most internists don't know that, but I've seen this disease before.

I return to the office thoroughly depressed. Why is the next bad outcome just around the corner for women like Florence? This is not karma; it's a political choice. This is women with health deficits barely eking by in circumstances bereft of resources. Following the arc of history, the healthcare system can only continue to hurt them. It's so frustrating, I want to scream. Shit!

Allison had already heard about Florence from Joyce.

"Hey, this isn't your fault," she jumps in immediately after she sees my face.

"That doesn't make it suck any less," I fire back, unwilling to be soothed. I want to throw things at the walls.

"You're just spinning your wheels. Won't help anybody, least of all you. She turns toward the door. "I'm gonna head over to Florence's place and talk to the dad to get his ideas about childcare. Hopefully, her mother will volunteer what she can do. I'm gonna lay it out that Florence could be in the hospital for a while."

"Wow, I don't even know if Florence has been told that. It's not the first thing a doctor tells a patient as they begin treatment in an ICU setting. Long term prognosis usually comes later, more near discharge. I don't know how familiar the internist is with postpartum cardiomyopathy. But maybe it's good to prepare the family for a chronic change." I'm sagging, uncharacteristically floored by the gravity of the moment.

A feeling of hopelessness is tugging at me, a riptide threatening to pull me under. What had seemed like a really good outcome, an uncomplicated VBAC and a healthy new baby, has suddenly become tragic.

I feel a little better after Damian calls to say that he'll be home for a long weekend. He sounds happy. No surprise, but still nice to hear. I think again what a genuinely nice person he is, and it makes me proud. Not that it's any of my doing. I'm not trying to claim any credit.

One thing that counterbalances my gloom about Florence is how seamlessly Dr. James has lightened my load. I don't often count my blessings, but the fact that he's performing the bulk of the postpartum tubals makes me giddy. He's so happy in the OR that he doesn't mind the hurdles it takes to get the surgeries done during postpartum hospitalizations. He simply smiles through all the headaches, making him the man that the staff and MDs all want to deal with. He's the hospital's newest star.

He's becoming one of the boys, not exactly a good ol' one, but some of the general surgeons, anxious to add their own procedures, have joined the effort he's spearheading to acquire laparoscopic equipment. None of them was ever willing to follow me anywhere. Put a scalpel in his hands, and he's happy as a clam. He's also introduced me to a faster, simpler method for circumcisions and assumed the majority of responsibility for performing them. He's engineered a plan to catch the ones we can't get done in the hospital by doing them in the office.

I hate doing circumcisions, the one bit of expertise I tried to leave behind in Philly. There's no way of making less odious a procedure done on a hungry two-day-old strapped down to a board screaming for the duration. I did them because I was swayed by the plight of the poor boys who would be forced to wait into childhood when a urologist would perform the operation under general anesthesia. That and the welcome stream of very generous Medicaid reimbursements. So Otis's near takeover of the procedures has come as a huge relief.

All in all, Otis is proving to be not only amiable but conscientious about building the practice from his own ideas. He doesn't share my passion for scouring the specialty's literature or hypothetical discussion, but few people do. Now that moving on to a fellowship is becoming more concrete, his presence makes me even happier. I realize that leaving Antioch high and dry without an ob-gyn worried me more than I wanted to admit. Otis seems happy enough to join the Antioch tradition of physicians who make Weavers Crossing their permanent home.

Florence has been scheduled for follow-up appointments with Dr. Fowler two weeks after her discharge. I have my fingers crossed for a full recovery over the next six months. I'm pretty cynical though; somehow it feels like the fix is in.

Chapter 26

STEPPING INTO UNKNOWN TERRITORY

HAVING MULLED THEM OVER FOR a few years now, my priorities for a fellowship program are clear as a full moon in a cloudless sky. First and foremost, I want to be immersed in ultrasound scanning with a high volume of potentially diagnosable prenatal anomalies and interventional antenatal procedures. Throughout the process of upgrading my ultrasound skills, I want to learn the impact of specific disabilities on affected children and their parents, study the range of pediatric treatment options, and gain the necessary tools for counseling patients effectively. And I want the latitude to return to the benchtop to develop the area of research I will use first for the required thesis for MFM board certification and then extend in my faculty position. I'm not wild about a steady stream of sleepless nights spent with residents in the hospital and the childcare issues that would entail. Daytime coverage of

L&D should be sufficient to satisfy the joy I find in teaching the art of obstetrics while I explore new ground. Those stipulations require a program where I won't be run ragged by too many clinical responsibilities. After all, a well-rested mind to ponder and explore is the pollen that produces the lushest fruit. It's not the pace of work in Weavers Crossing that bugs me; it's the lack of outlets for the pent-up energy.

Despite the mundane aspects of the application process, I'm getting excited. The UNC program has one distinct short-term advantage; we would have an in-state home from which Damian could finish at NCSSM. However, it doesn't offer the possibility for basic research, and their fellows' busy clinical schedules consume most of their time. At least, that's what I've heard through the rumor mill. So it was no great loss that I wasn't offered an interview to observe for myself. I'm happy to look exclusively in the South, not being an enthusiast of returning to snow and cold weather. Since Aaron's region is now headquartered in Atlanta, he just needs a city near a good airport. I have interviews scheduled at programs in Mississippi, Georgia, Alabama, and Florida. As a nontraditional applicant, I thought I needed to maximize the possibilities.

Aaron and I aren't discussing the process, let alone the details. I'm choosing programs, and he'll simply shift his home base once I'm accepted. Almost imperceptibly, like ivy creeping along a wall, the gulf between us is widening. At this point, I don't think either of us would mind living in different locations for a while. It's not an arrangement we haven't considered before.

We're not talking about much of anything beyond garbage pickups. We've run afoul of yet another area of diametrically opposing views. Aaron wants to apply for financial aid for

Damian's college even though we can afford to pay for his education, even a pricey one.

Under Aaron's careful management, Damian's educational fund has grown into a tidy sum since it began with his social security number shortly after birth. Beyond the savings, our income eliminates most financial aid except loans. There's some possibility of scholastic awards and scholarships specifically targeted for minorities, but those are typically small. The fact that the financial aid forms are tedious to complete, especially if it seems we aren't going to qualify, is not the point. For me, it's the principle of the thing. I'm passionate about not consuming limited financial resources that would then deprive other students who need them. Some of them could wind up missing out on a college education altogether.

Aaron still thinks like the kid who had to pinch pennies and work through high school and college. For him to admit that financially he's fairly well off makes him more like his family than the workers he's organizing. He's horrified at the prospect that someone will confuse him for his relatives' obsession with making more money than they can spend.

What were our exhaustive searches for every possible discount and the best deal for? Wasn't it to build financial security? We came by the money through honest hard work; it's a circumstance to celebrate, not one for embarrassment. That said, it's a difficult contradiction for Aaron to reconcile. For me, ignoring your resources is doing what self-absorbed rich people do—turn a blind eye to people who don't have what they have. And that's most certainly not who we are.

I'm adamant that I want Damian free to focus on his studies while having fun, unfettered by the need to work. He can sit back and enjoy the college ride. Aaron, on the other hand, is sure that working builds character. I want this to be our gift, an education without the long tail of financial debt that has dogged many of my former classmates. We can do this, and we should. At the moment, Aaron and I are deadlocked. And so we're doing what we usually do—avoid the topic like the plague.

I just can't flip through another medical journal tonight. I've underlined passages and dog-eared the pages of articles I'll tear out and file away in folders. I can still close my eyes and pretty much call up a vision of the page where I've read a particular bit of information, quite a useful talent in this job.

QVC is barely audible on the TV bolted on the L&D call room wall where I'm overseeing a labor induction. The channel has become a bad habit I use to provide mindless and redundant background noise when I've listened to all the music I can stand. Unfortunately, in my more dispirited moments, like after a fight with Aaron or a clinical setback, I have indulged my shopping bug to treat myself to a few items, mostly clothes and jewelry. A girl can't have too much sterling silver jewelry, and the network has a ton. With your first order you get an account, and *boom*, they've got you. It's a quick phone call away and you can return anything free of charge, no questions asked.

Bonnie Taylor was tired of being pregnant a week past her due date. There's an increase in neonatal complications with each week over forty, so we don't like to let women go two weeks over unless they insist on it. Few ever do. With a favorable cervix, she and I agreed that tonight is the night to have a baby.

Both Bonnie and I ate our dinners at home with our families, her last chance to have a meal before the baby comes. Bonnie, an underweight twenty-year-old with a carefree smile, had eaten with her mother and sister. She's very cute, with a thin brown face lit with neatly applied blue eye shadow and framed by well-pressed long, straight hair. She worked at the Walmart until her belly got in the way of lifting boxes to stock shelves. They fired her, but luckily, she was already on Medicaid because of her low wages.

We're still in the early stages, so it's time for me to settle into an uncomfortable sleep on the call room mattress. It's just like the ones in a patient room, not meant to be comfortable, just washable. I'll have to be up to check Bonnie's progress at some point during the night, or better yet, to deliver her baby, but I don't think that will come until tomorrow afternoon at the earliest. First babies take a long time. I drift off thinking about how to talk Aaron into bringing me lunch tomorrow since I'm not supposed to leave the hospital. McDonald's or Burger King or Long John Silver's maybe?

By the time I'm pouring my first cup of morning coffee, we're finally in the active phase of labor. Bonnie's contractions are coming every four or five minutes, and they're hitting her Stadol-hard. These are the times I wish we had epidurals, to change this experience from torture to something more like a strained back. She's going to be hoarse tomorrow. I have to remember to order some lozenges for postpartum.

Bonnie's labor stalls, despite increasing doses of Pitocin, about the time I'm finishing the fish and hush puppies Aaron brought me for lunch. I'm very tempted to call it quits and call in the OR team, just because I'm tired of being here. But that's more about me than Bonnie's labor curve, so I try to sleep out my impatience. By the time I wake, I wander into her room to check her cervix.

Constance, the nurse, is in triage with another patient. Her fetal monitoring strip is fine. As her mother helps me talk Bonnie through the contraction, I can announce that she's complete and she can start pushing. "Hallelujah!" her mother exclaims.

We're struggling to get Bonnie positioned, showing her how to pull up her knees with the start of a contraction, when Constance returns. Bonnie doesn't yet have that irresistible urge to push, probably because the baby's head still has a distance yet to come down into the pelvis. Constance will have her hands full as she weaves back and forth between her two patients, leaving Bonnie's mom to fill in as coach. I'm glad I hadn't thrown in the towel earlier as I head back to the call room.

We're in the delivery room now, Bonnie's mother at her side. She's draped, perineum cleaned. I'm gowned and gloved, yelling, "Keep it going. Take a breath. Get back at it. Keep it going. You can do this!" I'm the cheerleader I couldn't be in high school.

"That's it, baby," her mom joins in. "You can do it." The urge to cheer is contagious.

"Okay, rest up while we wait for the next contraction. I can see a little bit of the head, not too much hair yet. We're so close," I croon. "Maybe one or two more pushes. You got this; you got this."

Three pushes later, slippery and beige, she's in my hands as I hoist her onto Bonnie's belly.

"It's a girl!" We're all laughing, joyful, and relieved as I dry the baby with a blue cloth, action that both warms and stimulates her.

Constance brings a dry cloth as I double clamp and cut the cord. The baby squawks with the roughing up as Bonnie's mother gurgles ecstatically. I turn my attention to the perineum to assess the need for stitches. None needed.

The baby lies on the Ohio bed, dried, Apgars done, wrapped in a blanket with a cap firmly pulled on her head, all to stop rapid heat loss. Grandma goes over to carry the baby back to Bonnie.

A gush of blood signals the placenta has separated, so I pull gently on the cord, allowing the placenta to plop into the pan. But the bleeding isn't slowing, and her uterus feels more like a rotten mango than a firm cantaloupe. I begin massaging her belly through the drape with one hand without any responsive firming, so covering my hand with a surgical sponge, I shove it up into the uterine cavity to wipe out any residual tissue.

"This is going to be uncomfortable again," I warn Bonnie, who groans under the persistent pressure and pushes hard with her feet against the stirrups. "Your uterus is a little boggy, and we need to get the muscles to clamp down to stop the bleeding. I know it hurts, but it'll be over soon."

I order Constance to get a shot to help the uterus contract while we increase the Pitocin drip as well. Sometimes, after a long induction, the uterine muscles just tire out, but massage usually induces contractions, the organ's response to touch. I look over my shoulder at the placenta in the tub, but I'll have to use one hand to turn it over to examine if it's intact, no fragments left behind. Occasionally there can be an accessory placental lobe, but I hadn't felt anything with the sponge I'd used inside the uterine cavity.

I switch hands on top of the drape and insert the other in her cervix to basically bounce the uterus between my two hands. The blood from my gloves dragged across the drapes appears grotesque, like a Texas chainsaw murder is underway. The bleeding seems to be slowing, more clots than free-flowing red. Because clots don't form in rapidly flowing blood, their presence is an encouraging sign that the uterus is firming up. Constance jabs the shot in Bonnie's arm, barely noticed with the persistent pressure on her uterus.

Grandma has been anxious as she looks over from the Ohio bed where the baby is resting quietly. My gown is dripping with blood. My shoe covers are soaked as I step around in the maroon puddle that slid down the drapes and missed the sponge bucket at my feet. Ob-gyns ignore the copious amounts of blood and fluids as par for the course, but Grandma's eyes are encased in fear reflected in her tight grasp on the Ohio bed, as if she's plastered in place. Despite appearances, the crisis is over. Just as a precaution, I order some antibiotics to cover the intrusion of my gloved hand inside Bonnie's uterine cavity. Once I'm satisfied, we can pull down the surgical drapes and get everyone out of here. The nurse's aide will have quite a cleanup job.

Stripped of my gown and gloves, hands washed, I hug grandma, rubbing her back with an "It's okay. She'll be fine. We've got the bleeding under control, and she'll be fine" in the way repetition tends to reassure.

Disaster averted. I'm pumped from the intensity of it all, that automated program embedded in my brain that instantaneously clicks through the steps that need to be done. It feels good. We'll have to check Bonnie's hemoglobin tonight and again tomorrow to make sure she won't need a transfusion. Unless her count is very low or she feels lightheaded, three iron pills a day avoids the risk of HIV infection from a transfusion.

Baby, mom, and grandma are back in a curtained-off section of the triage room when I've completed the paperwork. I duck my head around the curtain to congratulate them again and tell them we're going to keep her IV going while she's on postpartum so we can make sure she's hydrated. Actually, while the fluids are good, we're keeping the line open in case a transfusion becomes necessary. I've told them about the possibility, but I suspect it got swallowed up in the mayhem. I'll see them tomorrow on postpartum. They don't have a name for the baby yet.

Bonnie looks even more droopy than I as the exhilaration of giving birth is replaced by the exhaustion from pushing after the hours of labor. She did all the work, and she deserves a long rest. I can't wait to get out into what I think is Indian summer weather, or at least the sun is shining. The adrenaline surge from the postpartum hemorrhage is dissipating into a fatigued hangover from intermittent napping.

I gather my journals from the call room and tease Constance that although I'll be at home if she needs me, I hope I won't hear from her again. We both laugh, knowing that it's unlikely, and that's the joke. I'm dreaming of a plump red tomato picked fresh from my vines as I lean my hip against the exit door bar and slip down the stairs. I'm going to need another nap. Maybe I'll sit on our balcony in the sun if the weather is like Baby Bear's porridge—just right.

Although the idea of throwing a party petrifies me, I have summoned the courage to throw a welcome shindig for Otis. My anxiety stems from the childhood trauma of a birthday party where nobody came. After that, all our birthdays were celebrated with family only. It didn't help that my parents seldom entertained, failing to provide a proper example, or at least, that's what I tell people about my phobia.

Aaron, on the other hand, is unruffled by playing host. He's planned all our children's birthday parties in an attempt to create the kind of do's that his parents didn't throw for him. As for adults, he's unconcerned about whether people enjoy themselves; he simply throws them in a room and lets it percolate, or not. I, on the other hand, am generally in knots throughout. I worry about having the details just right, as if there's some objective standard that defines what "just right" is, and I don't mean Amy Vanderbilt.

In addition to finally showing off our newly decorated house, this party is a bid to broaden our social circle beyond the Whiteheads. Phyllis is probably the closest thing I have to a best friend here, and we've established a rhythm of casual house visits around Geena and Abbie's comings and goings, sometimes including a meal and maybe a couple of movies with the girls. Aaron can't resist an opportunity to shoot hoops with Jonathan in either of our driveways. One of Aaron's biggest regrets in life is that he didn't grow taller and can't jump higher. I'm hoping that he will find some common ground with the husbands or PAs to overcome his general disdain for medical personnel, creating a pathway to more couples-based friendships.

To be fair, he hasn't had much opportunity to make friends locally. Occasionally, we'll take an out-of-town associate for dinner. The "we" is something of a misnomer; when the small talk fades, the conversation settles into intense discussion of work-related issues with no effort to include me. I sit ignored behind a genial smile like a ketchup bottle nestled beside the salt and pepper shakers. My own thoughts, like new protocols or research questions or whatever, drown out the names and places that swirl between the two of them about which I know nothing. Aah, the duties of the wife in a two-career marriage.

In the end, the pins and needles were all for naught. Sherrie Walcott, our real estate agent, popped through but didn't stay too long; I knew she couldn't resist a chance to see Dorinda's handiwork while schmoozing potential customers like Otis who's still renting. Likewise, Dorinda could be seen for a time in the midst of the decor she helped craft. Those two are about the only nonmedical women I know in town. Kelly, her husband David, and their baby; Allison Murray; Robert Pierson, the group's administrator, and his wife were among the Antioch staff. We had an assortment of other nurse's aides and clerical staff. Joyce wove her storyteller magic, unaccompanied by her husband who'd gone fishing. I hear she's married to a local muscle shirt type who hunts and fishes. She too enjoys the outdoors—part of the reason she chose to live here. It's hard for me to imagine a he-man who would marry someone like Joyce, clearly a woman who takes charge and gets her way. I imagine him as a former hippie who dropped off the grid. Oops, look at me throwing out stereotypes, which is only to say that we all do it. I had created out of whole cloth the image of a guy whose values would be consistent with hers. Pigeonholing people is a basic human instinct that helps our species navigate our environment. What we do with those stereotypical constructs is what counts.

Otis came with a date, a very attractive woman about my complexion, probably in her thirties. She's a teacher at the high school who demonstrated her command of proper English while code switching across the spectrum of guests. Damian hadn't been one of her students. Happily, Otis had a good time, especially when we brought out a cake decorated with, *We're Glad You're Here.* He practically blushed with embarrassment, evident more in his eyes than his face. His grin was as wide as a Cheshire cat's.

Most people were in and out of the pool, especially those with kids. We had badminton, ping pong, pinball, and video games. While we filled up on hotdogs and hamburgers, Aaron proved to be quite the host, joking over the grill with whomever was around. He can be pretty charming; after all, he's in the business of persuasion. I sometimes forget that. I can't remember seeing him laugh so much in a long time. Occasionally, I'd stop to watch the magic happen, even though I remained in a state of heightened anxiety until the end. Did we need more drinks in the cooler? How about more pickles? I couldn't help myself. Phyllis tried valiantly to keep my nerves in check.

Surrounded by citronella candles, we ended the evening dancing to music blasting from a boombox. Damian, home for the weekend, took charge. Max, the contractor, took a turn or two around the patio with his wife, looking bonded the way loving couples are supposed to. Eventually, I coaxed Aaron to join me. He's not a natural or confident dancer, but after he gathers the kind of courage that flows from a bottle or glass, he likes to dance with me. He's been doing essentially the same dance since college, probably a remnant from high school before we met. With the rhythm pulsing through my body, I was suddenly fifteen again, back in somebody's basement, at a party stepping to the sounds of The Supremes and the Four Tops. My girlfriends and I would break into the routines we'd practiced, everyone engulfed in playful competition trying to outdo each other. It's a cultural thing that automatically resurfaces as soon as the music starts. I am always happy when I'm dancing.

Chapter 27

A GLIMPSE AT THE FUTURE

THE INTERVIEW IN FLORIDA WENT well. The ob-gyn department is another 99 percent white work environment, including the nurses, administrative staff, residents, and fellows, not that it could be anything else in 1991 or into the foreseeable future. Okay, maybe a few programs are only 98 percent white, with South Asians and Middle Easterners beginning to rise in the subspecialty. For the most part, affirmative action has not penetrated the upper echelon of academic medicine. An occasional faculty photo is dotted with women at beginner ranks while the administrative staff that hang the frames on the walls are almost exclusively female. Nonwhite minorities are still less than one percent of medical faculties and barely more than that among medical trainees. In other words, I'd be swimming in an ocean of white faces like I usually am.

The faculty, while small, is not so buried in clinical responsibilities that they have no time to teach. There, fellows are not just cheap labor; the fellowship is specifically designed so that the fellow will not be essential to the delivery of clinical care. I'd be free to pursue research and delve into specific aspects of training or just sit and quietly contemplate when not involved in teaching residents during clinical assignments, classroom lectures, and conferences. It also means more time at home with the kids.

The program is an exception to a growing chorus of fellows' complaints that they spend their time covering the faculty's private patients, denied the opportunity to do the research needed to write and publish a thesis, without which they are ineligible for board certification. Given the near nonexistent possibilities to conduct research outside an academic setting, the portal to that piece of paper that identifies a bona fide maternal-fetal medicine subspecialist is padlocked. Essentially, they would have sacrificed two years of private practice incomes for additional training that gets them nowhere. I mean, my salary at Antioch is on the low rung of the ladder, and my fellowship salary will be about half of what I'm making now.

I was excited too by a small core of basic scientists who work with some of the same compounds that dovetail with my interest in preeclampsia—a happy accident. But I was most impressed with the prenatal diagnosis division, primarily Dr. Timothy Akerman. He's knowledgeable, methodical, and patient, bordering on obsession. His skills seemed magical as he chased a fetus through its various twists and turns in order to fix a static imaging plane. As I watched Dr. Ackerman struggling to define what appeared to be a cardiac abnormality, my frustration grew almost to the breaking point. I thought he should throw in the towel and just wait for a follow-up scan, which is the normal course of events until delivery. Of course, I kept my thoughts to myself.

My age, authored scientific papers from my days working in research labs, board certification in general ob-gyn, and experience in independent practice at Antioch all seemed to be appreciated by the faculty—in other words, less supervision and more clinical independence. Although it should not make a difference, my completed family means that maternity leave will not become an issue either. No doubt my brown skin doesn't hurt but rather will tick up affirmative action stats for the medical school, the hospital, and the university—a triple-double.

I have learned from colleagues to color every detail in its best hue. I no longer fear the affirmative action label because I know I don't control that narrative. Automatic assumptions about inferior qualifications have sometimes proven to be a useful secret weapon; a little underestimation can provide an edge. Sometimes, it has left room for me to explore my own agenda unnoticed. I find that over time, people will either change their assessment or they won't, and that's not up to me either.

No one should think for a moment that I begrudge the battle I'm fighting to be seen as a three-dimensional human being. I was born into this struggle, central to my core from my first breath. I would not be who I am if I wasn't striving every day toward being treated as an equal or, God forbid, acknowledged as having superior capabilities in some areas. I have been a trailblazer—*trail* being the operative word. The point is to open a way for others to follow. And as our numbers grow, the splintered edges of the path will break into a broad avenue. When that day comes, this "first" role is one I'll be happy to watch disappear.

I also know that I'll bring a different perspective to the room, whether they realize it or not. That may be my superpower. It's not simply that I and many of their patients share the same skin color.

My experience as a patient and a provider brings a different slant to routine medical interactions. My work in a poor, rural county, like much of Florida, will inform what I'll teach the residents even as I understand how unofficially Jim Crow continues to color small-town life in the state. While I may not have completely figured out patient interactions in Weavers Crossing, this will be a setting where I can continue to explore them. I'm asking questions about attitudes that most other providers aren't. If I find some providers that are too, maybe we can work on some answers together.

I'm pretty sure that the program faculty have little insight into my prowess in this area, primarily because their perspectives don't allow them to acknowledge that color infuses an experience that is different from their own. To acknowledge that would be to admit that America isn't the place they want to believe it is.

I wonder too if I'll have to return to dealing with whites who don't want me to provide their care and how the faculty here will deal with that. I haven't missed those interactions one bit. However, the power dynamics will have shifted. If I'm the attending, not the resident, on L&D at night, I'll be happy to inform the patient that they have me or they can go to another hospital. I want them to know that the white residents might be at the bedside, but as the faculty, I'm the one with the final decision-making authority. I want to see the reaction the next morning when the daytime attending has to react to the pushback from the patient, family, or nursing staff. Will it be appeasement or defense of something they've never seen before? Or maybe the patient will have chosen to leave, and the fellowship director will have to deal with the fallout. Hospitals don't like to lose business, and that's far more important than their lukewarm commitment against racial bias.

This round of applications has helped me realize that I'm an asset to any department, and I'm not going to be shy about showcasing that. The only question is whether they will appreciate it as beneficial to their departmental mission. This more objective appraisal counterbalances the weighty burden of bad outcomes in Weavers Crossing that feels singularly mine, unlike in residency where no single person was responsible for any one outcome. Otis's presence hasn't yet changed that.

The women, their children, their losses, and injuries are visible to me as part of the casual interplay of daily life. Intellectually, I know it's no reflection on my general competence, because outside the office, shit happens. Even so, the feeling leeches some joy out of the bright spots. But at least I look good on paper.

I have a recurring dream where Florence is drowning in a swift current. She flails in the water, desperate to resurface for air. She sinks again, her lungs filling with water, and then I struggle to wake myself up. Despite the progress with fellowship applications, I'm the one being silently dragged down by an undertow. And then a life preserver appears. The abstract that I submitted to the ACOG annual meeting about our VBAC patients has been accepted for oral presentation. This is a huge surprise. I had applied for a poster presentation, a report of preliminary findings from an ongoing study. Posters, usually displayed on rows of flip boards in the convention hall, provide early entry into scientific discussions for students, residents, and fellows. Many convey results from projects done under faculty mentors designed to teach research methods and enhance CVs for applications to the next level of training.

I'll acknowledge that while it's like much of the ob-gyn literature, it's not a good study. For one, significant studies are never single authored. It's retrospective and observational with a small sample size, none of those characteristics being a gold standard. With a small sample size, the absence of any cases of uterine rupture means nothing when it's expected to occur in one in two hundred women having a trial of labor. No ruptures is exactly what would be expected in less than a hundred subjects. Understanding that limitation, I folded several complications that could be anticipated to occur into one composite variable. Essentially, it increases the statistical probability of finding a significant incidence of potential harm. If found, that could suggest that allowing VBACs in a rural setting might not be as safe as in other places. If not found, it simply means that the risk of complications with VBACs remains an open question, not that the practice is a safe one, and that additional investigations are needed.

My selection is so unexpected that I'm overwhelmed by what feels like the special recognition embodied in this elevation to a podium. Not only will it be my first oral presentation at a national meeting, the abstract will be published in an issue of the journal, and a completed manuscript could become my first publication in ob-gyn. The fact that it was done outside an academic center is a solitary landmark that really makes me proud, even with the study's limitations. I don't know anyone else who has done that.

Not simply an "African American first" that will make my mother proud; it's something I've never seen before.

This kind of heady thinking reflects the ego inflation I'm feeling during this round of applications, so different from when I left medical school. I have a list of solid, if not major, accomplishments in the real world now that, in my view, make me a prime candidate. That nontraditional, older Black medical student ranked in the middle of the class who was trying to convince a residency program that they should take a chance on her has developed into a practicing physician who has shown initiative and leadership. I'm good at what I do. The tables have turned, and now, these programs should be competing to impress me. In the grand scheme of things, the upcoming presentation isn't that big a deal, but it never hurts to gild the lily. If you ain't tooting your own horn, who is? I'll have to let the fellowship programs where I've applied know.

Allison tells me that Florence Bivens has been lost to follow-up. Her medications had helped her resume normal activities, although at a slower pace, but her cardiac output is still lower than it should be. Now apparently she's slipped from Allison's grasp, no longer at the same address, which means that without visits for refills, she's probably stopped taking her prescriptions. We can only chase people for so long. Maybe she's found another doctor. Maybe her boyfriend has already moved on. Maybe she'll return. So many maybes. I was hoping that the young mother would heed that 50 percent chance of dying with each pregnancy and choose tubal ligation.

When Kelly, heavily pregnant with her second baby, steps into my office near the end of our clinic session, she unknowingly pitches a curveball.

"I have a patient who says she needs to talk to you about her daughter," she said.

I'm scheduled to give a CME presentation on fetal heart monitoring for the hospital nurses and don't want to be late to set up.

"Okay, I'll give her a few minutes." I plan to keep an eye on the clock.

"I'm so sorry, Dr. Hampton," the woman blurts out before she gets through the door. I note her chestnut-brown complexion with light brown eyes above a crisp white blouse and jeans. When she turns to close the door behind her, her beautifully polished nails stand out. I motion for her to sit down.

"We don't mean nothing by it. We appreciate you doctors, but we can't help it. We just need the money."

"I'm sorry. I don't understand. Maybe you should start at the beginning. What's your name?"

"I'm Cheri Winston. My daughter, Ella Johns, she, eh, eh . . . She passed a few years ago, maybe before you came. I got her two kids with me, but they won't, eh, give me the social security for 'em," she explains with a furrow forming in her brow.

"Can I interrupt for a moment to ask how I can help?" Even as I ponder the mystery unfolding, I'm getting antsy. I don't want to appear unfeeling, but I need to get going. "I'm sorry to hear about your daughter."

"Thank you. My other daughter, Lucy, eh . . . She, eh, lost her baby. A stillbirth, you know. You said she had high sugar. Eh, eh, so we had to get a lawyer. We just need the money. But we're gonna keep coming to the clinic. We like you."

I gasp, possibly audibly; I'm not sure. Is this woman saying that she's suing us? I haven't heard anything about it. I'm dumbfounded. I struggle to take in the narrative as she continues.

Cheri explains that because Lucy had been diagnosed with "high sugar" and her baby died, she was suing me, Antioch Associates, and the hospital for wrongful death. I'm not sure how to react to Cheri's insistence on continuing to patronize the group, not the norm when legal action is being pursued. Most clinics don't want to continue to treat litigious patients. Except, she isn't the litigant, so maybe I should thank her for her confidence in us.

Lucy, however, is a different story. It seems like an inherent rupture of patient-physician trust when a patient believes the doctor has committed malpractice. Right now, I just want Cheri to leave as fast as her legs can carry her. I will need a few minutes to recover before I can begin to prepare for the session with the nurses.

I rise from my seat to extend my hand to shake. "Thanks, Cheri, for letting us know. I'm sorry, but I have to run over to the hospital."

"Okay, Dr. Hampton. We're real sorry, but it's not your problem. Eh, the lawyer says it's insurance that's gonna pay."

I hope my smile appears sincere as I silently usher her to the door while suppressing my rising anger. Doesn't she understand that we're a small nonprofit struggling to keep the lights on, not a charitable foundation? Doesn't she realize that the insurance company's money comes from us? Shouldn't I care that she's accusing me of practicing bad medicine? Merely the filing of a malpractice case, no matter the resolution, has to be reported to the National Physician Database, which in turn reports them to medical boards for licensing and hospitals for privileges until I die. Most lawsuits end in a negotiated settlement that removes different parties by the size of their pocketbooks or, more precisely, their insurance companies' willingness to contribute to the pot. Even though the system operates more like a bingo game than a statement about physician practices, the idea that somebody out there believes you're a bad doctor is distressing. And thanks to the database, I'll have to keep reporting it on every privileging and medical license form for the foreseeable future, no matter the lawsuit's outcome.

Goddammit! Sitting behind the steering wheel of my car, I take some deep breaths and close my eyes. I try to process this development. An intrauterine fetal death? Did I do something wrong?

I've arranged this session on fetal monitoring because Stephens Memorial has very few opportunities for the nurses to garner continuing medical education credits useful for relicensing. Most of the nursing staff, all white of course, is homegrown with an associate degree at the local community college following their crappy education at the segregation academy. Their clinical rotations are completed at Stephens Memorial where I've witnessed the nursing instructors lay down "Do whatever the doctor tells you" as their first commandment. They transmit old wives' tales to both patients and colleagues, seemingly unfamiliar with anatomy and physiology gleaned from a less than optimal education that makes it much easier not to question the physicians, the real culprits in this saga. After all, they write the orders.

Even though nursing administration bears the responsibility to ensure that the staff remains proficient in interpreting fetal monitoring and the appropriate clinical interventions, you could drive a truck through the knowledge deficits on L&D. Since most neonatal outcomes are normal, the women have little practical experience with abnormal monitoring strips that end in harm.

A nurse, the only eyes on the monitor, has many other duties. She's admitting women and taking blood pressures and starting IVs and setting up the delivery room. She has to make sure the fetus hasn't wandered away from the tocometer that picks up the heart rate. A blank tracing is no information at all. That pile of paper by the bed is the sum total of what we know about the fetus. If the nurse has been away from the machine, she has to plow through the segments that have already been recorded to understand the fetal status. Her job isn't easy, especially when there's more than one woman in labor.

The nurse is the only person who can notify the physician about the strip. She has to present the information to the OB, who can then decide an appropriate response. The docs are completely blind to the tracing unless they come to L&D or ask to have it faxed, obviously cumbersome and time consuming. By the time it gets to the office, the strip may have changed completely.

I've slipped into my white coat as a transition to the professorial Laura Hampton, not the victim of Lucy Beaufort's legal assault. I miss teaching so much that I've created opportunities like this one, just like I created extra homework in elementary school. Aaron teases me about the "professorial tone" I automatically adopt when I try to explain stuff to him, mostly disapprovingly.

For me, it's important that a female physician who is Black has created this opportunity for them, unlike the two other male OBs who hold a loftier place in the patriarchy, regardless of the color of their skin. This activity pushes back against conventional narratives in the community. Maybe it will encourage the nurses to consider that their patients have the very same potential for knowledge and leadership, a momentous shift to viewing African Americans as a potential resource, not a burden. It sounds like an overly optimistic reach, but persistent interaction can alter perceptions enough to leave room for the benefit of a doubt, something Black people have seldom been offered. It's a lot like Aaron's house-to-house visits, one nurse at a time.

My motives aren't completely unselfish. The sessions allow me to both assess and manage the dialogue used on the other end of the phone to describe the monitor strips. My hope is to standardize the language to make the unseen descriptions more precise. In the exercise, I set out the standard definitions and ask the nurses to give their interpretations of sample monitor strips I have tacked up around the room.

By making the nurses more confident and well prepared, I hope they can be more aggressive about demanding the doc come in, not out of sense of their own inadequacy, but as an act of patient advocacy. It's a little subversive to encourage them to be assertive "bad" girls, pushing back against the all-knowing man in charge. I try to model the appropriate responses when I'm Johnny-on-the-spot if they ask me to look; better safe than sorry. I mean to be the change I want to see. Although I doubt that the other OBs know about these sessions, the word will eventually spread. It doesn't matter because nothing overshadows the fun. Being considered capable medical partners is something the nurses seldom experience, so they seem to enjoy it as much as I do, which earns me a lot of good will on the wards.

Of course I, as a physician, have authority over nurses, and I don't need to be anything else, not even competent. The same will be true for ob-gyn residents when I join some venerable institution's faculty. In my hands I will hold the power embedded in our merciless apprenticeship system, a cruel passage erected upon fear of ridicule and embarrassment. The faculty can, and does, do just about anything they want. For instance, a well-respected department chair in medical school threw instruments at people in the OR without any authorities batting an eye.

For my future trainees, it's equally important that they see this power wielded by brown hands. For one thing, they've probably never seen it before. More than that, Professor Hampton will step out of that inhumane paradigm to be equally proficient at providing residents with the tools they need through respect, not fear. There will be no tantrums or verbal lashings or accusations of stupidity. Even while I'll be a kinder, gentler professor, trainees are well enough immersed in the power dynamics. They will know that I can literally make or break them. A recommendation from me, enthusiastic or not so much, can mean a hire or a disappointment when they're looking for a job after residency.

Residency is an extremely intimate experience, difficult for an outsider to understand, but by the time my charges leave, they will go on to their practices and think, *What would Dr. Hampton do* when they face a complicated decision or an unusual situation. I'll be in their heads.

When I'm faculty, I can reach out to the handful of trainees who look like me. They can whisper their hurt in my ear. I can guide them through the quandary over when to react to offenses and when not. We'll commiserate over the lack of alternatives to the daily harms, large and small, and together, chart a path to highlight and potentially reduce them. Hopefully, I'll be able to recruit some of them to join academic ranks and do the research to answer questions about people who've been left out of the equation. We'll bring a different approach to lighting the way to better health outcomes.

I know my voice will be in the minority, if not singular, among faculty members, but we all borrow bits from different inputs. I won't influence every resident, but it'll be enough to have an impact, even if it's only a local one. That's still a lot of women seen over my trainees' forty-year careers. This is how I plan to begin to reshape medical care delivery.

Chapter 28

OUT OF THE BLUE

J OYCE SAYS WE HAVEN'T BEEN notified of a Lucy Beaufort suit, but her medical records have been requested, a sure indication that some lawyer is nosing around. If Cheri is talking about it using legal terms like "wrongful death," it probably means that one attorney has already signed on.

The tragic tale of Ella Johns, Cheri's now-deceased daughter, unfolds as a pokey response to an increasing crisis that ended in a preventable maternal death. The response at Stephens Memorial certainly sounds like the makings of a wrongful death complaint. Everything at the hospital took too long.

Ella, described as always cheerfully ready to help, suffered from systemic lupus, an autoimmune disease. Dr. Edwards had referred her to Greenville for prenatal care as her kidney function began to rapidly decline during her twin pregnancy. When she went into premature labor, the ambulance was compelled to bring her to Stephens Memorial.

When her blood pressure became stratospheric and kidneys began shutting down, Ella was moved to the ICU, where her condition was too unstable for transfer. Her acute condition, known as superimposed preeclampsia, can only be treated by delivery, which put the docs between a rock and a hard place. Preterm twins born at a hospital without neonatologists and a NICU is a recipe for neonatal disaster. The matter was settled when Ella had a stroke and died during an emergency cesarean.

Each new detail unlocked a cascade of fragmented images trickling from buried memories of the agony of a dying patient. Joyce's emotions were so ragged during the telling, she narrowly avoided tears. Over the phone, it was hard to know if she didn't shed some.

Barbara Edwards was shattered. She stood at the operating room table, slashing tissue as quickly as she could and watched the life slip from Ella. Her death wasn't a quiet one; the resuscitation team invaded the OR in a frenzy of arms and footsteps and machines, all to no avail. There is no crueler place to be when nothing else can be done. A deep hole opens up inside you that will never quite fill. Maybe Barbara was less taciturn and moved more quickly before what I suspect was her first maternal death, because they are so rare. Unfortunately, they happen more often in Black mothers than any other group in the country.

Devastated, Barbara must have felt trapped. No matter how conservatively she practiced or how far she distanced herself from high-risk patients, they could still appear on her doorstep and drag her into the abyss. She wanted a quiet, low-risk ob-gyn practice with an occasional not-too-serious complication, something like Bonnie Taylor's postpartum hemorrhage. She couldn't wait to leave the Antioch group the moment her obligation was over.

On the other hand, once I understood that there's no way to avoid complications, I was glad for every chance to fight them firsthand. Maybe it was karma that placed me under what people call a "black cloud," but nurses used to check the schedule to avoid working night shifts when I was on duty, fearful of some disaster. For example, I had three cesarean hysterectomies and a woman who survived an amniotic fluid embolism in a single month, all circumstances I hadn't encountered in the three years before. I accept that the natural course of disease can defeat our best efforts. But my patients, now and in the future, will benefit from these exposures because they've taught me well.

I don't understand why Cheri never filed a lawsuit over Ella's treatment. Clearly things went wrong, and the twins were robbed of their mother. It's tragic that she has to resort to the absurdity of the malpractice lottery to finance the support of her orphaned grandchildren.

Otis wastes no time in getting to the possibility of a malpractice suit when we intersect on the postpartum ward. He'd gotten an earful at church. It just took one good Sunday service. He had reassured the woman he's dating that it won't involve him. I can barely squelch the impulse to divert the discussion to where he takes his lady and what they do. For all I know, she cooks him dinner and they watch TV before they indulge in some carnal knowledge. That's what teens in the county do for entertainment, except they're in the back of a car after a bag of McDonald's. I'm sure Otis and his date have more comfortable accommodations.

Otis is quite a catch. Women in flower hats blossom with pies and cakes to fawn over an eligible bachelor who happens to be the newest doctor in town. Church ladies compete to cook their way to his heart, and he's basking in the attention.

Instead, I lash out, "I didn't do anything wrong. If anything, it was the patient's noncompliance that contributed to the fetal demise," as if Otis had touched an exposed nerve with the insinuation of malfeasance. I try to rein it in during our walk across the parking lot. We're headed in different directions.

I had reviewed Lucy's records to flesh out more of her story. I had diagnosed the fetal demise during an ultrasound in the office. I flashed on bits of memory—her face as I comforted her through her tears and arrangements for labor induction. Her story was littered with a series of unintentional errors, hers and ours, that ended in a tragic stillbirth. The problems started with a delay in flagging Lucy's abnormal one-hour glucose test followed by patient nonresponses, then more delays in additional testing, finally ending in a late start to a diabetic diet three weeks before her due date. She quit the diet despite being told to continue it and returned with a fetal demise. Joyce induced her labor and delivered the baby.

"Sorry, I didn't mean to hit a nerve." Otis leans back with his hands up in front of his chest as if to surrender. "Believe me, I sympathize with you. It was meant to be an icebreaker." And with a gleaming smile, he adds, "Just so you know, there's a rumor going around that Lucy is a big crack dealer, which probably means she's a user too. If it does become a suit, you may want to dig into that."

A gust of wind swoops through the parking lot, twisting and swirling litter up into the air as if to punctuate his revelation.

𝕴'm sipping another cup of coffee in my office in the late afternoon when the intercom buzzes.

"There's a call for you from a doctor in Florida," the aide says.

Shit. Is it a good sign or a bad one? Maybe they want clarification of something. The proper protocol is for the applicant to send a thank you note to the program director and the faculty who interviewed them. Mine contained the standard phrases like "I'm even more interested in the program now that I've seen it" and "I was so impressed with your facilities," etc., etc.

Since the Match algorithm favors the applicant, or at least that's what they tell us, applicants send their notes everywhere they apply to increase the chance that they will be ranked among the program's choices. Only when a candidate has completely lost interest in a program do they skip the cards. Program directors know the game, so they try to rank their choices by their impressions of an aspirant's sincerity, divined from additional phone calls by the faculty to the most desirable contenders. Their objective is to be able to brag in the next year's Match that they got their first choice, a plum that will make them more attractive to the next set of applicants. The process runs on its own logic.

Maybe this is a card follow-up, making it a good sign. They wouldn't call with bad news; they'd leave that to the anonymity of the Match Day announcement. Florida, above Alabama, Mississippi, and Georgia, had emerged as my first choice principally because of the research potential and their position as the only referral center in their region of the state, creating a steady flow of referrals with diagnosed fetal abnormalities and treatment in their pediatric subspecialty departments. It was everything I wanted.

"Hello. This is Dr. Hampton. How can I help you?" I'm wearing my friendliest, most professional face, invisible to the caller, but I hope it will filter over the receiver in the quiet confidence of my dulcet tones. The caller, the fellowship director, drops into a bit of small talk before getting to the point. After a burst of flattery, he offers me the position outside the Match, a kind of side deal where I would commit to coming there and drop out of the shuffle of the computer algorithm.

I'm almost speechless—a rare phenomenon. I sputter a thank you. ABOG discourages this kind of arrangement as an affront to the concept of fairness, seducing some of the most desirable candidates with a concrete offer that eliminates the element of chance. This time, my usual outlier position as one of a smattering of applicants leaving a practice may have worked to my advantage. Maybe I have Weavers Crossing to thank for this offer.

Here's an opportunity to leave the computer whirl and regain some control over my future. Most people my age are already well established in their careers, not still training to start it. I felt adventurous and brave when I started this career journey; now I only feel battered.

It is tantalizing. I, masquerading as a cool cucumber, thank him for their confidence in my abilities. The director wants a response within a week; I say it'll be less, after I discuss it with my family, which sounds appropriate but isn't completely true.

I assume that a "no" will send the director to their next most desirable candidate, automatically tossing me into the clutches of the second or third or fourth choice on my rank list. Not being selected by one of them is unthinkable. I'm completely overthinking this. I'll call the director tomorrow.

That decided, I'm out of my chair, pumping my fists and whispering a few quiet yesses. I start swiveling my hips and step through a series of smooth turns, my version of an end-zone dance. I'm not telling a soul until whatever required papers are signed.

Colonel Sanders's fare will grace the Hamptons' dinner table tonight. No cooking for mom, and for Abbie and Kyle, a celebratory non-burger fast-food meal without any pushback. They're unaware that we'll be celebrating my new job. In these moments, interacting with them feels at once grounding and miraculous.

One and done! My hesitation had been about skirting a system that forces everyone to maximize every advantage. I'm right to jump on this. Skirting the rules is certainly within my wheelhouse.

I didn't tell Aaron when he came home. Our lines of communication sputter like a radio too far away from the station's broadcast antenna. I'll tell him of the done deal when the time is right. Neither his job nor its location will be affected.

At some point, we had agreed that in recognition of his prioritizing my training, our final move would be his choice, and now that's Atlanta, home to the union's regional headquarters. Of course, Atlanta, while conveniently deferential to Aaron's needs, would be ideal for me too. Strangely, I feel like my day-to-day life is ruled by Aaron's prerogatives while he seems to think that his is a series of sacrifices made for my happiness. Unfortunately, his version of "my happiness" is essentially what he wants it to be rather than what I want, a topic over which we have consistently butted heads. At times, he insists that he knows better than I what makes me happy, and that's an infuriating non-starter for me. He's erasing my blackboard, my unique signature in the world. Me, who makes life and death decisions outside the house, is struggling to assert my own will within it. Lately, I've stepped out of the fray. My refusal to engage is certainly quieter; no raised voices or slamming doors. Much better for the kids. It's also probably a sign that I don't care enough to try. I simply do something, then wait for him to figure it out.

I welcome the room to breathe when he's gone. It would be unbearable without that. Those heady days when our idealism had infused our passion for each other have long ago dissipated. Our political passions have diverged even though the union movement and advocacy for underserved African Americans should commingle. And yet, somehow they haven't. Is it two decades of marriage and three kids that has dimmed our affection to this anemic ember? Can it be rekindled into a blaze that throws off a comfortable glow to last into our golden years? I wonder at times if it will quietly die before our final move.

Buoyed by my recent fellowship program commitment, the arrival of Isaiah Deacon, a seven-pound, five-ounce boy, feels somehow more joyous. It had taken a second page to ratchet me from between the sheets after I had lapsed back into a sound sleep. Aaron lay turned away softly snoring, completely undisturbed. My bedside clock read 1:06 a.m. Cootsie Deacon had been admitted in active labor, and by the time I first checked her cervix, she was seven centimeters.

The nurse was so overwhelmed by an unusually busy L&D that I decided to manage Cootsie's labor myself, like we used to do routinely as interns. Darting in and out of patient rooms to do the cervical exams instead of the nurses, there was something that bonded us with the women struggling to become mothers. Epidurals allowed us to have wide-ranging conversations with the families. We bonded in common battle, much like in the olden days when midwives coached women to the finish line in their homes.

And Cootsie's labor was just as much fun as then. We cheered with each push; Darryl patiently suffered her iron grip on his one hand while he supported her leg with the other. Her mother patiently wiped her brow. "C'mon, baby. You can do it" rang out in a chorus of voices. I screamed, "You got that boy, Darryl" when the baby swished onto my hands. The couple embraced and hugged and laughed while her mother cried.

"It's gonna be Isaiah," Cootsie yelled.

Our journey together had come to an end. Isaiah's birth had felt so organic outside a delivery room with legs dangling from slings amid sterile gowns and drapes surrounded by what look like instruments of torture. Still, no matter the setting, each birth is unique. Every birth is a small miracle. My sense of wonder never fades.

Suddenly, I realize how much I've missed the connections created through the labor management that I've left to the nurses until I swoop in at the end. I have to be in the office or the operating room. And I've got to be at home with my family in between. You can only be in one place at a time. It's sappy, I know. My turn toward research and teaching takes me further away from the immediate blush of new life, but we can't have everything. I'll have to make do with the reflected glow.

Chapter 29

I TAKE THE STAGE

IN WHAT FEELS LIKE THE blink of an eye, that talk at the national meeting is fast approaching. I've spoken a couple of times with the session moderator by phone, something I hadn't expected. What did I know? I've never presented at a big meeting before. I experienced it as something extraordinarily kind, not my run-of-the-mill experience in medicine. Anyway, the moderator probably checks in with all the presenters in his session.

For once, Aaron and I didn't have a major dust up before I left. Probably because he has no concept of how important this is to me. Still, I kiss this gift horse in the mouth. I'm grateful, but you can't thank someone for doing what they should normally do. Or for not doing what they shouldn't. That's fight territory.

Well wishes from Adrienne and Elise were a boost, but I'm not particularly nervous; I've done tons of lectures over the years. These things have a standard format. I don't expect this national audience to disrupt my established rhythm. My slides are formatted so that if worse comes to worst, I can read them from the screen. I'll speak extemporaneously like everyone does, even if it leads to some *ums* and *ers*. I figure I can't be worse than the range of speakers I usually listen to. Sounding like everyone else demonstrates that I understand the norm. Besides, I can't resist the impulse to reword or ad-lib a practiced script, so I might as well go with the flow.

The five-minute Q&A following my ten-minute talk is a bigger concern. That inculcated drive to always have the correct answer can trigger something called imposter syndrome. Will I be exposed as a less knowledgeable black mark on the audience's whiteboard? It's a reflex, this representing all brown-skinned people to an assemblage of low expectations. Even so, I've observed enough speakers to have good dodges for questions I'm unsure about, like "we've not looked at that. Thank you for your suggestion." Or, "I don't have the numbers right in front of me, but it's something like . . ." Of course, there's nothing wrong with a truthful "I don't know." I tell patients some version of "I'm not sure" about lots of things.

This event is a lot like the illusion that a high school prom is the most important event in your life. A few minutes in a dimly lit auditorium is a blip in my story. It's a matter of perspective. This talk pales in importance to the well-being of my family, for instance. No one in the audience is going to give me a second thought when it ends.

As reflections in the white looking glass, we don't have the luxury of defining who we are by what we do. But that's the tension, the tug of war between proving I belong despite the color of my skin and the vulnerable human beings we all are.

After I've registered, I stroll through the convention center, ego invested in the ID badge around my neck topped with a "presenter" ribbon. I pass through the familiar Big Pharma Wonderland of booths littered with a staggering array of trinkets, paraphernalia, and flashing company logos wherever I look, but I decide to circle back during the session interludes when vendors will break out their candy and cookies and logoed coffee mugs.

I arrive at the room assigned to my session about twenty minutes before the ten a.m. start. I'm wearing a pale pink blouse and a red suit, the power color that stands out in a sea of traditional navy and black. I look great, if I do say so myself. My shoulder-length hair, curled under in a pageboy and swept to the right, has replaced my usual ponytail.

Spotting the moderator's badge, I stroll down the long-carpeted aisle, smiling as if we're acquainted. Extending my hand as I introduce myself, the moderator appears jarred, leaning backward if only momentarily. Granted, I look gorgeous and much younger than my age, but I don't think that's it.

Shaking my hand, he seems instantly more formal, not the warm friendly voice of phone memory. He's ill at ease, perhaps embarrassed about the significance of his surprise, so he's erected a screen around his guilt. Quickly, he reviews the room's audio setup, the slide projector, the order of speakers, and his introductions and then politely moves on to someone else he's spotted in the room as if fleeing the scene of a crime. Did I imagine the speed with which he made his exit?

A familiar shadowy force had reared its ugly head. Hearing my phone voice, so free of an easily discernible accent, he had reflexively assumed the natural order of things. But when a nonwhite body appeared, the normal niceties of discourse quickly melted away. "Laura" is race neutral, as my parents intended. Hampton is Aaron's family name, one picked out of a phone book for its very non-Jewishness. Jewish quotas at universities had been an obstacle to his uncle's admission to the college of his choice, a bit of family history that drew Aaron into the circle of people who had been ostracized, excluded, and subjected to attempted extermination because of who they are.

The moderator must have thought the audacity of the work could only have sprung from the mind of someone who looks like him, the default in his universe. Not that he would have or could have acknowledged it as a bias. Nor is it consciously understood. Certainly, 99 percent of the time, he would be right; I am an anomaly in his sphere. But if the world were different, he would have been equally open to all possibilities.

Assumptions like those often cloud easy interchanges between people in groups unused to mingling with each other. I used to make a hundred decisions a week to either take offense or not, to acknowledge the affront or not, to refer to a neutral arbiter or not. How can I even characterize the flip of a friendly hand into a cold shoulder as an affront, although I suspect deep down it will pluck a chord in many a liberal, spinning them defensively into denial. Am I educating the individual by pointing it out in a way that will shape future perceptions? More often than not, I've found that additional effort beyond letting it slide is never worth it. They'll say I'm being too sensitive or they didn't mean anything by it or worse than that, they'll have me apologizing for accusing them of racial prejudice. I, like all Black people, traverse the landscape forever vigilant for the slight, insult, or a more aggressive takedown, because they will come, intentional or not.

I smile. Fooled 'em again. Thanks, Mom, for your dogged insistence on good grammar and diction. There is some perverse satisfaction in this confirmation that the world remains the same.

I take a seat in the second row to wait as the room begins to fill, pondering how much easier it is to confront already declared hostility because I know what's coming. Then I mount the podium steps to take the chair behind my name card. This little tête-à-tête slides away like rain rushing toward a storm drain. I wait through the two speakers before me and my short introduction. Then I step to the microphone.

"Thank you, and good morning. I'd like to tell you about . . ." The lights dim, and I click my title slide and begin.

I think the talk went well. People even stayed after the Q&A was over to ask more questions. Heading out of the room, decorated with this presenter ribbon on my name tag, I hope to run into some colleagues from other programs. After all, my sundry educational institutions have sprinkled graduates across others, and there should be some acquaintances among them.

Out in the hallways, teeming with people shifting between meeting rooms, I wind my way around clumps of folks, hugging in reminiscence. ACOG meetings are essentially alumni gatherings for folks who have passed through one or the other of the 120 medical schools, and often more than one of them as they climb training tiers. I smile and raise a hand when I spot my session moderator walking towards me, but before I can speak, he floats right by without a glimmer of recognition. I quickly redirect my hand to the back of my head as if rearranging my hair. Burned twice by the same dude in an extension of another familiar pattern.

I figure I should stand out like a buffalo in newly fallen snow, but it's the exact opposite, much like the slaves from which I'm descended. We were meant to be unseen and unheard unless spoken to. Ralph Ellison's *Invisible Man* got it just right: "I am invisible, understand, simply because people refuse to see me." It seems paradoxical. We come in such a wide variety of shades and physical combinations that should make it hard to mistake us, especially compared to the paler palette of people called white. So many times I've become another brown blob, even for people with whom I'm supposedly friendly.

Aaron is a happy exception. He's people-sighted, an eagle eye that doesn't miss details about any of the people he encounters. And he can often put a name to a face. Joyce is another.

I don't know why the *same ole, same ole* continues to surprise me, rather like the insanity that comes from expecting a different result from the exact same action. This invisibility cloak is what it is—immutable. The power to remove it isn't mine. The blind must miraculously gain sight before they can heal themselves, not that I can see that happening after several centuries. Me, I just keep putting one foot in front of the other.

Of course, we dark-skinned physicians have our radar up to locate other members of our tribe. We smile and speak as combatants in enemy territory. Often, we exchange contact information for future networking. Sometimes we commiserate over our stories, identical except for the names. This is the answer to that age-old question, *Why do all the Black kids hang out together?* an echo of antebellum suspicions about unsupervised gatherings of human chattel that elicited rumors of fomented rebellions. We're there to lick our wounds. We're there to be ourselves away from hostile white eyeballs. Later, I'll loop Adrienne, part of our tribe, into the goings-on over a phone call.

Occasionally there are some who adopt a less friendly air, stepping away from what the wider world might interpret as collusion. Often, more standoffish individuals speak with Caribbean or Afro-British accents. They're desperately trying not to be lumped in with native-born slave descendants. Their unusually spelled names confer higher status as immigrants, which affords them better treatment. Otherwise, they count on a change in attitude when their words fall out in a foreign accent. It's difficult to blame them; I don't wish this burden on anyone who can help it.

To my surprise, a science reporter wants an interview and photo for an article on the ACOG meeting. What, little ole me? As it turns out, the study's selection is a by-product of the intense effort by ACOG to sell VBACs to the majority of practitioners and secondarily to American women. My abstract got sucked into the middle of a political tornado before I understood that there is such a thing. Talk about serendipity! And maybe ACOG is savvy enough to kill two birds with one stone. While pushing their campaign about the safety of VBACs, they can highlight new members like me, which advertises the organization's dual progress in affirmative action for women and minorities. Whatever, I'm going to keep soaking it all in.

Through the afternoon, hoping to lure some reps to our clinic with samples to treat vaginitis and yeast and bladder infections, I wander in and out of our ob-gyn mart, although here again, the patents on most of those medications have long ago expired, and drug companies hand out samples of their newest market entries, not old ones.

At night, I join some McCune faculty and residents for a dinner that degenerates into a drinking contest. I casually showcase my successes: the research, the presentation, board certification, and the MFM fellowship—the application, not the deal outside the Match—all salvaged from what looked like a backwater holding pattern when I finished the program.

After all, I was the only resident in my class of six who was jobless at our graduation banquet. That had been a nightmare. I was truly embarrassed as I stood in that chandelier-lit ballroom when the director announced that I was still searching for a position. My face would have flushed crimson had it not been for the melanin in my skin. Mortified, I knew they were thinking this is what happens with people like me—failure to launch. Not my first rodeo.

My utter humiliation was only amplified by Aaron's absence. This most momentous night in my medical career had not been important enough to my husband for him to attend. What were they thinking about me and a man most of them had never met?

My copious alcohol consumption hadn't helped. I was self-medicating over the lost opportunity for the research fellowship I had been negotiating. I was soothing my despair over having to make a last-minute decision about a rural practice where I knew I didn't want to work. With the addition of that four-year detour from my chosen career path, it all swirled into an emotional tornado that whipped me out of control.

But tonight, I'm soaking up redemption with, once again, way too much wine, something I seldom do in the presence of academic elders. We ramble through a garden of memories made more humorous in the retelling. I spin stories of Stephens Memorial's missteps with the skill of Whoopi Goldberg. I relax into an alcohol-driven "I'll do me" mode, vaguely aware that no one important will probably remember it by the morning. The intensity of training together had created invisible bonds, made sweeter by the soft focus of time. For these hours, the group has the feel of a family reunion despite our unrelatedness—a dance among people who forgive each other even when they may not like each other. On this night, I emerge as an unlikely belle of the ball.

Chapter 30

THE RAIN ALWAYS STOPS

I HAVEN'T BEEN ABLE TO CRAWL out of the doghouse, even though I've tried. Laura seems to be increasingly distant. She's more quiet with me. She almost never talks about what's happening at Antioch or the hospital any more. To be honest, I don't mind that because I didn't much want to hear about it anyway and that always creates some friction between us. But she hasn't said much about our next steps either.

It all started with the trick she pulled when she left for that board exam in Chicago. I have to admit she threw me for a loop. A man makes a simple mistake and he gets pounced on. I was reading my newspaper and bam, she exploded. Whoa, this was something new. I was floored. Instead of giving it right back like I normally would, I took a beat. She was scaring me. I didn't get a chance to say anything else. Only after she stormed out did I start to rage. I mean, what a bitch! Who the hell did she think she was? Ordering me around! That can not happen in my house.

She can ask me but she can not tell me. I took that outside to the patio while the kids were getting ready for school.

And then came the silent treatment. Oh, Laura is a master at that. A total lock out. Maybe I can pry out a "yes" or "no" to a direct question but half the time she acts like she doesn't hear me. Her lips were sealed. Not a word after she declared the conversation was over. Not when she snuck into bed. No goodbye before she left. She didn't answer my phone call or call home the next night. Sometimes, there could be no communication for as long as a week, maybe more. Laura can be a bitch when she wants to be.

Ok. I forgot. It's not like I killed somebody. Let's be reasonable. I'm human. I've been busy. She can't expect me to keep track of her schedule. I have to put mine in a datebook and even then I sometimes forget. Besides, people are always trying to add to it. This thing comes up in one place and that thing in another.

So I messed up. I don't know where she expected me to find someone to take care of the kids. My secretary? My staff? She's the one who knows about this sort of stuff. She knows more people in Weavers Crossing than I do.

I'll concede that she was right to be mad. That test was obviously important to her. She says it's a must pass for her career. I guess I threw her off her rhythm and I'm sorry about that. I didn't mean to. I just stepped in the crap without seeing it. But I can't imagine that she won't do well because she's good at what she does. Still she had been studying a lot and running up the phone bill with hours of talking to Adrienne and Elise. That was a sign that she was worried. I don't know any details about the questions on the test, but she was spooked about it being oral and not written. Again, if there is one thing she is good at, it's talking, so I don't get it. In any case, I should have put two and two together. I should have sensed her anxiety and paid more attention to it. That's one of those things that she's always reminding me to do: listen.

But I don't hold grudges like she does. I'm always ready to move on after the blowup is over. How could I fix this? After all, it was only two days. I knew that Abbie would be fine with Kyle after school, but I asked Phyllis if the two could have dinner at her house Tuesday night so I would not have to worry about getting home before bedtime. That way, I could get to my scheduled meeting with one of our small factory owners to encourage him to stop violating our contract. We needed to up the pressure as only I can when I'm face to face. I had not planned to come back home originally, but a man has got to do what he has got to do. I'm one of the good guys.

I used my most earnest and contrite banter to convince Phyllis that I had screwed up and needed to be rescued. I can be pretty persuasive. I could handle most of the other stuff by phone on Wednesday with a fast food dinner of the kids' choice and Laura was supposed to be back on Thursday during the day, when I could resume my regular schedule.

By the time Laura got home, the kids were on their way to getting ready for bed. My reception was pretty icy. She asked Kyle, not me, how it went and then went with him to put him to bed. That was the last I saw of her. She went down to her office from Kyle's room and didn't even bother to unpack in our bedroom.

I knew I had some ground to make up so I didn't push it. I asked her if she was coming to bed and she shook her head. I left early the next morning, but I put an "I'm sorry" greeting card in front of the coffee pot that I had started brewing as I do every day

I'm here. I wrote, "I know you did great. Love you," No grudges. Back to business as usual. I waited for the thaw that I knew would come. And I thought about the next few gestures I could make to accelerate the defrost. I'm one of the good guys.

And so, we will move on to the next crisis that comes Laura's way. We had a nice celebration dinner for passing the board exam. I'm happy to bring her lunch or dinner when she asks for it if she is stuck in the hospital on the weekends. But I feel like something different is going on. It's not more cycles of the silent treatment. For some reason she's holding back, not talking about where to next or moving plans for instance. You can't say I haven't learned from my mistake. I made plans to take care of the kids for her trip to present her paper. I even remembered that a presentation was the reason she was going. No matter what, I will keep working to show Laura that I am one of the good guys.

Chapter 31

WINDING DOWN

ROOM 1 HOLDS PATSY LYNCH, not our run-of-the-mill prenatal patient. Clearly, she doesn't spend much time outdoors. Her pale hands laced with blue veins lie folded at the end of arms that are far too thin. Limp strands of dingy brown hair hang loosely in front of her ears to frame the sallow face of someone who's not getting enough to eat. I wonder why I haven't seen her before.

"Hi, I'm Dr. Hampton. How are you doing today?" I've finally stopped apologizing for the wait but instead launch into my routine battery of questions as I help her up onto the exam table. Her compact belly bulges completely in front, smaller than she should measure for thirty-eight weeks. This will be her fourth child.

"Looks like you haven't gained much weight. Are you getting enough to eat? Do you get food stamps?"

"No, ma'am. My husband don't believe in no handouts. We're fine."

"Would you like to talk to someone about diet during pregnancy? You know, how many calories you need and what kinds of foods you should be eating? You're almost ready to deliver, I know, but it's not too late to increase your caloric intake. I'll give you a script for Boost or Ensure. They taste like milkshakes. You could keep drinking them after you deliver, two or three a day."

"I don't have time today, ma'am. Maybe next week."

I offer it, but I doubt she will use it—the advice or the scripts. And since she's only had a few prenatal visits, she probably won't be back postpartum.

"Okay. I see you've signed your tubal papers. Are you still planning on getting the surgery soon after you deliver?" I ask as I write the script. It's only paper.

"Yes, ma'am. Four kids is plenty."

"Great. You might not still be pregnant by next week, but maybe I'll see you in the hospital with your new baby."

At the end of the day, I notice a white man sitting on the hood of a raggedy pickup, parked not far from my car. I'm thinking about what to make for dinner when I look up to find a rifle pointing at me. I stop mid step. He's not too close yet.

He spits out a liquidy, "Stop right there, you Black bitch!"

The odor of booze blended with tobacco and accumulated sweat wafts toward me from a soiled khaki shirt open to a sleeveless undershirt. Cigarette burns and irregular brown stains pockmark the front. A homeless bum scavenging in a garbage can has nothing on him.

"Don't you lay a finger on my Patsy! Don't even go near her!" he shouts from a snarling mouth, exposing tawny teeth that aren't all there. A sparse, dirty, brown comb-over flaps above his blotchy red face. "Ni*#@er! Let this be a warnin'!" he shouts, moving closer. "I'll kill ya if you touch her!"

I back up. It seems prudent not to point out that I've already touched his Patsy. That would be a match thrown on his vat of ethanol. His eyes lean closer to the rifle, and he shouts, "BANG!"

I jump.

I watch him back up towards his truck, still training the rifle on me. He walks toward the driver-side door of the pickup and places the rifle on the seat as he gets in. He turns to glare at me, finger pointed out the window, before starting the engine. A Confederate flag covers the rear window.

I don't know what to do. I stand motionless for an undetermined amount of time. Should I return to the office? Zombie-like, I walk to my car and just sit there. He seems to be gone.

I'm relieved to see Aaron's car in the driveway. He's heading out to swim his laps. I want to look calm as I walk in the door, but I don't think I'm very successful. I'm not sure how to play this—strong and dismissive or overwhelmed.

"What's wrong?" Aaron asks. "You look like death warmed over."

"Some cracker just threatened to shoot me," I begin.

"When, just now? With a gun? What the hell?" Aaron's gearing up. "Are you okay?"

It all tumbles out. I crumple.

"Did you call the police?"

"I don't even know who to call," I squawk. "Is it even a crime around here to point a gun at someone? Even if it is, I'm not sure they'd care. I don't trust them. They might end up charging me with something."

"Come on." Aaron paces back and forth like a tiger in a cage.

"You don't know anything about these sheriffs. Anyway, I can't prove he did it. There wasn't anybody around. He could just claim he wasn't there. He'll claim he doesn't know anything about it if they bother to question him. Who do you think they'll believe—me or one of their own? For all I know, he and the sheriff may be best buds."

"Then what do you want to do? We can't let him get away with it." He's stopped, hands posed to manhandle somebody.

"I think he already has. I'm not going near the cops. They're not here for me. We can be thankful that the man just threatened me and nothing more," I finish limply.

Aaron hugs me. "I'm sorry, so sorry. What can I do?"

I melt. "Just hold me."

I'm not going to deny that the gun rattled me. A lot. Both Otis and Joyce agreed there's no point in going to the sheriff. What isn't clear is what to do about Patsy. She exhibits the classic signs of a victim of abuse: meek and scrawny, sporadic prenatal visits, quoting the husband's demands. Has she been a victim of his rath again? Of course we can't do anything about that; she has less protection around him than any of us has. Obviously, I can't see the woman, much as I hate to give in to intimidation. Otis hasn't seen her yet; will he be safe? What set the guy off? Me? The tubal? The creep may be an ineffective drunk, but he could have friends. Both Otis and Joyce own guns, but that wouldn't bother that idiot, even if he knew.

Our choices are limited. Legally, a practice can't drop a patient without notification, usually by certified mail; otherwise it's considered legal abandonment. There's no other local practice to refer Patsy to; we're all nigras in this town. Besides, she's too close to her due date; no other practice would want to take her on this far along. Unsure if Allison would be safe, we agree that she should try to gather more information before attempting a visit.

After the kids go to bed, Aaron sits with me on the couch, a bowl of ice cream in his hand. He wraps his arm over my shoulder. We remain quiet in front of the TV. Reveling in the cold sweetness of the butter pecan on my tongue, those brief moments outside the office seem almost not to have happened, as if wishing them away could turn back the clock. Denial is one of the mind's most powerful tools. It wasn't the kind of violence I had feared—random, unprovoked acts of white supremacy by a boisterous gang of overheated white men riding out of nowhere. This attack was certainly against Blackness, but it was personal; a pitiful, drunken abuser perhaps fearing the end of his reign. In theory, this kind of thing could happen anywhere, in a city or a middle-class suburb.

I slept surprisingly well, maybe just from the shock of it. This morning, Aaron has all kinds of suggestions because he's a man of action, but I don't want to put any more energy into it. I've chosen to bury it. I'm so close to escaping. I will bide my time with no plans to buy my own weapon.

Some things have already fallen into place. I've arranged to begin my fellowship in August, rather than July 1 when all postgraduate medical programs start. I will wind up my duties with Antioch in mid-June, leaving time to organize the move and let the kids settle in. Hopefully, they'll make a few friends before school starts.

I lucked into a rental house situated in a quiet suburb not far from the hospital. The house is off a main thoroughfare within walking distance of Abbie's new junior high. Junior high seems like a good breakpoint to switch schools. I may try Kyle in Montessori. Damian did really well, but I'm not sure it's quite the way Kyle interacts with the world. He's too wiry, either hyper-focused or running amok. But you don't know unless you try.

My guilt over marooning Kyle in an educational desert comes from the knowledge that an educational foundation is built in the early years. I feel the need to go the extra mile for him, even though our dual-educator home functions as its own classroom. We've got older kids, books everywhere, bedtime stories, and letter magnets on the fridge. We go on fun educational outings. I'm hoping Montessori is another easy, well-established solution to enhance his experience.

Chapter 32

WAKE UP CALL

WHAT THE HELL? SOME IDIOT threatened Laura with a damn rifle! In broad daylight! Right outside the office! Something like that never crossed my mind. What can I do? I can't protect her when I'm not here. I can't protect her when I am. It is time to get the hell out of dodge.

Before the craziness, I was still living the dream. Still riding that wave of momentum into a couple more factories. Not all our campaigns have succeeded, but I don't expect that. At home, I've got my pool maintenance routines and weekend yard care on a schedule. For entertainment, I was happy to take everybody to see Alvin Ailey in Raleigh. Sure it was the B touring troop, but Laura was thrilled to see probably our most favorite dance company. She was bobbing and weaving so much through "Revelations," I thought she would come out of her seat. She says she knows every move from seeing the piece so many times. And Abbie was over the moon when I took them to see the musical Les Misérables, her current favorite. I napped through most of it. I have no idea why she likes it, but kids get hung up on things. I have a lot more fun taking them to the zoo in Richmond, which I will do at the drop of a hat. Of course, this close to DC, it's crazy not to take the kids for a day. There's always more to explore, including another great zoo. I'm one of the great dads.

But this shit is another level altogether. I'd be happy to leave tomorrow if it would keep my family safe. But Laura will not even consider it. She insists on working into June. At least she will work in town and not drive to any of the other clinics. No long drives on roads with few other cars. But the guy pulled the gun on her in town so I'm not sure how that helps. She wants to pretend like it didn't happen but that's just stupid. It's easy enough for the guy to come to the house one night. And what about the kids? Let's just hope he's as harmless as Laura wants him to be.

In the meantime, all I can do is try to be home more, and I know that's nothing. I hate feeling powerless. So I'm concentrating on expediting the move. I don't remember talking with Laura about it, but I'm staying behind to sell the house. I've always handled the house buying and selling, so it just makes sense. One of my strengths is handling the details. But Laura has been making arrangements without talking to me first—not the way we usually do things. I think she's trying to show me how independent she can be. It's almost like she doesn't care if I come or not. I'm a little worried that she's on her way to calling it quits. I don't want to be kicked to the curb. I can't imagine life without her. But I need to get her out of this town unharmed.

Maybe this crisis can change things between us. She seems distant, not wanting to say anything about what happened. Is she blaming me? I can't see how. I want her to lean on me, not shy away. This should be the time we harden our united front, the two of us against the world. That world just got uglier. Instead, we don't joke or share laughs anymore. We almost never touch anymore, even when we're standing next to each other. If I come into a room, she quietly disappears. She spends more and more time in her little office. She's got her fellowship. What's she doing? She says she's making sure she has all her data before she leaves the practice. She says she's writing a paper. It's like she's thrown up a brick wall.

𝕴 don't think I can put the house on the market until after Laura and the kids go. Things will be too chaotic to try and show it. I'll swim as long as I can but then make sure the pool is closed down for the winter and the yard is maintained. I might hire a cleaning lady to keep the house looking presentable because I'll be on the road. Living in a neat house is important to me, but with Damian coming back and forth from working as a camp counselor at Climbing Higher, I can't count on it. It's like pulling teeth to get him to pick up his clothes and make his bed. He's got a whole intellectual rationale about why beds don't need to be made that drives me up a wall. This is one of those "I said so" tasks that I shouldn't need to argue about. I got tired of the fighting, so we settled on keeping his door closed so I don't have to see in. Despite all this turmoil, I let Sherry Walcott know we're looking to sell if something comes up. We need to keep a North Carolina address until October so Damian can finish his senior year at NCSSM, but I bet the house will still be on the market when he graduates.

NCSSM has been great for him. Unlike Laura, he doesn't want to be the smartest kid in the class or get the best grades. She's unhappy that he's not living up to his full potential, but his grades are fine. He's more social, like me. From what I can tell, he's pretty popular. He's playing on the school soccer team and in an intramural league. Soccer has always been his sport. I've been to a few games; he's good. I'm so proud of him.

He's pretty adaptable. He could probably handle a school transfer just fine, but in your senior year, that has got to suck. He won't know a soul while everyone else will already be in a crowd. That's tough. And a better school than NCSSM doesn't exist, so Laura and I will make sure he stays put, whatever it takes.

I will handle the whole sales process: the assessment, the inspection, the works. Laura won't need to lift a finger. I don't want any last-minute snags, and I'm not sure that she's aware of all the ins and outs. I'm uncomfortable about arrangements when I'm not taking care of them myself. Laura and I could be butting heads, but she seems happy to leave me on my own. She will only have to sign the paperwork when it's all done. She doesn't realize what a gift this is, so she'll never thank me for it. I am one of the good guys.

North Carolina is more central to my region than Florida, so I'll be flying and driving more once I relocate. I can't see any way around leaving home on Sunday and returning on Friday. I might need to rent an apartment in Atlanta when I'm in between locations. I can fly anywhere in the South from there. That's a major reason the union decided to put the regional headquarters there.

I don't think Laura realizes how hard it's gonna be on me. There are too many places to be. I'd like to spend some time with Damian so he doesn't feel stranded when we've moved to a different state. Maybe she doesn't care that I will only see Abbie and Kyle two days a week. I don't think she's thought about the kids at all. They'll miss me; they need their dad around. Maybe she wants it to be hard. I feel like she's writing me out of the family. But I'm not leaving. I'll do anything to stay.

In the end, I think being separated so much will work in my favor. I think she's going to miss me. I know she loves me; she just has trouble admitting it. Somewhere deep down under the nagging, the put downs, and the silent treatment, she loves me. She'll never find a man who will treat her like I do. She'll realize that I'm one of the good guys.

In the meantime, I'm battling the Ice Queen. Or maybe Fudgesicle Queen is better. What? I can make that joke, if anyone can, because part of what I love about Laura is her brown body. I haven't seen much of it lately. I still think she's beautiful. I get excited just thinking about her naked. But she's tired. She's not in the mood. She doesn't wake me up when I've fallen asleep on the couch. Again and again with so many excuses. I think she's trying to punish me for something; what, I can't figure out. It's not going to work. I'm not going anywhere.

I'm sure, in the end, we'll be fine because I'm one of the good guys.

Chapter 33

A PARTING SHOT

THE FUTURE IS ALMOST HERE. My emotions bubble up at the strangest moments, often in different directions. Sometimes, I'm as eager to acquire new knowledge as a freshman in the front row of a chemistry lecture. Other times, I'm reluctant to slide back into a student desk and relinquish a role that's more like the school's dean. They say power corrupts, and I like this feeling of being heard and followed. And while I'm really excited to leave this sabbatical in the wilderness to rejoin a circle of professional colleagues, my thoughts about my legacy here are fraught with contradictions.

I can't remember what I expected this place to be like; I knew so little about it. You think things will just fall into place, but I seem to have made a mess of it. I hovered above and around an invisible impenetrable dome without a portal to slip through. Tranquility, a state that should blossom quietly within a home, seems to have eluded mine. Well rested with too much time on my hands, I was always thinking ahead, never able to slow down enough to be present in the moments and enjoy them.

No question this has been a bumpy ride, an emotional roller coaster hurdling into deep plunges when women suffered complications, then thrown into the sharp curves of administrative setbacks, up the inclines of successes in office ultrasound and board certification, only to plummet again and again from yet another bad outcome for a mother or a baby before coasting home on fellowship acceptance. I just can't shake this sense of failure that overwhelms not just the ordinary things but the successes as well. I know intellectually that they're not failures so much as the alchemy of diseases and circumstances in Stephens County. But my mind hasn't convinced my heart. What I needed on this crazy run was a companion next to me screaming loudly when we dropped, grabbing me in the curves, and celebrating with arms waving above our heads when we slid into the finish. The seat next to mine has been empty.

I ask myself if, in five years, anyone in Stephens County will remember Dr. Laura Hampton? Sure, I delivered about three hundred babies, so their moms probably will. And maybe, just maybe, a few women got pregnant when they wanted to, and others didn't because of OCP samples and tubal ligations. Doesn't sound like much.

Hopefully, the people at Antioch at least will remember that I originated our office ultrasound service, because I believe that does make a real difference for our patients while it helps keep afloat an organization operating on a financial razor's edge all the time. Of course, their financial future depends on Medicaid benefits and so many other variables completely out of the group's control, but Otis seems an able guide. While the more generalized use of spinal rather than general anesthesia for cesarean is a check mark in my column, I hope that with time, surgical and labor epidural analgesia, my epic failure, will come to pass in the near future.

But Dr. Hampton has probably been more reshaped by this place than she reshaped it. Women brought medical problems and complications that I'd only read about. And when they did, they nourished my self-confidence as elements in my list of differential diagnoses shifted and expanded. I will forever be indebted to these women for making me bolder as a caregiver and educator.

I'm proud of my part in nourishing the Antioch group's idea of wraparound care, lurching along as best we could from one financial divot to another. Imagine trying to maintain a business through the point when Medicaid had exhausted its allocation by June and simply stopped paying any providers until the new fiscal year began in September. Over 80 percent of our income dried up for three months, but our payroll, rent, and supply bills arrived like clockwork. It's just crazy for a state to care so little about both the patients and the providers. That is the fate of the politically impotent whom most of the general public don't know and care even less about.

The economic constraints of the business of medicine busted my brain like a sledgehammer explodes a watermelon. Our dysfunctional apparatus for perinatal transfers is the result of the scramble by physicians and rural hospitals to hold onto reimbursements for patients who would get better care somewhere else. They think they have to squeeze every dollar out because, as with all things in this culture, dollars are more important than people—the capitalist spear that rips through people's lives. Is it any wonder the country has higher perinatal mortality and morbidity rates than any other country with an advanced economy? Juxtaposed against the superiority of greenbacks, I've grown from someone who knew nothing about what anything cost to someone who's engaged in minimizing the cost for every patient I see.

My patients allowed me into bits and pieces of their lives where I saw the enormous toll of poverty I hadn't known still existed in the US. I found people practiced in the art of survival, their lives filled with the joys that those of us who are better off assume are our right. Undefeated by knowing they've been left out and left behind, they remain forever hopeful that a better day will come.

Caught in the cross currents, I've been forced to reexamine my assumptions made through my middle-class lens. Going forward, I must knit strands from the impressions and interactions in my daily life into a broader understanding of our multilayered cultural environment. And I'll have to keep diving deep as different economic and political realities present themselves. It's not just the details of diagnoses and treatments that I have to consider if I want to effectively serve my future patients, colleagues, and students.

Maybe it's the intermittent glances that leave me unsettled. I run into Fanny Hoskins from time to time at Walmart. She went on to have an eight-pound, nine-ounce baby boy by C-section. Turns out she had pregestational diabetes, and now Joyce is taking care of that. But I worry about how Melissa Spurling's daughter will grow up and the futures of Florence Bivens and Lula Hubbard, whom I never saw again. Maybe, fingers crossed, she was right about Big Jonah. I worry about how Monica Jackson's life will be upended by trying to tend to her two children at home while shuttling back and forth to Chapel Hill to visit her twins. And Patsy Lynch who simply disappeared; we have no idea when or where she delivered. Not that I'm sorry that her old man vanished. To some extent, the loose ends are not unlike the life of an academic perinatologist who may see a mom-to-be in consultation without a glimpse into her outcome. Many of the patients will come for only one pregnancy and, even then, be shared with other providers in the department. My interactions here more intensely link me to these families, and so I should know what happened. Maybe that's what's so disconcerting—to chafe against the small-townness of the place and yet have it frame my sense of obligation.

I'm grateful for Joyce's and Phyllis's support while I've been here. So far during my career, I've probably worked with more medical personnel who were hostile to my presence, if only subtly, than were welcoming. Neutrality, the refuge of many, is merely a mirage for abetting, like Josh when he didn't bat an eye at my being mistaken for a housekeeper. At the same time, I've seen how my competence can win in the end, if grudgingly. I'm confident that because I'm smart and capable, I will continue to do so. I'm armored like a tank to make the journey, my sensitive radar scanning the environment for incoming artillery.

What I haven't been so savvy about is letting my dislike of individuals interfere with professional interactions. Many, probably most, people work with people they don't like personally. Perhaps the most important lesson from Stephens Memorial is that unholy alliances will have to become part of my future if I want to accomplish my goals. I've transitioned from being an underling to a leader in charge of others. I have a practiced professional persona designed to get me in the room with the powers that be, and I can't allow personal animus to interfere with the goal.

Fittingly, Florence Bivens fires one last parting shot. I'm rounding on hospital inpatients when I spot her in one of the rooms, sitting up in bed. She's hunched over a little but lifts her head in a smile when she sees me. I wave from the hallway, genuinely happy to see her. Then it hits me why she must be here.

"Hey, Florence. What are you doing here?" I inquire cheerfully. "Is there a problem with your heart?" It's an oblique question. This is the antepartum ward, so she must be pregnant.

"I can't keep nothin' down," she says a bit breathlessly.

I come closer to sit on the edge of the bed, face to face, not wanting to imply some kind of "boojee" superiority by looming over her.

"Why didn't you come back to see us?" I ask, probably a bit too pathetically.

With her eyes downcast, Florence replies, "I didn't want y'all to know. I thought you was mad at me."

I'm a little hurt. I thought that we'd taken good care of her, and instead, it appears we managed to shame her.

"Oh, Florence, I don't get mad at patients. I just want you to get the best care." I want to back out of this hole quickly. "You know, your medical history is pretty complicated, so your doctor needs to know as much detail as possible. Who's your doctor now? I can talk to him about you."

"Dr. Nwachukwu."

Ugh. I shudder to hear the absolute worst choice, but I obviously can't say that. My reaction probably shows on my face, but hopefully she doesn't catch it. On second thought, what difference does it make?

"And how's the baby? Getting big, I bet?"

"She's doing real good."

"I bet she's really cute. Do you have a picture with you?"

"Yeah. In the nightstand."

I open the bottom drawer and put the purse that I pulled out onto her lap. While she rummages through it, I add, "By the way, I'm leaving town soon. Dr. James is staying on though. Did you meet him . . . Oh, she's precious!" I coo as she shows me the picture. In this moment, we're just two moms shooting the breeze. "Anyway, get better now. Good luck. I'll go look for Dr. Nwachukwu."

I turn before walking out the door, sad and fearful for her and that cute baby. "Really, Florence. I wish you all the best."

Maybe her failure to return meant that she had wanted to avoid any recriminations for ignoring our recommendations. Or maybe she moved and lived closer to Nwachukwu's office. Or maybe a friend had recommended him. I believe that continuity of care produces the best care, but we've failed to convince women that staying with the same provider is better care. The memory of past medical encounters, or at least a continuing medical record to clear the cobwebs, makes for more informed medical decision-making. If you ask a woman about continuity of care, you'll be met with a blank stare. But even if they know what it is, they're not buying it. I remind myself again that this stuff isn't personal.

I panic. I worry that maybe Florence's nausea is a symptom of elevated levels of digoxin, a cardiac medication, not pregnancy-related nausea. Had Nwachukwu ordered a drug level, which would provide a clue to what he knew?

Dressed in a scrub suit and white coat, Nwachukwu walks up as I'm closing her chart. The rapid pace of my speech seems to overwhelm him, and I realize, somewhere midway through my exposition, that the words are spilling out like a firehose putting out a fire. I pause, regroup, and slow down.

"I know that Florence is probably not the best historian," I restart. "She may have been confused about the medical terms and conditions."

He seems totally in the dark about her postpartum cardiomyopathy and residual cardiac failure. Okay, I did go off the deep end. He's not giving her any digoxin, so it's not an overdose.

"I've admitted her for hyperemesis," Nwachukwu says flatly, apparently offended by the audacity of a female to meddle.

Hyperemesis gravidarum is basically excessive nausea and vomiting in early pregnancy, which he's treating with antiemetics and IV fluids. Sometimes the diagnosis is the simplest one. But as the man sidesteps questions about her previous OB history, I want to shake him. I mean, sometimes when a patient has a two-volume hospital chart, it's worth a quick scan for the juicy bits. I'm frightened of his incompetence. I fear Florence will join the trail of mothers and children across the county that he's damaged. I want to help him sort it out, but I doubt that his ego will let me.

I take my frustration with me before it boils over and call Joyce to let her know that Florence is in the hospital. She thinks Florence couldn't afford her meds without the Medicare disability they were in the process of applying for when she disappeared. Would getting Allison involved be treading on Nwachukwu's toes since Florence is technically no longer our patient? Maybe the hospital social worker will help with a disability application, although they will have Medicaid coverage for this hospitalization. Florence, though, needs the disability payments to live on.

What am I doing? Florence's hospital admission by a different practice is emblematic of the tangle of threads that have interlaced my tenure here. She had passively resisted the pressure to contracept. My world is relatively safe, so out-of-kilter odds scare me half to death. Maybe Florence thinks her life is perilous whether she's pregnant or not.

I don't know what will happen to Florence Bivens. Lady luck hasn't been kind to her. I'm hoping that maybe she'll find her way to Greenville or UNC. Her best hope is that some emergency will result in a hospitalization that will require transfer to Chapel Hill where she could get consistent prenatal and cardiac care during hospitalization. Who would be taking care of her child during a prolonged stay is a whole different question. I leave her in the hands of her Maker. I hope I'm wrong and that she and her children will live long, fruitful lives.

The shadowy contours of a gun barrel sometimes wake me in a sweat. Thankfully I haven't looked down the real thing since, but the specter lingers. It's the green hidden between red light flashes.

Time to go.

Lately I've been walking through the house idly selecting items to take in the move. Our rental is smaller than this place, so we'll need to get rid of some stuff. We're leaving my beautiful central kitchen island flooded with sunlight behind for a more compact, crowded space with a small window. The subtle refreshing sparkle of the tiny, slightly iridescent calla lilies on the master suite's wallpaper will brighten another couple's day when the sunlight hits it just right. And I don't know where I'll fit a desk for my Mac Classic or piles of medical journals in the new place.

The losses pale in comparison to the potential on the horizon. On my first visit to the new house, everything just seemed bright. This is a city, with restaurants that serve alcohol, movies, shopping across a myriad of name-brand stores and boutiques, bookstores, concerts, and music in bars, a couple just down the street. As I watched an armadillo amble down the suburban lane, I felt safer sitting in the front yard. The sunset spread vibrant colors across the sky that reverberated through the trees, quieting imagined white sheets and pickup trucks on dark kudzu-overhung roads. Visions of rifle barrels will fade. The mosquitos, possibly more ferocious than those in our backyard, drove me back indoors though.

𝕀 wonder if by working this summer as a camp counselor, Damian's opting out of the chaos of moving once again. My fears resurface that he'll never live at home again, perhaps because home keeps shifting like the desert sands, and he can't locate it.

Aaron and I have pretty much accepted the idea that the sale of the house might not happen before graduation. Is his remaining behind a sacrifice for our son or a statement about the state of affairs between us?

Once he joins us, Aaron's thinking he'll routinely leave the house on Sundays and be back on Fridays. This isn't terrible; it's more a relief that allows me to organize family routines for the week. We can save weekends for family fun, time to enjoy the things we've missed for four years. But what does it mean for Aaron and me?

The tapestry that shielded us against the world has slowly come unraveled. I'd love to believe that Aaron will come to miss me, the Laura Hampton he fell in love with. Except I'm not her anymore. That love-struck girl who would do anything to please her sweetheart has grown into a woman who's thought a lot about what she wants, and I'm not sure Aaron can see that. Or maybe he can and he doesn't like what he sees. So I guess I want Aaron to be in love with the Laura Hampton I am today. Is our shredded tapestry irreparable?

Will Aaron's absence make my heart grow fonder? Will I roll over in bed and be glad when he's beside me? Will I soften to the allure of his touch? I honestly don't know. Maybe with some relief from the daily recriminations, the assaults on my confidence, the sense of butting heads, I can shed my armor, that second skin that protects me from revealing myself. Maybe I can cobble together a friendship circle where I can share my vulnerability. Maybe I won't need to lean on Aaron to be my sole support, building resentment when he repeatedly disappoints me. Disappointment permeates our relationship. Maybe he harbors his own disappointments in me. Maybe our mutual disappointments are the cocoons that close us off from being unguarded and vulnerable with each other.

Aaron and I have an opportunity to reset. Marriages are like ships at sea; they rise and fall in waves that crash against their bulkheads just like partners grapple with the different circumstances surrounding them. We've invested a lot in our vessel, not to mention the three great human beings riding in it. There must be a way to continue our voyage. Both of us have to commit to creating a Laura-and-Aaron space, beside and within the family, a cozy intimate nest nurtured by our years of common history. I don't know that we've ever had that. We've spent a lot of time running in different directions. It's possible that we need a navigator to steer us through those unchartered waters—someone to help sculpt our hardened, impenetrable edges. But neither of us has time for that, at least not in the near future.

A snake shedding its skin seems an apt metaphor for leaving one place for another. The tattered scales are left to decay, like memories of people you'll never see again. Even if you keep in touch, you'll never share the same space. Refreshed, the snake slithers on to new challenges to its survival. I like the idea of starting over in a new place unmoored from the past. Maybe that's why I train in different institutions where old baggage can be sloughed.

We watch the moving van pull out of the driveway. Abbie and Kyle are settled into the car. A quick quiet kiss. Aaron waves. We're heading for the flashing red light, a tap of the brakes away from merging into the interstate stream of northeasterners flowing south to the Sunshine State.

ACKNOWLEDGMENTS

I am forever grateful to my Tuesday night critique group: Linda, Tony, Alex, Ann, Jill and Jim for graciously reading this work and taking time to help me mold it. Finally, I want to thank Elias Altman, who I doubt remembers me from our single encounter almost ten years ago. I was pitching a book proposal for a nonfiction exposition on racial bias in medical education and healthcare disparities, when he suggested that I write my life story, an usual one about the child of two Black middle class parents with graduate degrees who goes on to a career in academic medicine. Years later, I chose fiction as the medium to present a story about healthcare disparities combined with the anguish experienced by every Black physician I've read about or met when confronted with racial bias.

ABOUT RIZE PRESS

RIZE publishes great stories and great writing across genres written by People of Color and other underrepresented groups. Our team consists of:

Lisa Diane Kastner, Founder and Executive Editor

Joelle Mitchell, Licensing and Strategy Lead

Cody Sisco, Acquisition Editor, RIZE

Benjamin White, Acquisition Editor, Running Wild

Peter A. Wright, Acquisition Editor, Running Wild

Resa Alboher, Editor

Angela Andrews, Editor

Sandra Bush, Editor

Ashley Crantas, Editor

Rebecca Dimyan, Editor

Abigail Efird, Editor

Aimee Hardy, Editor

Henry L. Herz, Editor

Cecilia Kennedy, Editor

Barbara Lockwood, Editor

AE Williams, Editor

Scott Schultz, Editor
Rod Gilley, Editor
Kelly Ottiano, Editor
Carolyn Banks, Editor

Evangeline Estropia, Product Manager
Pulp Art Studios, Cover Design
Standout Books, Interior Design
Polgarus Studios, Interior Design

Learn more about us and our stories at
www.runningwildpublishing.com

Loved this story and want more? Follow us at
www.runningwildpublishing.com/rize,
www.facebook.com/runningwildpress,
on Twitter @lisadkastner @RunWildBooks @RwpRIZE

RUNNING WILD

RIZE